Conflicts

of

Interest

DIANE KESSLER

CONFLICTS OF INTEREST

This book is a work of fiction. The characters, incidents, and dialogue are drawn from the author's imagination and are not to be construed as real. Any resemblance to actual events or persons, living or dead, is entirely coincidental.

Quotations are from the following sources:

J. Neville Ward, The Following Plough (London: Epworth Press, 1978), pp. 79 and 22.

Raymond E. Brown, The Community of the Beloved Disciple (New York, Mahwah: Paulist Press, 1979), p. 109.

"Lead, Kindly Light," by John H. Newman (Boston: The Pilgrim Press, 1958), Hymn No. 215.

Printed in the United States of America

First Edition

Cover and interior design: Jason Davis

Library of Congress Control Number: 2020914272

ISBN: 978-0-578-76474-0

This book is dedicated to my parents:
Dan, who loved a good story, and
Martha, who listened to a lot of them

'Tis the gift to be simple, 'tis the gift to be free
'Tis the gift to come down where we ought to be,
And when we find ourselves in the place just right,
'Twill be in the valley of love and delight.

Joseph Brackett (1797-1882)

Shaker Dancing Song

Chapter 1

When Piper Mangan walked into my office, the first thing I noticed were his shoes. My father had worn shoes like that—sleek black leather loafers with double stitching, no buckle, shined to a high gloss, not a scuff mark on them. I knew the type. High rollers. Developers on the make. I'd seen them at the State House often enough, strolling the halls in their camel hair coats, looking like they owned the place. Which, in some instances, they probably did.

At least my father had been handsome. In the case of my potential client, his shoes were the only sleek thing about him. They supported a pear-shaped body, a bulbous nose, and a face that had been ravaged by acne around forty years ago. He was pigeon toed. He didn't walk, he waddled.

Piper Mangan was outside my normal clientele. The energy-producing businesses for which I lobbied were headed by upstanding, civic-minded citizens. They donated to the Museum of

Fine Arts, stepped up whenever Boston Children's Hospital came calling, put their names on buildings at dear old Harvard. Voluntary charity was their *metier*, but they despised corporate taxes.

That was my area of expertise. The arcane nuances of investments in subsidiaries, tax credits, and loss carry over deductions energized me. Boston isn't New York, but everyone needs oil, gas, and electricity to heat their homes and cook their food—especially in New England, where temperatures in mid-winter can drop below zero for days at a time. My clients all had a stake in state tax policies. When some liberal legislator started making noises about increasing the business excise tax by a quarter percent, I'd spread the word, a lunch was arranged for a select few at The Union Club, and *voila*, the idea vanished as quickly as the dessert macaroons. White gloves only. No fingerprints anywhere.

Protecting the interests of energy companies in Massachusetts was how I earned the hefty retainers that, until recently, had kept me in cashmere. I was good at what I did, and I intended to keep things that way.

I had agreed to see Piper Mangan because, although only my administrative assistant Maura knew it, we needed the cash. My biggest revenue source had been gobbled up by a corporate giant based in Texas. Twenty percent of our income walked out the door with that merger. If the trend toward consolidation in the energy business continued, I could lose more clients. Then where would we be? Not only that, the cost of real estate had increased exponentially since we'd settled into Rowes Wharf. Some days I felt like I was dog paddling in Boston Harbor in four-foot waves with no life raft in sight.

I invited Mangan to take a seat in one of the wingback chairs I had placed by a brass-rimmed glass coffee table. It was understated, not too feminine. Nevertheless, it spoke. I had spent nearly

$3000 on that table, a sum I couldn't afford when I launched my business in '97, but the table fit right in with the view overlooking the harbor. It said I was in the game, I was successful, a woman in a man's world.

I'd been forty then. Now I was approaching the big five-0. Maura said any birthday ending in five or zero was significant. I didn't want to admit it, but I had to agree.

"So, Mr. Mangan," I said, "you've had some interesting encounters with Representative Whately recently." To create the right atmosphere—professional, not too intimate--I sat at an angle across from him, knees together, legs crossed at the ankles. I smoothed out my skirt and pushed my hair away from my face. It had a few gray streaks in it, but the dark brown still was dominant. I chose the word "interesting" to scc how he'd respond.

He squirmed in his seat. His hips flanked the sides of the generous chair. "I thought I could handle things. I've got a good track record, don't you know."

This was an exaggeration, but I let it slide.

Then Mangan launched into his pitch. He said he wanted to build an upscale suburban village for fifty-five and over residents, with houses ringing a golf course. The property he was after required the purchase of three family owned farms, but the farms were being considered for conservation land in a public-private partnership. That's where I would come in, he said. The "private" folks hadn't been able to come up with enough money to close the deal. Without the "public" part of that partnership, the dream of the conservationists would be dead on arrival. Mangan wanted the bill authorizing state funding to help purchase the land killed and entombed. Then he could sweep in, use leveraged capital, and scoop up the farms for a bargain price.

Why he was interested in doing this in a New England climate where golf was out of the question four months of the year, I didn't know, but that was not my problem. He would need approval from state regulatory agencies with initials as long as the alphabet (also not my problem). He stood to make millions if the deal went through. Unfortunately, he said, the farmland happened to be in Representative Whately's district.

Whately was chair of the Joint Committee on Environment, Natural Resources and Agriculture. The rumor was that Mangan and Whately had gone toe to toe over environmental land-use in a private meeting gone sour. If Whately was opposed, Mangan's development was going nowhere, at least while Whately was in office.

"I've never had problems with his committee before, never any problems," he said. "But somehow Whately's gotten an environmental bug up his butt. I need outside help."

I knew he did. But should I be the one to give it to him? I may have tiptoed right up to the edge on occasion, but thus far, I'd not toppled over. I had a reputation for being straightforward. But I knew from experience, Mangan traipsed over the lines without a backward glance.

I offered him a bottle of Poland Spring. He waved it away. I twisted off the cap, poured myself a drink, and glanced out the window. Pellets of sleet were pinging against the glass. Seagulls were tossed aloft in the fierce wind. What else could you expect on a February morning in Boston?

"When Maura told me you'd called, I did a little research," I said. "As I'm sure you're well aware, you've got a tough slog ahead of you. Whately will be running for re-election next fall. The environmental groups in his district have added some muscle since Mrs. Tannenbaum left the bulk of her estate to Environmentalists of Central Massachusetts."

"Why couldn't she have given her dough to the Worcester Art Museum? Heaven knows they need it."

"I hear she was an avid birder."

"Birds. All I know from birds are the Canada Geese that leave their poop all over my golf courses."

I offered a smile of acknowledgement. I didn't know anything about birds, either, but you couldn't miss the geese. They had invaded the Esplanade where I took my Saturday morning jogs. The previous spring one had almost nipped me when I got too close to her goslings.

He leaned forward, his beefy hands between his knees. "I'll be frank with you, Miss Petersen, completely frank."

He was definitely from the old school. It actually had been Mrs. at one time, but that was over a quarter century ago and it hadn't lasted more than eleven months—not even worth a footnote on my resume. I had been attracted to my prospective husband because he was a real gentleman, the antithesis of my father. Whereas my dad's parents were German immigrants, Alan grew up in Wellesley, boarded at Phillips Academy, got both his BA and MA in art history from Harvard. He could make the most obscure eighteenth century French Baroque painting come alive in just a few sentences. Turned out, however, that was the only life in him. My new husband's refinement as an aspiring art critic came with a price—no action between the sheets.

Moral to that story, check out the goods before you make a purchase. In freshly minted feminist zeal, I had kept my maiden name. It was a good thing. It would have been a real hassle to change everything back. Besides, who would want a last name of five syllables? I must have been temporarily deranged even to consider it.

After that debacle, I channeled my passion toward work. My

friend Barbara said I was compartmentalizing. Nevertheless, my vocation as a lobbyist had carried me through more than one bad patch over the years.

"Claire. If we work together, we'll talk regularly. Call me Claire."

"I'll be frank with you. I've come to you because you're a woman."

He glanced at my legs for a second too long. I was tall and my legs were one of my best features, but I didn't appreciate overt ogling. I crossed my arms and leaned back in my chair. Mental note: wear pants suits around Mangan.

One side of his jowly cheek puffed into a slight grin. He must have spent a fortune on dental work. His teeth were too perfect to be real.

"I gotta tell ya, Miss Petersen, you may have been around the block a few times, but you look like you're thirty-five."

I resisted the urge to roll my eyes. I'd put up with a lot over the years, but the idea of Mangan leering at me was grotesque. If I took him on--still a big if--it would require deft footwork. It would be a one and done, for sure.

"And you have a reputation for being able to close a deal," he said. "The reps aren't used to seeing you take up bills related to land-use."

He was only half right. I wasn't a goo-goo environmentalist, but sometimes I took a detour on my way to the office from my Back Bay condo and walked through the Public Garden. They called it part of "the emerald necklace" for a reason. Those sprawling Pagoda trees were spectacular. Springtime flowers made me pause, grateful for the vibrant colors and lush greenery.

"You'd be a fresh face on this issue," he said, "a fresh face. I think we need that now. And because you're a woman, you'd give a softer image to real estate development."

After those remarks, that $3000 coffee table would seem like a Walmart bargain compared to what I'd charge him for my services. It wouldn't make up for the twenty percent missing from my bottom line, but if I snared two more big clients, doubtful in the midst of a recession though I had been trying, then I could stop having nightmares about zombie calculators eating my brain. I had an obligation to keep the business afloat not only for myself, but also for Maura. We were a team. She had been with me since the launch of Petersen and Associates.

We talked for another fifteen minutes. Most of the time Mangan ventilated about all the campaign contributions he'd given to Whately and other members of his committee over the years. Occasionally I threw out an approach that might help move Whately out of the box.

When the conversation began to circle in on itself I pulled it to a close.

What I should have said, but didn't, was, "Mr. Mangan, I'm a respected lobbyist. My clients have solid reputations. Yours is as tarnished as my father's old 5-iron."

Better yet, what I would like to have said was, "Mangan, take one of those titanium golf clubs you hand out to legislators and shove it up your ass."

What I actually said was, "Normally, I don't deal with land use issues."

I twisted a gold chain bracelet around my wrist. "Tell you what. Let me think about it, talk with a few people, do a little more research."

By then I was ushering him into the reception area. "I charge a flat fee for a retainer, plus expenses. My administrative assistant Maura—you met her when you got here—she'll give you that information." I nodded to Maura, inclining my head slightly to the left. It was a special signal she and I had. She knew which fee schedule to give him.

I shook his hand. "Thanks for coming in," I said. "Why don't I call you—say, on Wednesday, after I've had a chance to assess the situation."

After he left, I asked Maura to come into my office with the accounts ledger. With her round eyes, fair skin, freckles and short curly red hair, which she maintained with the aid of Clairol, she looked like a forty-three year old version of Orphan Annie. Her feet barely touched the floor when she sat in the straight-backed chair next to my desk. The niece of a state rep from Dorchester, she started work in his office right out of high school. She'd befriended me when I was an underling, still learning the ropes; used to let me hang my coat in their office when I needed a place to park it; offered me a cup of coffee if I looked particularly weary at the end of a day. She was smart, should have gone to college. Her uncle announced his retirement from the state legislature just as I made the decision to start my new firm. When I asked her if she'd like to take a chance on me (there were no guarantees that I would be successful), she agreed on the spot.

"I'm trying to decide whether to take this character on," I said. "He may be more trouble than he's worth."

"How much is he worth?"

"He couldn't begin to replace that twenty percent hit we took, but it would buy me time to attract some new clients. And we haven't raised our fees in four years."

"Expenses keep rising," she said. "Those companies you represent don't hesitate to increase their rates. My heating oil bill—Mom and I are on a budget plan—went from $290 to $325 a month this year. That's a twelve percent increase."

Beyond the outrageous rent I paid for our office space, Maura's salary was my biggest expense. I thought I was being generous by giving her a 3% raise in January, but now I wasn't so sure. She and her aging mother lived together in the same Dorchester triple decker where she'd grown up. She had been spending too much time on the phone with her mother recently, but I was willing to cut her some slack. She was fiercely loyal, and she was a meticulous bookkeeper.

"The copier is on its last legs," she said. "I've had a repairman in here once a month for the past few, and that doesn't come cheap."

"Can we nurse it along for a while more?"

"I suppose so, but we're throwing good money after bad."

That settled it. Two days later I gave Mangan my decision and fleshed out a strategy. I encouraged him to postpone decisive action until after the November election. Whately was by no means a shoe-in. He'd alienated too many people in the business community with his new-found environmental sympathies. In the meantime, I would see if we could at least stall, if not derail, movement on any detrimental land use legislation by throwing it into an omnibus study. That would be a sure way to kill any threatening bills for at least a year.

He resisted. He didn't like my timeline. But since he hadn't been able to come up with a better approach—at least one I was privy to--he grudgingly acquiesced. We settled on a retainer that was acceptable to him (it certainly was to the Petersen and Associates' bank account). He agreed to bring in a check and sign some papers.

"I know you've been in business for many years," I said, "and you have an operation you can be proud of."

The last part was bullshit. With the indiscriminate use of fertilizers to keep his putting greens pristine, he'd assaulted the environment from the south shore to the Berkshires. But like my father, I was a people pleaser. Always leave 'em feeling good. It was useful in my line of work.

Chapter 2

When I walked out of my office to check on the Friday mail, I almost tripped over a big box on the floor next to Maura's desk.

"What's that?"

"It was outside the door when I came back from lunch."

She handed me some articles about Representative Whately she'd clipped out of the Worcester *Telegram and Gazette*. "It made me a little nervous. It could have come from those tax reform zealots you talk about, but with the name 'Erich Petersen' on the return address, I figured it was personal."

The box was brown, its previous use obscured by black magic marker.

"It's from my Uncle Erich."

"You sound surprised."

"He's my father's older brother. Always sends me cards at Christmas and on my birthday. He must be nearly ninety, a bit of a recluse, never married, lives in Ohio. I haven't seen him in years."

"Lost touch, huh?"

"Uncle Erich learned to play poker when he was in the Army. Unfortunately, when he came back home he taught it to my father."

"So that's where it all started." She knew about my father's gambling problem.

"Don't you want to open it?" she said.

"I don't have time to deal with this now. I'll sort it out later. I've got a meeting with Mr. Mangan's opposition." I stuffed the newspaper clippings into my briefcase. "Let's stick it in my office closet. Do you want help?"

"No, it's bulky, but not heavy. If you have a three o'clock you'd better get a move on."

"Thanks. I don't know what I'd do without you."

"Speaking of which," she said, "could you spare me for a couple of hours on Monday afternoon? Mother needs to go to the doctor and she shouldn't go alone. I thought if things weren't too busy here…"

"I hope it's nothing serious."

"I don't know. Last Saturday we were heading out to the grocery store and she couldn't find her list. Looked high and low for it but couldn't find it. You'd think she'd misplaced the crown jewels. She never could remember anything without writing it down. But she was obsessed, just obsessed with finding that frigging list. Something's going on, and we've got to get to the bottom of it."

"Why don't you take the whole afternoon? Treat her to supper afterwards. I've got a gift certificate to Mama Maria in the North End. If you can use it, you can have it."

I didn't have anyone to go with, anyway. I'd had an occasional date thanks to my friend Barbara's determined efforts to "round out my life," but none had been interesting enough to follow through.

I'd almost convinced myself that I liked it that way. Fewer complications.

I grabbed my coat and headed for the door.

Richard Truitt was executive director of the Massachusetts Environmental Coalition, a position he had held for about a year. MEC's fifteen member-organizations were united "to combat climate change and protect the environment." One of the members, Environmentalists of Central Massachusetts, was causing Mr. Mangan's agita.

Truitt was the environmentalists' new darling. Occasional television interviews with young female reporters had helped burnish his image. I wasn't sure what he had done before then, but after he began work with MEC he started showing up at legislative committee hearings. We had a nodding acquaintance. Both of us roamed the halls of the State House, made small talk if we happened to be standing in line at the fourth floor coffee shop.

Richard had called and asked for a meeting, said something about being the "new kid on the block" and wanting to get to know more of his colleagues. If that was the real reason, it would be a first. My antennae were up.

He'd suggested we have coffee at Sal's Diner at 2:30 on Friday. I was late.

Sal's was like dozens of funky restaurants tucked in the sidestreets of Boston. The façade needed a face-lift. The place smelled of French fries and tuna fish. A list of deli sandwiches was posted on a billboard above the cash register. I waved to Richard as I dashed in the door, ordered a mug of coffee, handed over two dollars and threw two more in the tip jar. The waitress, whose gray roots were showing through her black dye, looked like she could use it.

Richard was sprawled in a booth, playing with a menu. I added cream to the coffee, cradled the mug across the room, put it and a supply of napkins on the table, tossed my coat and briefcase into a corner, and slid onto the Naugahyde seat.

Richard looked at the napkins. "Wouldn't one or two be enough?" he asked.

"Hello, Richard."

"Hi, Claire." His right eyebrow automatically raised when he smiled.

"Look, I have a habit of filling my coffee cup to the brim, then slopping the contents when I carry it to the table. The napkins are insurance. I'm not going to take down a whole forest with 'em. Besides, aren't they biodegradable or something?"

Richard leaned into the corner of the booth. He was tall, lanky, and tan, whereas I looked like I'd been stored under a terrarium for the winter. He also was sexy, all the more enticing because he wore it as comfortably as the beige corduroy jacket with leather elbow patches he often sported at the State House. Although I guessed that he was about six or seven years younger than I, flecks of gray were interspersed with his wavy chestnut brown hair. He could have used a haircut.

"Rough day?"

"Sorry I'm late," I said. Mangan had called again and I'd had to rehearse my proposed strategy once more—an ominous sign for our relationship. "I was on a call with a potential client. You can't rush these things."

I wasn't going to tell Richard that I'd taken on Mangan. That would put us in direct opposition to some of his members. He'd find out soon enough. Maybe he already had. I wouldn't put it past Mangan to boast he'd landed Claire Petersen and Associates.

"You've been hanging around the environmental committee hearings lately. I wondered if you'd had second thoughts about seeing me. Are your energy clients nervous about something?" The eyebrow went up again, a grin followed.

If I was having second thoughts, it wasn't for the reason he was suggesting.

I poured a yellow packet of sweetener into the brew, stirred it with a wooden stick, and took a sip. The coffee was good, and I hadn't paid $3.95 for it.

"You know, Richard," I said, "you could be having second thoughts, as well. My clients tend to be pro-business and anti-regulation, whatever the cause. Some would say you're consorting with the enemy here."

"You know what they say. 'Keep your friends close, your enemies closer.'"

Was he teasing or serious? Perhaps a little of both.

He took a knife, cut a cinnamon scone in half, and pushed the plate in my direction. "Here, have a piece. They're surprisingly good."

"No thanks."

"Are you sure?"

"I had a late lunch."

"Besides, we share the risk, although I'm more likely to bump into a member of my board here than you are one of your clients."

He was right. His members probably wore LL Bean hiking boots, jeans, and flannel shirts--a unisex outfit, one style for all occasions. My clients were Brooks Brothers types.

"Spotting one of them at the State House is like a rare bird sighting," he said. "I pay close attention when it happens. I know them by their plumage: navy camel hair coats, red power ties, and tassel loafers."

Was he referring to Mangan?

"That's why they pay me the big bucks," I said.

"And that's why I bike to work, weather permitting—along with being environmentally responsible."

"Biking around Boston is an act of hubris, faith, or insanity."

"Maybe it's a little of each. But not blind faith. I do wear a helmet."

"You already have demolished one of my stereotypes about liberal do-gooders. They always seem so serious and single minded. You have a sense of humor. I'll give you that."

"You mock me," he said.

"So why'd you want to meet?"

"That's it. Get down to business."

Actually, I was attracted to tall men, and I wanted to nip that impulse in the bud. Richard, I was sure, was all nuts and berries. His organization took principled stances, you had to respect that, but he was not my type. Though I no longer was sure what my type was.

A few years ago I'd had a disastrous affair with a lawyer in the public charities division of the attorney general's office. He allegedly was separated from his wife, but I later found out that she was on an extended stay in Nebraska with her dying mother. He looked like he'd stepped out of Central Casting—six feet two, ears close to the head, nose well-defined but not dominant, riveting blue eyes, wispy brown hair over a high forehead, closed-lipped smile that never wavered. He breathed politics. He recited poetry. I soaked it up like a rainstorm in the Sonora desert. Maura noticed me singing in the office. I had been so charmed by him that my palms grew sweaty waiting for his calls, and not just my palms. When we weren't together, we talked on the phone late into the night. Next thing I knew, he'd dropped me. No explanation. The singing stopped, replaced by mournful brooding late into the night over pints of Häagen -Dazs Rocky Road ice cream.

That was the third great deception I'd suffered at the hands of a man. The first was my father. The second, my husband, hardly counted, in or outside of bed. A virgin when we wed, I initially blamed myself for his indifference. I must have been doing something wrong, right? Then I found a love letter from someone named Gordon tucked among postcards from the Metropolitan Museum of Art. I was flattened. How could I have been such a poor judge of men? Afterwards my friend Barbara said she thought I'd been more focused in the idea of being married than being married to Alan, but she didn't say so at the time. Even if she had, I wouldn't have listened. I'd had more than enough of living with Mother. Alan offered a way out. Security. If I'd picked up any signals, I'd ignored them. Then came Mr. Public Charities.

I kicked myself for being so gullible in affairs of the heart. After Mr. Public Charities, I vowed to give up men for Lent--a celibate existence that now had lasted almost seven years.

"I'm a no nonsense kind'a woman."

"OK. I thought it might be in our mutual interest. One hears rumors, you know. You're an influential figure on the Hill," he said, "so I pay attention. Thought I should check it out."

"I wanted to scope out the scene," I said. "I've had occasional conversations with Representative Whately, but I don't have a good feel for him. You must deal with him all the time. What's your take on the guy?"

I had worked with Whately on a quirky issue affecting solid waste disposal in the Berkshires, and his chief aide was someone I knew from college, but I wanted to see how much I could get out of Richard about MEC's legislative priorities. I was listening for whether land use in central Massachusetts surfaced during the conversation. Bottom line: he wasn't giving anything away. I'd have to work for it.

We talked another five minutes. Then Richard steered the conversation from the professional to the personal. He said he lived in the upstairs of a duplex in Cambridge. He didn't mention anyone co-habiting. At that point, if I'd been having an MRI, all sorts of impulses would have lit up brighter than a pinball machine.

"That's a high rent district."

"I own the place, rent the first floor unit. Well, co-own it with my folks. They made a shrewd purchase during one of the dips in the housing market. It was a real fixer-upper, but that didn't stop 'em. They were amazing. My parents were teachers at Cambridge Rindge and Latin. Mom taught home ec and Dad taught shop in voc ed. She painted walls, sewed curtains, restored second-hand furniture. Dad handled the rewiring and put in new plumbing. As soon as I was old enough, he put a wrench in my hand and taught me how to use it. Not a day goes by that I don't think of them when I walk through the door."

"I'm impressed." And I was. My father thought you used a hammer to pound screws.

"They aren't there anymore?" I asked.

"No. Packed up and moved to Florida after they retired. I miss them, but they love it there. Mom tutors special needs kids. Dad's always working on some project or other to improve their condo. We call each other pretty regularly. You know how it is. If my mother doesn't hear from me, I hear from her. The umbilical cord never gets completely cut."

I didn't know how it was. With my parents, like it or not I'd been spared the experience.

Richard wasn't wearing a wedding ring, but that didn't mean anything. I wondered if there was a Mrs. Truitt. If little Truitts were running around the neighborhood.

"So how about you? Do you live in one of the suburbs, or are you a Back Bay kind of girl?"

"I grew up in Newton," I said.

The eyebrow went up again.

"It wasn't like that. My Dad died of a heart attack when I was thirteen. It was a real struggle. But Mom was determined to keep me in Newton schools, said education was my future."

"I like the energy of Cambridge," he said.

"Everyone in that city looks like they've been frozen in adolescence."

He laughed. "You've got a point. But on any given weekend I can find more things to do than I have time for. You ought to give it a chance."

I usually could tell if a man was hitting on me. I wondered if the subtext to this conversation was different from the one I had brought into the room. I left disquieted, and not just because I saw a battle looming over land use.

Chapter 3

I'd squeezed in a seven o'clock breakfast with my friend Barbara. I was usually free early in the morning. Barbara didn't work. Cooperative to a fault, she accommodated my crazy schedule. So that was when we met.

"Let's go to The Four Seasons," she said. "My treat."

"That's not necessary."

Neighbors until we were thirteen, we'd been inseparable even after I had to move and she'd gone to a private middle school. At age sixteen I'd been invited to keep her company when her family went to the Bahamas during spring vacation. At twenty-two I'd allowed her father (of necessity) to pay for my dress when I was maid of honor at her wedding. I could pay my way now, and I was determined to do so.

"Well, whatever," she said. "We can fight over the check when it comes. It'll be good to see you. It's been too long."

If she were trying to induce guilt, she'd succeeded.

Barbara was an only child. She had been born not only with a silver spoon in her mouth, her whole crib glittered. She had been the kind of kid who always did her homework before she went out to play, whereas I had been a tomboy, ready to test late February ice-covered puddles despite previous experience with soaked socks and shoes. Together, we were yin and yang.

We sat in upholstered chairs at a window table. The Four Seasons was one of our favorite venues because the dining room overlooked the Public Garden. Boston was enjoying an early spring. It was only March 4th, but the trees were beginning to bud. Yellow-green weeping willows leaned over the water. It was too early for swan boats to be skimming along the lagoon, but in mid-April, the young crew would begin pumping up their leg muscles as they paddled tourists around the swans' nesting island.

Barbara hadn't even put the pink linen napkin on her lap before she started complaining about her husband. This was something new. She never uttered an unkind word about anybody, least of all Caleb. The two of them were in that ten percent of couples who belonged together without qualification. I wondered if post-menopausal hormones were disturbing her equilibrium.

"After I got pregnant and gave up my career, we agreed on a division of labor," she said. "I take care of the domestic side, he's the provider. It's worked. At least it used to."

"Not anymore?"

Barbara, who was pencil thin, ignored her oatmeal and put a raspberry the color of her fingernails into her mouth. She chewed contemplatively.

"Things have changed."

"That's a predictable part of life. It's always changing."

"So you're a philosopher now?"

"The service is gratis." I was trying, apparently unsuccessfully, to lighten her mood.

"These days Caleb seems so, well, so preoccupied. And Timmy doesn't need me like he used to." She stared out the window. "Sometimes I'm just bored. I wonder if you made the smarter choice. Your life is consequential. You help craft laws, for God's sake. I use *Robert's Rules of Order* for the Garden Club."

Consequential? Lately I'd wondered if I had been deluding myself about how significant it was. How much did it matter if, after several protracted meetings with the head of the Governor's Office of Administration and Finance, I had succeeded in protecting Wilmington Gas and Oil from a quarter percent tax increase in the sale of its petroleum products?

"Now that we're empty-nesters," she said, "well, at least part of the year, I want us to spend more time together. Otherwise what was the point in sacrificing my career?"

This was new. I hadn't heard her use the word "sacrifice" before, though at the time, that's what I'd thought she had done.

In many ways, Barbara was a throw-back to an earlier era. Caleb was a senior level asset manager at a firm that handled funds for old Boston Brahmin families and high net worth individuals. They lived in a huge multi-million dollar Victorian in West Newton. She had all the accoutrements of affluence—household manager, Mercedes SUV, pants suits from St. John, membership in the Country Club passed on from her maternal grandparents. Between her family and her husband, she was set for life.

I'd seen what happened when she had a June wedding, got pregnant in September, and chucked her position as a marketing specialist at a big-name investment firm. She said she wanted to be a stay-at-home mom and give her kid a good start in life. With Caleb's salary she could afford to. After that, all she talked about were the joys of breast-feeding, Timmy's first words, and the latest children's book to receive the Newbery Medal. I adored Timmy, too, but I thought she'd misplaced her brain somewhere back in the financial district. It wasn't pretty.

Nothing was handed to me. I had to work for everything I owned. Yes, I was making a six-figure salary, though nothing close to a half million. Until recently I had a part- time intern (thus, the "Associates"), plus Maura. I'd been able to support the office and pay the mortgage on a million-dollar condo overlooking the Esplanade in the Back Bay. But I knew from experience that it could vanish in an instant. That kept me focused.

"He can afford to ease up now," she said. "He's well established."

"He has a good reputation around town. I've referred a few clients to him."

"At home he either has his nose in a book or in the *Wall Street Journal*. And on weekends, he goes golfing with his buddies."

I picked at my breakfast. I didn't know what to say. Was he having an affair? If Caleb had fallen, all hope was lost. He didn't strike me as the type, though after what I'd seen, I wasn't sure there was a type. Maybe he was having his own mid-life crisis, complete with a bimbo on the side.

I wondered if I was dealing with mid-life angst, as well. My father hadn't made it through middle age. Then my mother, in her 51st year, died of a cerebral aneurism. She went to work with a splitting headache. The next thing her boss knew, she was sprawled out on the floor in a coma. She didn't even make it to the hospital. I'd been absorbed by work, never took the time to know her as a person in her own right, and BAM! She was gone. The memory made my intestines do a fandango.

"I know what you're thinking." She brushed some crumbs off

the table. "Maybe you were right. But I loved being a mother," Barbara said. "Still do."

"And I love being a surrogate auntie."

A waiter refilled our coffee cups.

I told myself that Barbara just needed someplace to ventilate.

"How's Timmy?"

A junior at Yale, it was hard to believe that I would watch him graduate in a year. He was the closest I would come to having a child of my own. I'd witnessed, second-hand, every stage of his development, from two-year-old tantrums to a ten-year-old obsession with comic books to teenage acne. When he was in the midst of adolescent rebellion I thought I had made a lucky escape from the challenges of parenthood, but I loved that kid more fiercely than I ever could have imagined.

She brightened. "Do you want to see the latest pictures?" She fished a pocket album out of her chic black leather purse. "These are from parents' weekend. Right now all his energy's focused on the MCAT. Wants to get into med school at Harvard or U Penn. Just think of it! He's got his whole is life mapped out."

"All the energy you invested is paying off. You're very lucky that way."

Barbara put the pictures back into her purse.

"I know," she said, "I don't have any right to complain."

"If that's what you're feeling, you have every right. At least you can tell me."

She dabbed her lips with her napkin. "Actually, a maiden aunt in Missouri just died and left me a little bundle. I'm not sure what to do with it."

"Such a problem," I said in my best Barbara Streisand accent.

"I'm thinking of putting it into a donor advised fund. Maybe we could name it after my aunt. I'd like Timmy to learn about charitable giving. That would be a way to teach him. Maybe we could make a big gift to Oxfam or Doctors Without Borders or UNICEF."

At twenty-one, he might be more inclined to give to the National Organization for the Reform of Marijuana Laws, but I didn't tell her that. Barbara had a naïve quality that I was reluctant to puncture. It was one of her endearing traits.

"How much did she leave you?"

"About three million dollars."

"Three million!" As my German-born grandmother would say, this was like having *Schlag mit Schlag*. "With that kind of money, you could fund a whole school in Malawi."

What I could do with three million dollars! For starters, invest it, protect my business from more unanticipated disruptions, maybe even find a little chalet in Vermont where I could retreat on weekends. God knows, I had plenty of unstructured weekends.

"You've got a great sense of humor," she said. "It's one of the things I love about you."

"You might want to tuck a bit of it away. I mean, God forbid, what if something dire happens—not that it will, mind you, but we women can never be too careful. You're used to living well. You wouldn't know how to cope with a reversal of fortune."

"You worry too much. But I understand. If I'd had to go through what you went through, I'd feel different, too."

She knew my history. After my father died, mother discovered that he'd borrowed on his insurance policy. His IRA contained a paltry $55,476.10. Not only that, he had taken out a home equity loan to pay for renovations that mother said were essential to make their Victorian the "show place it yearned to be." Also, for gambling debts, though we didn't discover that until after the funeral. He was addicted to high stakes Saturday night poker. Some of the boys were his buddies, but others were more unsavory. It was pay up or else. The pressure must have gotten to him. My gut still quivered when I thought about it.

Net result: we couldn't live in our house anymore. We had to move. We couldn't even afford a post-World War II bungalow in the Oak Hill section of Newton. We had to get an apartment in the Italian working class neighborhood where mother's former cleaning lady lived. And Mother, who never had worked a day in her life, got a job as a clerk in a candy store that specialized in hand carved dark chocolate confections for all occasions—birthdays, religious holidays (Easter was a blow-out), civic celebrations (like when the Celtics won NBA championships). You wouldn't believe what people could come up with.

So there we were, squeezed into a two bedroom apartment with so much oversized furniture I felt like a munchkin in Oz. No more nice clothes. No more celebratory meals at The Ritz. We grocery shopped at the discount food store, looked for yesterday's fresh baked bread, fruits and vegetables beyond their sell-by dates. I was so embarrassed. I envied girls whose fathers let them take horse-back riding lessons at stables in Weston, who went with their mothers to a salon every two weeks to get their toenails done, and who got to go to places like St. Barts for their winter vacations.

Mother did the best she could with the hand she'd been dealt, but self-absorbed teenager that I was, I couldn't see it at the time.

God bless her, Barbara stuck by me. She'd invite me over to play records. We'd listen, over and over, to "If Loving You Is Wrong I Don't Want to Be Right" and "I'll Take You There." The only problem—what she didn't understand—was that I could look out her window straight across the street to my old bedroom. I never did let on how hard that was.

Not long after we'd moved, I remember staring at a pile of

cashmere sweaters that Barbara had tossed on a chair in the corner of her room. My mother had made me give up most of mine. When I came home from school one afternoon, they were gone. She said they were too bulky, and we had to conserve space. I picked up "Alone Again (Naturally)" to put on Barbara's turntable, brushed it against the arm of a chair, and put a huge scratch in the vinyl. The record was ruined. Barbara said I shouldn't worry, she could buy another. I apologized profusely, but was it an accident? I vowed that when I grew up I never would live the way Mother and I had been forced to. And I'd made sure I hadn't.

Barbara freshened her lipstick.

A woman was walking by our window at a fast clip, leaning into the wind, one hand holding her briefcase, the other tucked in her coat pocket, collar turned up against her neck. She looked like she was on a Nordic Track. I checked my watch. It was nearly eight o'clock. I had to get to the office for a conference call.

"I've got to go soon. I have an 8:30."

"That's all right. I understand."

"Look, you've been out of the job market since Timmy was born. I know it would be hard to pick up and slot right back in, but maybe you should put out some feelers. Offer your marketing talents to one of those non-profits your family supports. It might give you the kind of lift you need right now. Caleb might even like the new you."

She startled.

"Not that he doesn't like you as you are. I'm just saying. Think about it, will you?"

"I will. I promise."

But I knew she wouldn't.

"Here I've been rattling on but we haven't talked about you," she said. "Are you OK? What are you up to?"

"Same old same old."

"That doesn't sound very stimulating."

I finished my shirred eggs. She pushed her cold oatmeal, practically untouched, toward the side of the table.

"Thanks to a big corporate merger I've lost one client but I've taken on another. He's outside my ordinary business-types. That should prove interesting—not, I hope, too interesting."

"Come on, Claire. How about the rest of your life?"

"You know me. Work is my life."

"I'm going to keep after you."

"Just don't try to invite me over to dinner with one of Caleb's newly divorced office buddies. All they know how to talk about is the latest meeting of the Federal Reserve and how it's going to impact the market. It's too much like work."

"He was a decent guy. Don't knock me for trying."

"Oh, Barbara, what would I do without you?"

I finished drinking the last few sips of coffee and dabbed my lips with my napkin. Our waiter arrived with the bill and I whipped out my platinum American Express card before she had a chance. We hugged, air kissed on both cheeks, agreed to get together again before too long, and I grabbed a cab to the office.

Nothing really bad had ever happened to her. She couldn't conceive what it would be like if it did. A thin wedge of envy edged into my heart.

Chapter 4

I needed to go to the State House for a hearing. It was raining, a steady mid-March shower that promised magnolia and dogwood blossoms all along Beacon Street. When I opened the closet door to get my umbrella, Uncle Erich's box was in the way. I pushed it aside with my foot, vowed I would deal with it on the weekend, and dashed out of the office.

The State House guards saw me so often we were on a first name basis.

"How's that new baby, Curtis?" I asked as I put my purse, briefcase, coat and dripping umbrella on the scanner belt. "Are you getting any sleep?"

"Not much, Claire. Hey, thanks for the card you sent. You wanna see a picture?" He pulled a photo of a wrinkly newborn out of his wallet. "My mom took it when we got home from the hospital." His grin encompassed his whole face.

"What a handsome fellow. He's got your eyes."

Any maternal impulses I had were directed toward Timmy. I doubted that I could have juggled the demands of work and family, though unlike Barbara, I'd never been faced with the choice.

I grabbed my stuff and headed down the stairs to Gardner Auditorium. Located in the basement of the old building, the walls were a drab green. The place needed a coat of paint.

Richard was standing outside the hearing room. I hadn't seen him since our conversation at Sal's diner. He had the same tousled hair. It was even more unruly—the kind of hair a woman wants to run through her fingers.

I'd made discrete inquiries. He had been married, no children. He was too young to be a widower, but there it was.

"Hey Claire, what brings you here?"

"Remember I told you I was thinking about taking on a new client? Well, I did."

"Are you going to tell me who it is?"

"Sure. Piper Mangan."

"Come on. The golf course guru? Isn't he outside your normal client base?"

"Everybody's entitled to a bite of the apple."

"He tends to go after the whole barrel and squeeze cider out of the remains."

I looked around to see if anyone else was listening. "Surely you exaggerate." I shifted my briefcase from one hand to the other and hiked my oversized purse onto my shoulder.

"Not by much. Do you know what kind of a reputation he has around here?"

"He's a developer."

"But not just anyone has to represent him. Not you."

I wondered what that said about my status on the Hill. I

thought of myself as being tough, straight-forward, clean, but not a purist. I liked to win.

I lowered my voice as I pulled open the door to the hearing room. "Well, we're not interested in any particular bills before the committee right now. I thought I'd stop in, show my face, scope out the scene. See you around."

He walked in after me, took the stairs to the balcony, found a seat toward the back, and nodded at Senator Fitzgerald who had arrived late and was inching behind colleagues to take her place at the end of the dais. The auditorium smelled of damp umbrellas and stale cigarette smoke.

I walked across the back of the room and stood in a far corner. A representative from Western Massachusetts, seated on a table in front of the committee chairman, was testifying about legislation he had filed to protect farm viability—a key issue in his district. As an example, he cited a co-operative of dairy farmers who prided themselves on producing hormone-free milk. "The cows are practically part of the family," he said. "They get breakfast before the farmers do." This produced a mild chuckle from Rep. Whately.

That probably was why Richard was in the room. Most legislative business of consequence would take place out of sight, but in Massachusetts, every one of the thousands of bills filed each biennial session was entitled to a hearing by a joint committee of senators and representatives. Richard was savvy. He wouldn't testify, but Representative Whately and Senator Fitzgerald would note his presence. Sometimes when you'd been around for a while, visibility was enough to send signals later clarified *sotto voce*.

One senator and four representatives from the committee were at the hearing. The rest had absented themselves for "urgent business." Senator Fitzgerald was from Holyoke. She was paying attention since legislators from the western part of the state were outnumbered by the heavily populated areas east of Route 495. They knew if they wanted to get anything for their districts, they needed to stick together. Representative Whately paid attention, at least most of the time, because he was chairing the hearing. The other three, respectively, were checking an iPhone, conferring with a legislative aide, and fighting sleep. It was a typical morning.

I decided if these hearings needed to be monitored, I'd send Maura. I had no intention of spending hours listening to stories about broods of bovines.

A young woman in one of the plush theater style seats in the auditorium was taking notes. I sat down behind her. With her well-scrubbed face, neatly trimmed hair, suit jacket and skirt just above her pink knees, she looked fresh out of college. She reminded me of myself when I was her age.

I'd worked my ass off in high school, got a full tuition scholarship to U Mass Amherst, had three jobs while I was there, two in the summer. That barely paid for books, room and board. My last summer job—my ticket up and out--was as an intern researcher in the office of state representative Jeremiah Dunleavy, recently installed as the new Speaker of the House of the Massachusetts General Court. He'd known Daddy. They'd played poker together. He had bumped into Mother one day when he was picking up a chocolate confection in the shape of the State House with its golden dome (yellow-tinted white chocolate for the latter), and as fast as you could wield a gavel, Mother, in her typical "don't ask questions, just do it" manner, told me I had a summer job. I was too inexperienced to think about the implications, I just needed the work.

It didn't take long before I realized that could be my ticket out of penury. I would become a lobbyist. But not just any old lobbyist. I would create a boutique firm handling industries that paid well to outsource concerns they didn't want to handle in-house. I'd always been good at math, so I would become the expert on corporate tax policies, especially ones affecting utilities. A lot of money was sloshing around there.

My first job, thanks to Speaker Dunleavy's impressive contacts, was working as an assistant to Big Tom Callahan. He was a legend in the business. He knew every legislator in the State House. Not just their names. He knew the names of their wives, their children, *and* their mistresses. And if they didn't have wives, he knew their girlfriends. Boyfriends, if you prefer. As the saying goes, he knew where the bodies were buried. And he didn't mind unearthing them from time to time if need arose in order to get what he—no, what his clients—wanted. That's how the game was played.

My job was to trail around with him in a short skirt, show a little leg, distract male legislators (despite the feminist revolution, it worked), and make them think about the benefits of voting for something like House Bill No. 2367, "a bill to lessen the harmful tax burden on community banks." I didn't have to "put out," as Big Tom indelicately phrased it. The Speaker would not be pleased.

What I did do was write up summary fact sheets with talking points in bold so busy legislators didn't have to strain their eyeballs reading a fifty-five page bill, and provide a list of reasons why it would benefit their constituents. We somehow forgot to mention how the bill would also help our clients.

Twelve years later I graduated from Big Tom's tutelage and started my own firm, "Petersen and Associates." At first there was only Maura, but I liked the sound of it. Later I'd added a couple of interns. And I had dreams, big dreams. One day I'd be the most successful lobbying firm in Boston, a pioneering woman in a man's world, the go-to girl if you wanted to close a deal at the State House.

The representative had finished testifying. After the ritual courtesies ("Thank you, Representative Whately and members of the Committee for taking me out of turn." "Thank you, representative, for your testimony," etc. etc.), Representative Whately looked toward the back of the room where five people stood in line, waiting. "Are you here to testify on the farm bill?" he asked. Two people nodded. "All right, why don't you both come down in front and we'll hear you next before we move on to House Bill 8359."

Spending more time at the hearing was a waste. As I walked toward the exit, Richard smiled and waved from the gallery. I pulled the straps of my bag over my shoulder, nodded in his direction, and hurried out the door. As long as I was handling Piper Mangan's account, I'd need to do a delicate dance where Richard Truitt was concerned—both feet on the floor, the illusion of connection, no touching.

Chapter 5

By the time I got back to the office it was 5:30. Maura had gone home where, at last report, her mother still was putting dinner on the table by 6:00 sharp, which they consumed while watching the evening news on Channel Five.

I kicked off my shoes and eased into the oversized chair behind my desk. I'd had that chair for ten years. I loved the feeling of the smooth soft leather against my skin, but I kept shifting my rear against the seat in search of better back support. Maybe it was time for a new one. On the other hand, if we couldn't afford a new copier, I certainly wasn't going to spend money on a new chair. Perhaps if I brought a pillow from home—my decorator had insisted on scattering them around "to add character," it would solve my back problem.

Maura had put a copy of last month's accounts payable and receivable on my desk. I wanted to see if I could wring any more savings from our fixed costs. I ran my finger across the columns for a year-to year comparison of expenditures. Our expenses had increased an average of three percent for each of the past five years. Utility costs had gone up the most, ironic since they were my primary clients. In one hand, out the other. I knew they were making gobs of money thanks to my diligent efforts to avoid business tax increases. If their income was going up, maybe I should increase my fees, though they already were at the high end for local lobbyists. No leeway there. One of our smaller clients was four months behind. I'd ask Maura to get on them.

I rarely drank liquor, but I kept a small stash in the office. That evening I poured a thimble of Maker's Mark into a Waterford tumbler, added a couple of ice cubes from the office fridge, swirled the caramel brown mix with my finger, and sipped. The sharp taste burned my throat and warmed my chest.

The place was quiet—no beeping phones, no fingers tapping on a computer keyboard, no muffled voice from the outer office. I kept thinking about Richard's comment. "But not just anyone has to represent him. Not you."

Why did he care? Did it matter?

Uncle Erich's box was in the closet. It emitted a low hum from somewhere under the coats and umbrellas, or maybe the sound was from a water cooler in the outer office. I hauled it next to my chair. A letter was taped to the top. I couldn't remember ever having received a letter from him, let alone a box. Only greeting cards.

My grandfather had died during the Depression when the two boys were still in school. When Uncle Erich came home from Germany after the war, he'd had some kind of breakdown. He lived with my grandmother and paid rent to help with expenses. Together they hobbled along. When Grandma died, she left both the house and its meager contents to Uncle Erich. If Grandma had had any money, mother and I could have used it. But she didn't.

Daddy hated that house, said it brought back too many memories. When I asked, he said "That's all in the past, chickadee." End of story.

How much had my mother told Grandma and Uncle Erich about our situation? She could have said "Do you know what that S.O.B. did to us?" But that wasn't in Mother's character. She brooded in silence. I'm not sure they would have understood anyway.

"Dear Claire," Uncle Erich had written in flowing, cursive script. "I was cleaning out my attic and I found an old sewing tin with stuff belonging to your Grandma. It's probably been there since she passed away. I'd forgotten all about it. With my bum knees, I don't go climbing up there very often, but I'm getting on in years, and my doctor says I need to move into a retirement facility before my arthritis gets any worse. So I've sold the old house."

It couldn't be worth very much. I wondered how he could afford the move.

"I don't need any of it," he wrote. "I thought you might like to have some of her things. Grandma always had a tender spot for you. She kept your picture right by her bed."

I must have been around seven when that picture was taken. My parents and I were heading for vacation on Cape Cod. They had argued as we crossed the Bourne Bridge. My father used language I'd never heard before. Mother cried. I huddled in the corner of the back seat. Later that night, when Daddy was tucking me into bed, I asked if they were going to get a divorce. Daddy laughed, rumpled my curls, told me not to worry, that adults got mad at each other once in a while and needed to let off steam.

In retrospect, Mother and Daddy never seemed like a couple. I related to each of them, but not both of them as a unit. They were in a contest with each other and I was the prize.

"I'm sending it to you along with a few other things. Use whatever you can. I hope you're well and that your life is good. Love, Uncle Erich."

He didn't say "Write to me," or "Why haven't you stayed in touch?" or "Can you send me some money?"

Uncle Erich was my only living relative. I should at least get his forwarding address.

A knitted comforter in pastel pinks, greens, and yellows was on the top of the box. Underneath, encased in freezer bags, were five handkerchiefs and a set of pillowcases, all with crocheted edges in delicate patterns. Tucked in one corner, wrapped in tissue, was a cheap Chinese paperweight. Grandma used to keep it on a little table in her living room. When I was a child, I liked to see how the light from a nearby window streamed through the tiny multi-colored glass flowers and made a rainbow on an adjacent wall.

I put it on my office desk, positioned it so it would catch the morning sunlight, finished the bourbon, and called a cab. I'd haul the box home and deal with the rest of the contents later.

I didn't sleep well. My satin sheets looked like they'd been through the rapid spin cycle. Eventually I surrendered and got out of bed. It would be another half hour before the *New York Times*, the *Wall Street Journal*, and the *Boston Globe* were delivered, so I decided to go jogging. I was determined to stay fit. I didn't want to drop dead prematurely. Too much of that had happened in my family. I put on gray sweats and new lightweight running shoes and headed for the door.

The concierge hadn't yet come off the night shift.

"Watch your step out there, Ms. Petersen," he said. "It rained hard last night. Could be slippy."

"Don't worry, George. I won't take any chances."

Enough people were out, even early on a Saturday morning, so I felt safe. The paved trail bordered the Esplanade. I had a favorite route, just three miles along the Charles River—one and a half down, then back the same way. Most of the time I could do it in thirty-five minutes or less. I had no ambitions to run the Boston Marathon.

I kept thinking about Grandma as I jogged along. What would it be like to abandon everything you knew and come to a country where you didn't even speak the language? Could I have done it?

When I came home from sixth grade with an assignment to write a story about my grandparents, Daddy had put me off. He seemed embarrassed by the circumstances in which he'd grown up. He mocked his mother's fractured English. He criticized his brother, "a momma's boy who was afraid to leave the nest." A year later, Daddy was dead.

After that, mother and I were so preoccupied we rarely saw them. I was getting ready to leave Big Tom Callahan and branch out on my own when Mother called to tell me that Grandma had died. I never made it to her funeral. I called my travel agent to explore non-stop flights to Cleveland, but I was scheduled to sign a lease on a modest two room office. I'd awakened at 2:30 for seven nights straight, worried about the financial obligations I was assuming. In the end, I stayed in Boston and Mother represented the family—what was left of it.

I should have gone.

I wasn't paying attention to the wet surface of the pavement. One minute I was jogging, the next I was on my ass. I landed in a puddle. Cold water soaked through my terry sweatpants. Another runner came up behind me and stopped.

"Claire! Are you all right?"

It was Richard. He looked down at me sprawled on the path, rubbing my right ankle.

"I think so." My ankle felt like it had been jolted with a cattle prod.

He squatted beside me. "Want me to take a look?"

"No thanks. I'm just a bit discombobulated."

"You look a little pale."

I remembered. I hadn't put on any lipstick.

"I'm all right. Really. I have weak ankles. Sometimes one turns on me if I hit some uneven pavement. I'll be OK if I sit for a minute. I don't think anything's broken. Maybe bruised." I tried a laugh. "Like my pride. The concierge warned me that it might be slippery. Do you think I listened?"

"It could happen to anyone."

I continued to massage my ankle. "What are you doing here? And so early?"

"I could ask you the same thing."

"I had trouble sleeping," I said. "Thought if I came out it would clear my head."

"Plotting some new legislative strategy?" He put out his hand. "Here, let me help. Get you out of the wet. Rest a few minutes."

I winced as he pulled me up. I hobbled to a nearby bench. He took off his windbreaker, placed it on the seat, and motioned me to sit on it.

"I can't sit on your nice jacket."

"Don't worry about it. I can throw it in the wash and it'll be good as new. Everything's still damp from last night's rain."

"Tell me about it." My tush was wet as a baby's diaper.

He sat beside me, pulled a handkerchief out of a pocket, and wiped his forehead. I caught a pungent whiff of masculine sweat.

"Are you a runner?" I asked.

"I started about five years ago. My doctor suggested it as a good way to relieve stress when my wife got sick."

I turned to face him with what I hoped was a "You can tell me about it if you want to" look.

"Did it help?"

"Not really."

I adjusted my throbbing ankle and waited. Tires squealed on the wet pavement as cars exited Storrow Drive and rounded the sharp bend toward Beacon Street.

"She had breast cancer. She died on November 12th, 2004." His upper body shook slightly. I doubted that the shudder was from the temperature of the air.

"I'm so sorry. Had she been sick for very long?"

He took a deep breath. "She was diagnosed in 2002. They thought they'd got it. We were so hopeful. But a few months later, symptoms began to recur. From then on, she went downhill steadily."

I noted his use of "we." "You must have loved her very much."

"I still think I'm going to walk in the door at the end of the afternoon and see her sitting at the kitchen table grading papers." He looked away.

I didn't know what to say.

"For months afterwards," he said, "regardless of the weather, everything looked gray. Thank God that's changed."

The MIT dome on the other side of the river was obscured by a diffuse cloud of mist. A couple of joggers, a middle-aged man and woman, passed us, running side by side. I shifted my position to relieve the pressure on my right side, and my hip touched Richard's. I moved back.

"Now I run most Saturday mornings," he said. "It gives me energy. I take Memorial Drive, cross over to Boston at the Mass

Ave. Bridge, go to the Hatch Shell, reverse course and head back to Cambridge."

He leaned forward, resting his elbows on his thighs. His hands hung loosely between his knees. "I didn't know you were a runner."

"I'm not, really," I said. "I go jogging occasionally, weekends mostly, but I'm not very consistent. And as you can see from this episode, I'm not very accomplished, either."

"We had a soaking rain last night. The leaves are treacherous. I almost slipped myself." He looked at me. "You're shivering. Look, I've got time if you want me to walk you back to your place."

"That's very nice of you, but seriously, I'll be OK. Go ahead. Finish your run."

"You're sure?"

"I'll be all right in a minute or two. Really, I'm more embarrassed than anything. If I take it easy, I should be able to make it without a problem. I don't want to keep you."

"Nonsense. It's no problem. Even if your ankle is only mildly sprained, you shouldn't put much weight on it. Do you live far from here? I could get you a cab."

"Just a couple blocks. I'm over on Beacon Street."

"Well when you're ready, I'll either call a cab or escort you home. I won't take no for an answer."

I didn't like men bossing me around, so that was enough to make me want to get up and leave immediately, but I was hurting more than I would admit.

A group of sailboats were docked in a row not far from where we sat. The rigging clanged against the aluminum masts as they rocked back and forth in the wind. Richard told me he had learned how to sail in the community boating program. He'd signed up for the $99 trial period, loved it, and every year since had gotten a full membership. He made it sound appealing. He asked if I'd ever been out. I said I hadn't had the time or the inclination. My nervous stomach would have been tested by the waves.

Fifteen minutes later I limped back to my condo, Richard walking beside me. He had found a sturdy stick about the right height, peeled twigs and leaves off the sides, and improvised a cane to take some weight off my ankle. It had quieted to a dull ache.

"This is where I live," I said.

"Nice digs."

"It's convenient for work."

"If that ankle doesn't feel better by this afternoon, you should get it checked out. You need to be in top form. We can't have you limping up and down the State House steps."

"I will."

"Promise?"

"Promise."

Eager to disengage, I put out my hand. "Thanks so much. It was a piece of luck, you running by when you did."

His handshake was firm, the palms calloused.

"Glad I could help. Take good care."

Before he rounded a corner toward the river, he turned and waved.

I clung to the railing as I inched down four steps to the automatic glass door. George wasn't at the front desk. I was relieved. I didn't want him hovering over me after I'd ignored his warning. I made my way to the elevator. When I got to my condo I limped into the kitchen, pulled a bag of peas out of the freezer, and applied them to my sore ankle.

I smelled of sweat. I couldn't tell if it was mine or Richard's. I thought about tossing the stick into my fireplace. Instead, I stuck it in an umbrella stand.

Chapter 6

The peas worked—that, a dose of aspirin and a good strong cup of coffee. I sat on the living room sofa with my leg elevated while I looked at the morning papers. I re-read one paragraph about "contented singles" four times. Whether he'd intended to or not, Richard had maneuvered his way into my psyche, and I was anything but contented.

After a passing attempt to fill out the Saturday crossword puzzle, I declared an end to my rehabilitation. The ankle was tender but serviceable. I needed to do something.

The box was sitting in the hall entryway. I pushed it into the living room, put it on the coffee table, and opened the flaps. The contents smelled of petroleum and old newspapers. After Uncle Erich had had Grandma's furnace converted from coal, the house took on a distinctive odor. Every February I received two birthday cards, one from Grandma, the other from Uncle Erich, each containing a dollar with that unique scent.

Some embroidered goods slipped out of clear plastic bags, followed by a baptismal gown, the white aged to cream, the sleeve pointing toward me. Grandma had saved it over all those years, and for what? No marriage, at least none that stuck. No family. I was a darned good lobbyist. I used to think it was enough. Was it?

The rest of the contents were pathetic—a ratty wooden Christmas tree ornament with peeling paint, "made in Germany" stamped on the base; an ersatz silver coffee set; two German books with pictures of mothers and infants (what was I supposed to do with those?); and a few postcards of bucolic German countryside and a palatial buildings, some with writing on the back in indecipherable German script.

I'd studied Spanish in high school, ignored languages in college. Barbara had encouraged me to learn Italian and reward myself with a vacation in Rome and Florence, but I had never followed through. Instead I'd built my client base. The only German words I knew were filtered through Grandma's fractured English. She called me her *kleine liebe*.

The last object in the box was wrapped in copies of the *Oretown Sentinal* and secured by masking tape. My fingers were covered in black ink by the time I undid the layers. Inside was Grandma's rose pink candy dish. Made of cheap molded glass, it was imprinted with nondescript flowers. Grandma had kept it filled with white peppermints. I used to try to sneak some, but I couldn't lift the lid without a tell-tale clinking sound that evoked a prompt appearance from my mother. "Sugar's bad for your teeth," she'd say as she snatched the pieces from my hand. If Uncle Erich overheard, he'd put a finger to his lips, motion me to the front porch, and slip one into my hand.

I lifted the lid. Candy dust had left a faint peppermint smell.

I tossed the postcards on my desk. The books went on the bottom shelf of a bookcase. I put the rest in an empty plastic bin that used to store sweaters recently donated to The Salvation Army.

The candy dish, however, felt like a living object. I rubbed my fingers across the design. The glass warmed to my touch. I decided to fill it with peppermints so its purpose could be reclaimed.

The bag of frozen peas lay melting on the rug. I threw them into the garbage. That fall had rattled my brain as well as my ankle.

Thank you notes are almost a lost art. Mine were hand written on fine blue edged Crane and Co. stationary. People noticed. They remembered. And that often proved useful.

So it was out of habit that I started to write Uncle Erich on Saturday evening. I sat at my bedroom desk and leafed through the old but undated postcards. One was of an imposing three story residence. A small independent structure—a gate house?—was on the right. A tower, taller than the rest, was attached on the left--perhaps a later appendage to the main building? The house reminded me of a refrain from one of Grimm's fairy tales: "Rapunzel, Rapunzel, let down your hair."

I picked up my pen, put it down, picked it up again.

Dear Uncle Erich,

It was thoughtful of you to take the time to send me some of Grandma's things, especially since you must be very busy as you prepare to move to a retirement community.

I chewed on a ragged nail.

Before writing this, I was looking through the postcards. They made me realize how little I know about Grandma's history. Maybe sometime after you get settled in your new place,

I almost wrote, *I can fly to Ohio and you can tell me more.* Instead I said

I will call you and we can have a good talk. Will you send me your new address and phone number?

I especially liked the pink candy dish. Do you remember how I tried to sneak peppermints from it when I was a kid?

Take good care of yourself. I hope you are content in your new surroundings.

Love, Claire

I poked around my desk to find a stamped postcard I could enclose, wrote my home address on it, included my phone number on the back, and put the note in my briefcase.

On Monday morning I posted it in a mailbox on my way to work.

Chapter 7

Maura and I had an agreement. Whoever got there first made the coffee. When I arrived, Maura was sitting at her desk, picking up messages from the answering machine. A sweet sharp smell was in the air.

"Is that a new blend? It makes you stand up and take notice."

"It's from a deli in the North End. They were having a special. I thought we should try it." She pushed the pause button. "How's your ankle?"

I stopped in mid-pour. "How did you hear about that?"

"The first message on the machine was from Richard Truitt." She handed me a pink slip. "He wanted to know if your ankle was better. What did you do to it?" She grinned. "And how did he know about it?"

I outlined the embarrassing story.

"Lucky he came along."

"I could have made it back by myself," I said as I escaped into my office and hung up my coat. "I just needed a few minutes to recover."

"Well, it was nice, anyway," she said, projecting her voice. "Are you going to call him back?"

"I've got a lot to do this morning."

Maura swiveled around in her chair, folded her arms, and looked at me over her glasses through the open door. "Not enough to keep you from returning that phone call. Look, we've worked together a long time. From what I've seen, you've had no life beyond this office for ages. It's time you get one."

I set the mug down with force. Coffee slopped over the rim and onto my desk blotter, which was beginning to resemble an abstract painting.

Maura knew about Mr. Public Charities. She'd seen me ashen faced when I discovered his duplicity. I prided myself on being a skeptic in all my political dealings. Why I'd suspended caution with him continued to baffle me. In retrospect, I probably wasn't the first to be seduced. He was a real charmer.

For three solid weeks after that debacle, first thing in the morning Maura presented me with a fresh mug of strong coffee, cream, one sweetener, just like I liked it. Didn't say anything, just brought the coffee and put it in front of me on my desk along with the morning papers.

Now Mr. Public Charities was trying to propel that charm into a new electoral office. The previous September, when his boss said she was retiring after an illustrious career as attorney general, he announced that he was going to run for the spot. I shouldn't have been surprised. He deserved an award for his creative use of news releases. No matter was too trivial to be memorialized. When I saw the public relations roll out—big family man, pictures of the perfectly coiffed wife and two handsome children—I shuddered.

"Richard is younger than I am," I said.

"All the more reason to call him back."

"Your imagination is working overtime. He probably wants to tell me some disparaging tale about Piper Mangan."

"Didn't sound like it to me."

I was curious, but I wouldn't give her the satisfaction of saying so.

"Give him a chance" she said. "You've been out of circulation for too long, if you ever really were in it."

I flinched, but she was right. "Maura, that's going too far." I could have said that the same was true for her, but that would have been petty. At least she had a mother at home, even if she had become somewhat burdensome.

"I'm only saying you should give it a chance."

"You sound like an advertisement for the Middle East peace process."

"I intend to keep after you."

"OK. I'll call.

"Good. That's a start."

And with that, I closed my office door.

Was Richard trying to seduce me or defuse me? He didn't seem manipulative, but I'd made that mistake before. Mr. Public Charities had a PhD in manipulation, and I was still in junior high.

I started scrolling through a hundred emails, deleting the irrelevant ones. Thoughtful responses eluded me. What would Piper Mangan think if he knew I was consorting with the enemy—and not just figuratively? Yet I had to admit I was intrigued. Most men backed off when I had on my authoritative game face. Richard just brushed right through it.

I decided to return Richard's call and get it out of the way.

Then I'd be productive again.

"Thanks for checking up on me, Richard. Maura said you'd called."

"I tried over the weekend but your number's unlisted."

"Sorry about that."

"So how's your ankle?"

I reached down and massaged it.

"It's fine, thanks. I used a cold pack and elevated it." I envisioned the sodden bag of peas lying on my carpet. "It was a bit sore on Sunday, but I walked to work this morning and it seemed to be OK."

I had moved more slowly than usual, but I wasn't about to tell him that.

"Glad to hear it." He paused. Did I sense hesitation? "Say, I was thinking, would you like to get together for supper some evening? Do you like Thai food? There's a great little Thai restaurant not far from Harvard Square."

So Maura was right. Now what should I do?

"I don't know much about it." Oops. That sounded so provincial.

"Well, you could let me introduce you to some of my favorites. It's not a very big place and it's kind of funky, but it's fun."

Not the Four Seasons. Brown paper napkins in a chrome dispenser. Unlike Mr. Public Charities, Richard apparently eschewed the high life.

"Sounds interesting."

"So what would work for you? Except for Wednesday, my evenings are free all week."

"Let me look at my calendar."

I opened the desk drawer, pushed some pens out of the way, found the calendar. I could hear Richard breathing through the receiver.

"I still use paper calendars. I think they're faster than iPhones."

"I know what you mean."

After five o'clock, white space was on every page. "How about Thursday?" Friday sounded too much like a date. Tuesday sounded too eager.

"Thursday's great. What time works for you?"

"6:30?"

We agreed to meet at the restaurant. He offered to send me directions.

Immediately after the light on the phone went out, Maura walked in, glasses on a chain around her neck bouncing against her ample bosom. If she were trying to live vicariously through me, thus far, she'd been disappointed. Or maybe forewarned.

"So," she said, "do you have a date?"

"I thought these rooms were soundproofed. Did you have your ear on the door?"

"Well, do you?"

"I guess so. It looks that way."

"Good work."

"I didn't do anything."

"You must have done something. Keep an open mind about this."

"I'm not sure I want to complicate my life, and after getting burned like I have, it pays to be cautious." I leaned back in my chair. "Look, I'm out of practice, though I've got to admit, he's intriguing."

"Don't cautious yourself out of an opportunity." She said. "What's his marital status?"

"I checked. He's a widower, apparently unattached."

"That's a step in the right direction."

"And he knows how to fix a leaky faucet. At least that's what he says."

"On a scale of one to ten, he just passed six."

Maura handed me the rest of the messages and strolled out the door.

Why had I suggested Thursday? It was only Monday. I'd have most of the week to obsess about what I was letting myself in for.

Chapter 8

I intended to leave the office early so I could shower and change into something less professional, but Piper Mangan called at 4:45. The conversation did not go well.

"Thought I'd call my gal and see what kind of progress she's making in getting our bills sidelined."

I was so used to the "my gal" language from old pols that, even though it rankled, I didn't make an issue of it. Women were considered fair game in that testosterone laden environment. I took a stand on egregious offences—a head tilting too close to cleavage, wandering hands. First offence: a stern rebuke. Second offence: a hard jab to the forearm. Thus far I hadn't had to descend to more strategic locations.

"I've met with Representative Whately's chief of staff several times to explore options." I didn't tell him that one was a chance encounter at the State House coffee shop, where all conversations were guarded lest they become fodder for political rivals.

"Good, good. So can I start sleeping at night again?"

I wondered if there was a Mrs. Mangan. He'd probably been married to the same woman for forty years, had five grown kids, all teed up to inherit the golf course business.

"Look, Mr. Mangan, I was just about to head out the door to a meeting on your issue. It's complicated, but I see a promising way forward. Can I call you tomorrow morning?"

"I know it's complicated. That's why I'm paying you the big bucks—to un-complicate it." He breezed right by "just about to head out the door."

"Let me give you the broadest outline of a potential way through your situation." My foot tapped out a drumbeat on the carpet.

"*Our* situation, Claire. *Our* situation. As long as we're working together on this, it's *our* situation." The "ours" rumbled around in the back of his throat. He must be a smoker.

"Sorry about that, Mr. Mangan." The speed of the drumbeat escalated. "Of course it's our situation. I was just distracted because I'll be late for my meeting—about *our* situation."

"OK, so give me the short version."

"Here's the bottom line. The state is facing a budget deficit."

"I know, I know. I saw the head of Administration and Finance at a fundraiser the other night, and he was grumbling about it."

"That offers a potential path out of our dilemma. The conservation land purchase that's getting in your way would require an outlay of public funds when both chairs of Ways and Means, as well as the Governor, are looking at every line item to reduce the deficit." In the midst of campaign mania, they had been foolhardy enough to pledge they wouldn't raise taxes. That was a relief to my corporate clients, a problem for the social services sector. Now the commitment was hanging around their necks like a noose ready to snap.

"If it comes down to helping the environmentalists buy land versus helping developmentally disabled children," I said, "the kids will win."

"So they should, Claire. So they should."

Mangan didn't care about disabled kids any more than chocolatiers cared about obesity in children, but I wasn't about to tell him that. I looked at my watch. If I caught a cab, maybe I still would have time to go home, change, and make Cambridge on time, but it would be close.

"So the governor's budget woes could turn out to be our salvation. This is only a preliminary assessment. Don't hold me to it. I need to have some more exploratory conversations." I looked at my watch. "And now, Mr. Mangan, I really do have to go. I'll call you tomorrow and we can discuss this further, OK?"

"Right. You're my gal." He disengaged. Telephone etiquette was not in his arsenal.

My stomach was in knots. I called Richard.

"I'm so sorry. I might be running a bit late. I just have to stop off at home for a few minutes, then I'll grab a cab and be right over."

"Thanks for the heads up. Don't rush. We don't want you slipping on any more wet leaves."

"That was a one-off. I'm not usually so clumsy."

"I'm sure you're not. Take your time. I'll find us a quiet spot near the window."

"Sounds good."

Did it really? Here I was thinking about what I was going to wear on our first date, if that's what it should be called. Was I heading for another Mr. Public Charities fiasco, with an exploding crescendo followed by a churning denouement?

"You've got the address, right? For the Bangkok Gardens on Mass Ave?"

"I'm all set. See you soon. And thanks."

I threw three different outfits on the bed. One—my ESCADA casual—was way too elegant for a Thai restaurant in Cambridge. Another, my loose Saturday outfit, wasn't distinctive enough. Finally I decided on tailored light brown Italian wool slacks, a simple cream silk blouse with a soft neckline, and a dark brown cashmere sweater in case the restaurant was chilly. A simple strand of Mikimoto pearls and matching earrings completed the ensemble. I felt good in it, and as relaxed as I was going to get.

It was an atypically humid evening in early spring. I was already sweating as I walked out the door of my condo. The first six cabs that barreled up Beacon Street were occupied. When one finally pulled up I told the cabbie if he got me to Porter Square in fifteen minutes he'd receive an extra ten bucks on top of a twenty percent tip. The cab hurtled around the corner.

I checked my make-up in a compact. I hoped the mint green eye shadow was subtle. I'd chosen it to pick up the green flecks in my brown eyes. Other than that, lipstick—an orangey pink to complement my dark brown hair—and a dab of subtle perfume was all that was necessary. I'd never been a sun worshipper, so even at age forty-nine my skin was flawless. Neck and chin, not perfect but passable. I wasn't ready for camouflaging scarves yet.

When I walked in the door of the restaurant, one look at Richard let me know that he approved. He stood up and pulled out my chair.

"Sorry I've kept you waiting. I was on the phone with a client. You know how that is."

I placed my Coach purse under the table on the side by the

window wall to protect it from an easy grab and run. Despite the outdoor humidity, my hands felt cold. I was glad I'd brought my sweater.

"Have you tried the interrupted phone call technique?"

"What's that?"

"As you're talking, you gently press down on the disconnect button, as if through no fault of your own some untoward electrical malfunction broke the connection."

"With what my clients pay, they would expect my phones to work."

He leaned back in his chair and chuckled.

"Actually, I was hoping we could avoid shop talk this evening."

"Good idea." I didn't want Mangan leering over the proceedings.

"I told you a bit about my background. I'd like to get to know the non-working Claire Petersen."

I wasn't sure there *was* one. Maybe if I encouraged him to talk, he wouldn't notice. That technique usually worked with men.

A young waitress appeared and filled our glasses with water. A couple of ice cubes sloshed over the side. Richard picked one up and chewed on it—something that would not have been done at The Four Seasons. The paper napkin I put on my lap barely covered one knee. The waitress gave each of us a menu and said she would be back to take our order. A plastic tag on her apron said her name was "May." Richard spoke to her in a language with an oriental lilt. She beamed as she walked away.

"What was that?"

"Thai. I served in the Peace Corps after I graduated from Northeastern. Taught English as a second language, helped in community development. I'm pretty rusty after all these years, but I remember the basics. If you tried to engage me in a serious conversation, though, I'd be lost."

When he was in Thailand, I already was working for Big Tom Callahan, inching my way up the greasy pole.

"Sounds impressive to me. At least you'll be able to guide me through the menu." It was written in Thai and in English, but that didn't help.

"Why don't I order for you. We can get several dishes, share, and you can see what you like. Is there anything you can't eat? Allergies to shellfish, peanuts, that sort of thing?"

"No allergies. Yes, that would be nice. And I love peanuts— probably harkens back to those peanut butter cookies my grandmother used to make."

May reappeared and he rattled off an array of items.

The swinging doors to the kitchen whooshed open whenever a waiter plowed through with a platter full of aromatic dishes.

Richard slid a spoon back and forth across the white table surface. The silence was approaching awkward.

"Do you live around here?" I asked.

"Close enough. The house is tucked in one of the side streets about a half mile from here. It's one way. Discourages traffic from racing through. The system works."

"On street parking?"

"I actually am lucky enough to have a garage."

"Do you rent it? You could make a fortune. A parking spot on the Back Bay—a parking spot, mind you—recently sold for $360,000. Can you imagine?" My condo came with parking privileges, for which I paid an additional sum each month to keep my Volvo off the street and safe from vandalism.

"That's scandalous," he said.

Before then, I only had thought about the lucky recipient of all that cash, but Richard was right. It was scandalous.

"I only use the car for an occasional trip to Vermont," he said. "I love the Sugarbush Valley area around Waitsfield and Warren. Do you know it?"

"My parents took me skiing in New Hampshire once when I was a kid, but I haven't been for years and I never could get the hang of it. Skis in, pizza? Skis straight, French fries? I just wanted to go back to the lodge and drink hot chocolate." That had been shortly before disaster struck.

I looked out the window as a sixties-something couple ambled by with a big German Shepherd. The man held the leash. She had a small plastic bag, presumably to scoop up the poop. The woman kept touching his arm as she talked.

Mother never touched Daddy like that.

May appeared with the first course—a soup with shrimp and mushrooms swimming around in a creamy beige broth.

I swirled the spoon around and took a sip. "This is heavenly."

"Coconut soup. It's one of my favorites. I love the taste of coconut milk, but the curry paste and ginger are what give it a kick."

"I could live on this alone."

"Just wait. There's more to come."

And not just with the food. He was luring me in, spoonful by spoonful.

Richard continued to ask me questions—about what I was reading (newspapers), movies I liked (I couldn't remember the last one I'd seen), any siblings (only child), parents (I dodged that one). I felt like a rather dull date.

May reappeared carrying plates laden with steaming chicken, shrimp, and vegetables in exotics sauces.

Casting around for a topic that would make me sound more interesting, I told him about the box.

"My grandmother had a real talent for needlework—embroidery, crocheting, things like that. She used to crochet the edges of handkerchiefs and pillowcases and give them as gifts."

"People treasure those things," he said. "My wife used to knit scarves, sweaters, hats. It's practically a lost art."

A cold draft swirled around my ankles.

"Yes, I guess so. I never thought about it like that."

"You're fortunate. My grandparents were all dead before I was born."

I told him about sneaking peppermints out of the pink candy dish.

"In our family," Richard said, "the forbidden treat was English toffee covered in chocolate. My mother used to make it around Christmas. I was allowed to have two pieces when I came home from school and one for dessert, but I pilfered extra ones and snuck them into my bedroom."

"Couldn't she tell?"

"Of course. The chocolate made smudges on the bedspread. I've tried to duplicate her recipe, but it doesn't taste quite the same. And she resists sending it up from Florida, says the chocolate would melt. I think it's her way of trying to get me to visit during the holidays." He pulled another paper napkin out of the chrome dispenser, wiped his mouth, wadded up the napkin and tossed it in an empty serving dish.

That's what living alone could do to a man.

"Laura and I used to go, but I've stayed close to home the last couple of years."

I played with a piece of shrimp on my plate.

"Florida in December could be nice," I said.

"Often it is, though last year they had a freeze and half the orange crop got killed, so you never know."

Just then a young couple maneuvered through the restaurant

door with a bulky stroller. Richard moved his chair to make room as they wheeled it past us. The occupant, a pudgy curly-haired toddler wearing miniature red-rimmed sunglasses, waved to enchanted patrons as if she were a princess. A waiter produced a highchair and seated them at the table behind ours. The sound of a metal soup spoon slapping the Formica table immediately followed. So much for a quiet spot in the corner.

"I brought you here for the food, not for the ambiance," he said.

"The place has its own charm."

I meant it. You'd never get that communal feeling in the Harbor Hotel.

Richard leaned across the table and in a conspiratorial tone said "I don't think that kid is going to turn into a musician. Her rhythm's off." When Richard smiled, the skin crinkled around his dark brown eyes.

"Maybe she'll be Speaker of the House," I whispered. Although the odds of that happening were remote. The old boys weren't about to give up the perks of their leadership positions.

Then I told him about the postcards that Uncle Erich had sent.

"Did they have any writing on them?"

"A little, but it was in German. I couldn't make a thing out of them."

"I studied it in college. I can't guarantee anything, but I could take a pass at them. Would you like me to try?"

I wondered what I would find out. They probably were anodyne messages, "wish you were here," that sort of thing, but I was curious, and not just about the postcards.

"If it's not too much trouble."

"Tell you what." He looked down at his plate, then up at me. "If you like, after we're finished," he paused and I wondered what was coming next, "I could go with you back to your condo and you could show them to me. If I need to, I'll take them home and dust off my old German dictionary."

I used my knife and fork to maneuver the tail off a piece of shrimp, chewed it, swallowed. There he was, tan Oxford shirt with sleeves rolled up, bits of chest hair peeking out of the tee-shirt underneath, wavy dark locks, long legs stretched out underneath the table, feet almost touching mine. He'd tossed it off as a casual offer. Was it?

I could have demurred, said I needed to get back home to do some work. I could have, but I didn't.

"Sounds like a plan."

The table banging behind us had increased in volume and intensity, followed by a piercing wail and frantic movements of both parents to calm their unhappy child. This stopped any meaningful conversation. Richard asked if I wanted dessert or coffee. I declined. He motioned to May to produce the bill and asked that the remains be boxed for take-out. He paid with cash and what looked like a hefty tip. When he opened his wallet I caught a glimpse of a snapshot of a woman with long blond hair who I assumed was his wife. The wallet snapped shut before I got a good look.

I was great at picking up signals in the political arena, but I'd been out of circulation so long that I felt like I was trying to read 8-point type in the dark without a flashlight. Was I ready to jump back into the game? Was he? As Barbara was fond of saying, more would be revealed.

Chapter 9

It took me a minute to fish the key to my condo out of my purse.
I fumbled with the lock. When I opened the door, my collection
of Waterford crystal goblets, bowls, and vases gleamed in the soft
light. My decorator had recommended that we install glass fronted,
back-lit off-white wooden cabinets with wine red backs to "create
a statement" at the entryway. Even though it had cost a fortune, I
never regretted the expense.

"Wow! Impressive!"

"They give me a lift whenever I walk in."

"I can see why."

He walked across my plush oriental carpet to the picture window. Facing the Esplanade and the Charles River, it was one of the
chief attractions of the unit.

"You have a great view."

"On the fourth of July I have box seats to the fireworks without all the crowds."

"You should throw a party."

"Somehow I've never gotten around to it."

I could put together a list of professional contacts, but beyond Barbara's family, my circle of friends was a dot.

"Coffee? Tea?"

"Coffee would be nice."

Richard trailed me into the kitchen—a narrow space not designed for collaborative cooking. I rarely prepared meals anyway. I was so tired by the end of the day that I usually bought take-out from a neighborhood deli or ate cottage cheese and fruit. My housekeeper kept the refrigerator well-stocked with the essentials. When the apples turned brown or the peaches puckered, she threw them out.

He leaned against a cabinet while I retrieved coffee beans from the freezer, put them in a grinder, and deposited everything in a French press. When I pulled two mugs out of the cabinet, I bumped into him. I could feel my cheeks warm. "Oops. Sorry."

"No problem." He adjusted, but only slightly.

"Would you put these on the coffee table? I'll get the postcards."

"Where's that candy dish? Have you re-supplied it?"

"As a matter of fact, I did. I'll get it. That can be our dessert."

We sat next to each other on the sofa. I sipped my coffee. Richard flipped through the postcards. He separated them into two piles: ones with writing on the back and ones without. While he surveyed the postcards, I surveyed him. What would it feel like to run my fingers through that curly hair? My palms started to sweat, and it wasn't from the caffeine. It had been a long time since I'd entertained such fantasies.

"Have you ever been to Germany?" he asked.

"I went straight from U Mass into a job at the State House and didn't look back. I haven't done much traveling."

"Maybe your grandmother is sending you a sign."

He picked up a postcard and held it next to the light from a table lamp. "If she had used an old German script I might have trouble reading it, but this is quite clear. She's written 'the Wartburg where Luther translated the Bible.'"

I took the postcard and ran a finger over the faded black ink. "Grandma was devoted to her church. Daddy said they had to go every Sunday. Most of the service was in German so he amused himself by counting the number of times the pastor scratched his nose while he was in the pulpit, or kicking his brother under the pew, where he thought Grandma couldn't see him."

"Typical boys."

He swiveled around. Our knees touched. He swiveled back.

My skin was alive. We sat so close to each other that I could almost feel the hair on his arm. He popped a peppermint into his mouth.

"Nice perfume," he said.

"You like it?"

"On you I do."

I was getting warm. I took off my sweater.

"Look at those timber framed buildings. Aren't they magnificent?" he said.

"Look at this one." The building was identified as 'Sachsendorf.' I fumbled over the word, but his pronunciation made it sound sensuous.

"We should do a little research and see if it still exists."

I noted the "we."

My sweater had slipped to the floor. I bent over to retrieve it.

Just then he turned his head toward the hallway leading to my bedroom. "What's that?"

"What's what?"

"That sound."

"I don't hear anything."

"It sounds like a running toilet."

I had two bathrooms—one a small powder room off the hall entryway; the other next to my bedroom.

"It's probably nothing."

"Would you like me to look? If it isn't anything, no harm done."

"That feels like a lot of trouble. If there's a problem, I could call the plumber on Monday."

"In the meantime you're wasting water."

"You're the water conservation police?"

"Sorry. It's just that it could be something simple and I probably could fix it in a minute. I don't mind. Remember what I told you about learning from my dad?"

"Well, I guess, if you're willing."

"I think it's coming from down there." He pointed toward my bedroom.

I walked down the hall. Richard followed. The hissing sound grew louder as we approached. My bathroom was small. He squeezed around me and pulled the lid off the tank.

"Just as I thought. The fill valve needs adjusting. Do you have a screwdriver?"

"I might, somewhere in the kitchen. Let me see if I can find it."

I hunted around and returned with what I hoped was an appropriate implement.

"Will this do?"

"Perfect."

He fiddled with something inside the tank. The hissing stopped. "That should take care of it, avoid unnecessary usage."

He put the screwdriver on the sink and started to wash his hands. It rolled over the edge and behind the toilet. I dove down to retrieve it. Richard took my hand as I got up. I felt an electric spark, and it wasn't from static. Instead of releasing it, he drew me toward him and kissed me. Our teeth bumped. His mouth tasted like peppermint. The whole movement was so spontaneous, the venue so absurd, that we looked at each other in the mirror and started to laugh.

"You have an unusual approach," I said.

"It wasn't premeditated, but I liked the result."

"So did I."

I looked toward the bedroom. What would it be like to co-mingle our bodies, two dueling lobbyists, coupled under the covers? Unless he thought it was a clever stratagem to undermine the opposition, Mangan would have a stroke. I took Richard's hand and led him back to the sofa.

"I'm not sure this is a good idea," I said. "Piper Mangan's picture is probably on a dartboard at Environmentalists of Central Massachusetts." I could feel my better judgment wavering even as I said it.

He stiffened, ever so slightly. Had I made a strategic error of major proportions?

Then he scooped up the postcards. "I'll see what I can make of them and we can talk about it on our next date." The sentence ended somewhere between a period and a question.

"Let me get an envelope to put them in." I went into my bedroom and pulled one out of the desk.

When I returned Richard was standing by the door. He enfolded me in his arms. I felt the hair on the nape of his neck. That kiss had danger written all over it, but I wanted more. He whistled as he walked down the hall.

Chapter 10

It was a sunny Saturday with a light breeze. I could have been with Richard. Instead I was at Logan Airport waiting for a flight to Washington D.C. I knew what lay ahead of me—boring panel presentations, making nice to clients, and most important, scouting for new business.

The previous week I had received a call from a lawyer in one of the big Las Vegas casino operations, sounding out whether I would be interested in taking them on as a client. Casino gambling was illegal in Massachusetts, but the industry had upped their game in the state legislature. They wanted in on a pristine market. Their business could have solved my problems.

Oh, I thought about it, spent four nights losing sleep over it, but after seeing the damage my father's gambling had caused, I said no. I couldn't have lived with myself if I had taken them on. It was a hard call, but it was the right one. That, however, still left me in search of new business. I hoped that the time spent in Washington might help.

Richard had called just as I was getting out of the shower. I ran into the bedroom to answer the phone, naked, hair dripping.

"Did I catch you at a bad time?"

"No, I was just reading the paper." Water seeped into the rug around my feet.

"Did you go running this morning?"

"I thought I'd give it a rest this weekend." I grabbed a towel to wipe my face and neck.

"I haven't finished work on your postcards, but I wondered if you'd like to go sailing with me this afternoon. It's a beautiful Saturday. You could see what your condo looks like from the water."

"Oh, I'd love to, but I'm leaving for a conference in D.C. this afternoon." The idea of being with Richard was appealing, though the prospect of sailing on anything other than water smooth as glass made me queasy. While wrapping the towel around my waist, I dropped the phone. It bounced on the plush carpet. "Oops, sorry," I said. "Are you still there?"

"I'm here. Are you free next weekend? I could show you my place. I'll cook. And that would give me a target for translating the rest of the postcards."

So that's the way we left it.

Saturday afternoon, I wandered in and out of my closet, spread four different outfits on the bed, finally decided on weekend casual--designer jeans, a soft white cotton blouse, and a simple silver necklace. I debated about how many of the blouse's top buttons should be left undone. One was enticing; two were outright suggestive. I left it at one.

Earlier in the day I'd walked over to Charles Street and chosen a few things to bring—green tomato chutney, hand-made in the English Lake District; black olive tapenade; and because I couldn't resist, hot fudge made with Baileys Irish Crème. I also bought a six pack of German beer that the proprietor assured me was the best. I didn't want to show up empty handed.

The taxi deposited me on a quiet, car-lined street at Richard's Cambridge duplex, one of several that looked like they had been part of the neighborhood for decades, if not a century. Two doors, numbers 14 and 14 ½, were side-by-side. Richard had explained that a young couple occupied the first floor, while he had the second.

The front yard was small. A maple tree on the curb lawn, as tall as the house, had sprouted fresh green leaves. Well-manicured white rhododendrons and pink azaleas were in full bloom. The place looked so homey. As I climbed the wooden steps, Richard opened the door to a small alcove.

"Welcome!" He kissed my cheek, his lips brushing my skin.

"I was in the living room when I saw your cab," he said. "Come on upstairs. Do you want me to take that bag?"

"These are for you. Just a little something to put in your refrigerator."

"It looks like more than a little something."

Barbara thought I'd overdone it. "It's a hostess gift," she'd said, "not groceries for the homeless."

When we got to the top of the stairs, Richard opened the door and swept his arm into the hall.

"Let me take your jacket," he said.

Pegs on the wall, an olive green raincoat on one, a plaid flannel jacket on another. No coat closet.

"What's that wonderful smell?"

"Roast chicken with a few vegetables thrown in around the edges. My wife's old recipe. It's easy and it tastes good."

So she was a good cook. If this were a competition, I would lose in the culinary department.

He led me through the hallway and into a large kitchen, lined with ugly brown wood cabinets. No upgrades here. They reminded me of ones in the old apartment my Mom and I had moved to after Dad died.

"German beer!" he said. "What a terrific idea."

So I hadn't miscalculated. "It goes with the theme. German postcards, German beer."

"I'll put it in the fridge in case we want some with dinner. And look at these!" He hurriedly pulled out the jars and almost dropped the tapenade.

Was he nervous?

"We'll have to save the hot fudge for another occasion," he said.

I noted "another occasion." He wasn't wasting any time.

"For dessert," he said, "I picked up some apple strudel from a bakery on Mass. Ave."

"I guess we both had the German theme in mind."

"The chicken won't be ready for a while. Would you like me to show you the place?"

He offered a running commentary as he guided me from the kitchen into the dining and living rooms. An old upright piano stood in one corner of the living room, a stereo in another.

"I grew up with a lot of the furniture you see here," he said.

Although the overall effect was unmitigated clutter, I envied him living in the same house where he'd grown up. He seemed to have an uncomplicated relationship with his parents—so different from my own.

"Do you play the piano?" I asked.

"Not really. That was my mother's," he said as he patted the top. "She loved to play show tunes. I used to hop around in time to the music when I was a toddler. Whatever rhythm I had then disappeared when I reached puberty. I can't dance."

That was a relief. I was no Ginger Rogers. I couldn't dance forward, let alone backwards.

A set of wood-framed glass doors led onto an alcove in the front of the house. It contained a bookcase with titles like *Environment: Science, Issues, Solutions*, a spacious desk with piles of papers, and a computer.

"Do you work from home very much?"

"When I have to write anything that requires careful thought, I do it here."

I'd searched online for MEC policy statements. They were well developed—clear, persuasive, occasionally eloquent. I suspected he had written them. He was so articulate.

"Our office is small, with staff running in and out, frequent phone calls. You know how it is."

"I don't deal with volunteers, so I probably have a quieter time. Maura runs interference for me."

"Yes, we had an interesting conversation when I called to see how you were after you hurt your ankle."

He had charmed Maura. That much was clear.

A hallway ran the length of the unit. One side was lined with more books, the other was covered with photographs in cheap plastic frames—pictures of weddings, babies, school classes, family picnics, young Richard standing by his mother next to a snowman, teenage Richard on his bicycle, a group, probably relatives, gathered around a Christmas tree. I couldn't imagine what it would be like to be engulfed by so many people.

"I may have been an only child," he said, "but the house was always alive with folks coming in and out."

His face softened as he looked at a cluster of photos of a woman I assumed had been his wife. In the largest one, she was walking barefoot on a beach, pant legs rolled up, long blond hair lifted by the wind.

"That was my Laura. We married the month after we came home from the Peace Corps. I went to work as an environmental engineer for a Cambridge consulting firm. She was an elementary school teacher. She loved kids, but we never were able to have any."

We'd entered tender territory. "It doesn't seem fair."

"No, it doesn't," he said. "But life isn't always fair."

"Don't I know it." My ship had left that port a while ago.

"I need to go into the kitchen to check on the chicken. I'll be right back."

I couldn't take my eyes off those pictures. Standing next to Richard, Laura looked petite, almost fragile. She had an oval face with dimpled cheeks and full, sensuous lips. In one, Richard was pushing her on a swing. In another, they were standing in front of a Buddhist temple—in Thailand? She was smiling in every photo.

When I heard Richard coming back, I turned around and pretended I had been looking at his books.

"You've got a lot of room here, Richard."

"It made sense when I was married. It's more than I need right now, but it's the family home."

He'd said "right now." What about the future?

Richard concluded the tour with the master bedroom. He stood at the door and turned on the light. A queen-sized four poster dominated the space.

"The place isn't always this neat. I picked up a lot before you got here."

If he thought this was neat, I wondered about his interpretation of messy. A chair near the door was piled with books, newspapers and magazines were stacked on the floor.

I didn't know where to focus. Two large oriental rubbings of dancing figures in bright cobalt blue hung side by side above the bed.

"Those are beautiful," I said as I moved closer to examine them.

"They're hand rubbed from an ancient Buddhist temple. The government has stopped the practice now, but then you could buy them cheaply."

"I love the color."

"We brought them back from Thailand."

And they were side by side, right above the bed. I hastened back toward the chair by the door.

"So what are you reading?" I said.

"You might like this book by Alan Furst." When he pulled it out of the pile several others fell to the floor. He hastily stacked them up again. "It's set in the Second World War. He does a terrific job of putting the characters in their context. You come away with a much deeper understanding of what life must have been like during the occupation."

"Uncle Erich was in the Army, I don't know where."

Richard handed it to me. "I just finished reading it. Why don't you take it?"

I couldn't remember the last time I read a book for pleasure. "It might be a while before I return it to you."

"Keep it. I'm done with it."

I eased back into the hallway.

"Let's go into the kitchen," he said. "I need to do a few things for supper. Would you like a beer? Or a glass of wine?"

I opted for the beer.

The kitchen was warm, with an inviting fragrance of rosemary. When I offered to help, Richard placed me at a table with a scuffed, soft surface that doubled as a cutting board, and hauled out ingredients for a tossed salad. I tore lettuce into bite-sized pieces and sipped my beer. Richard, shirtsleeves rolled up, shuttled from kitchen to dining room, taking swigs of beer along the way. Occupied with dinner preparations, he didn't seem to mind the silence.

Barbara would have pronounced the scene cozily domestic. It was almost too comfortable.

During dinner Richard asked me questions about Uncle Erich. I was embarrassed by how little information I had.

"Why don't you take some time off and visit him in Ohio? He's getting up there."

I picked at my salad. His suggestion hung in the air. It had been years since I'd been to Ohio.

We went into the living room for dessert. To make room for the strudel, Richard moved some newspapers off a wooden coffee table. The finish, completely worn off on the edge nearest the sofa, looked like it had survived years of feet propped on it. No male feet would dare plant themselves on the furniture in my living room.

As we devoured forkfuls of strudel, Richard told me what he had learned from the postcards. Bottom line, not much, but two of the postcards, with vistas of a town called Grimma, had been signed *deiner liebe schwester* Anna—your dear sister Anna. One, dated 1925, announced the birth of her second son, Leopold. The other, dated November 1947, was a plea for any clothing and food that my grandmother could spare. The messages were brief and poignant.

Richard suggested that we look for information online. He sat in a battered office chair with stuffing poking out of the leather arms. I perched next to him in a chair he'd retrieved from the dining room. When a map of Grimma popped up on the screen, I pulled my chair closer to get a better look.

"Founded in 1170? I can't believe it's that old!" I said.

The town was situated on a river. Several photographs showed that when its banks had overflowed in 2002, major flooding had occurred. Richard scrolled through photographs of a church, a sawmill, a high school, the *marktplatz*.

I knew nothing about where my grandmother came from or who she had left behind. Had she grown up there? So many questions, so few answers.

"Would you like a cup of coffee?"

"If I have any more I'll be up all night."

We returned to the living room and sat on the couch. I leafed through the rest of the postcards. Several were from Grimma—the same market place we'd seen on the internet, the river snaking beside the town. Others were from Bremen and Colditz. Why had Grandma had saved them? What had they meant to her?

The room smelled of apples and beer. I adjusted a pillow. Richard put his arm around my shoulder. His hand gently rubbed, back and forth, back and forth.

I forgot the postcards.

We kissed. Then he began to stroke my neck and chin, softly, rhythmically, like you'd stroke a cat. The touch was so delicate, so sensual, that my whole body vibrated. Our kisses, tentative at first, were increasingly insistent. They unleashed a hunger I hadn't realized was in me. We were explorers eagerly acquainting ourselves with unfamiliar terrain. When Richard pulled back with a questioning look, I didn't think. I nodded a silent assent.

He held my hand and led me into bedroom. Little light filtered through the windows. I was glad for the dark. I hadn't made love in years. I'd stayed in shape, no stretch marks, flat tummy, but I was almost fifty. What would he think of my body?

We threw our clothes on the floor and I welcomed Richard on top of me, his strong frame pressed against mine. I almost felt dizzy with passion, lost in the soft hair on his back, the musky masculine smell, the sounds from deep in his throat. There was nothing long and lingering about it.

Richard kept saying "oh, baby, oh, baby, oh baby," and then, just at the crucial moment, he exploded with "oh, Laurie."

It was like a sharp slap. At the very least, I had expected warm caresses, soft words, cuddling. Not this. I felt pole-axed.

Perhaps I could have forgiven him if he had taken me in his arms and tried to make amends right away. Instead, I still was stretched out, my head on a pillow, my skin tingling, when he jumped out of bed and pulled on his boxer shorts. I couldn't see his face.

Then I noticed it on the nightstand on "his" side of the bed. A painted rock, the kind of thing a kindergartener would have made in art class, a third blue, a silver line in the middle, a third red, pink on the end with two orange dots and a silver mouth stripe. A gift to the teacher? Laura may have been small in stature, but at that moment, she loomed large. I sat up and pulled the covers over my breasts.

"I wish I smoked," he said as he disappeared into the bathroom.

"Whatever do you mean?"

"It's the first time I've been with a woman in two years."

I almost spit out "How did you like it?" but that clearly was not called for.

His voice echoed off the tiled bathroom walls. I strained to hear. "I'm sorry, I'm sorry, I'm sorry. I thought I was ready. I still miss her."

I didn't want to say how long it had been since I'd been with a man. I certainly wasn't going to tell him about Mr. Public Charities, that was none of his business. The wariness crept back like a rat squeezing under a basement door to get out of the rain.

"Well," I said, giving the sheets a sharp kick, "planned or not, it happened. You probably would have been better off at a Holiday Inn—something generic and inherently innocuous."

He came out of the bathroom with his socks and t-shirt on. Richard clothed made me aware of my nakedness.

"You can see the humor of even the most uncomfortable situation," he said.

Was that what this was? From Richard's perspective, maybe so, but I wasn't laughing. I decided to make a quick exit so he could ponder his "situation." It looked like I would have a lot of time to reflect on mine—yet another disappointment at the hands of a man.

This was one too many. You just couldn't trust them.

"I didn't realize," he said, still not looking at me, "how starved I was for simple human touch."

Nothing more? As soon as he said it, he must have known how that sounded because he added, "and you were wonderful..."

"Maybe choosing this bedroom for your first post-marital encounter wasn't such a good idea."

"I hadn't exactly planned it."

"Well, planned or not, it happened." As I scooped up my clothes and ran past him into the bathroom, I stubbed my toe on a chair--the perfect ending to an aborted evening.

I looked at myself in the mirror. My lipstick had worn off. My hair was disheveled. I buttoned my blouse all the way to the top.

By the time I'd dressed and re-entered the bedroom, he, too, was fully clothed.

"But now," I said as I fastened my belt, "It's time for me to go. You need some space, and so do I."

"I didn't intend for it to turn out this way."

"I know." I wasn't sure what he meant—didn't intend for us to end up in bed? Didn't intend for the post-coital remorse?

I walked toward the hallway. My toe was throbbing. Richard trailed behind, tucking his shirt into his pants. He retrieved my coat from the peg and helped me put it on.

He stood in the doorway, shoulders slumped.

Only after I'd grabbed a cab did I remember the postcards, still lying on his living room coffee table.

Chapter 11

When I arrived in my office on Monday, a floral bouquet was sitting on my desk—yellow roses and white lilies the size of saucers in a small square vase from a premier shop in the Back Bay. The accompanying card said "Forgiven? Richard". I knew what their arrangements cost. He'd spent a bundle.

Maura waltzed into my office. "Good weekend?"

"It's not what you think."

"He sent you flowers, didn't he?"

"Life is never that simple."

"Couldn't get it up?"

"If we hadn't worked together so long, I'd fire you on the spot."

She knew I didn't mean it. She inched toward the door. "Sorry."

"Let's let it go for now, OK? I've got a lot of work to do."

"I know. Piper Mangan left a message on the machine. He's in a lather. He wants you to call him 'pronto.'"

"Sometimes he acts as if he's my only client."

"Should I call him?"

"Let him stew in his juices a bit. I don't want him to get the idea that I'll jump at his command."

"Got it."

"And now I'm going to wrap my head around what I need to do today."

But I couldn't.

My professional motto had been, prepare for the unexpected so it doesn't leap up and bite you in the butt. Why couldn't I apply the same maxim to my personal life?

Saturday night's rising action was more than satisfactory, yet I hadn't foreseen the denouement. So much for my capacity as a strategic thinker. Had I completely misjudged him? Did Laura still have a firm grip on his heart? Was I hungrier than I could admit? Time to squash that impulse.

I picked up the phone. Barbara answered on the first ring.

"Hey you, what's up?" she said in her cheeriest voice.

"Are you free for lunch at the Harbor Hotel sometime this week?"

"Lunch? Sure. I love that place." She paused. "What's wrong? You never schedule a personal lunch on a workday."

"Nothing serious. I'm just a bit confused, that's all."

"If *you're* confused, it is serious. Must be a man."

"Well, yes and no."

"I thought so."

"So can you? When are you free?"

"I can meet you there today. What time? Don't want you to change your mind."

"Would 12:30 work? I'll reserve a table in a quiet corner."

"Hmm. This must be very serious."

I was getting irritated. She'd used the word "serious" twice.

"Nobody's dying or anything like that. I just need a listening ear."

"Got it. I'll be there. Remember, the Chinese say the opposite of crisis is opportunity."

"I prefer to avoid crises and forego the opportunities."

"That may be safe but it's also bland. Well, see you at 12:30."

Barbara wasn't particularly insightful, but at least she could provide some support while I heard myself talk. I looked at my watch. Four hours until lunch. I'd better get focused.

The phone beeped. "Piper Mangan is on the line," Maura said. "Should I stall him?"

"No, put him through. Otherwise I'll just have to call back."

"Mr. Mangan," I said in my brightest tone.

"Claire." None of this "my gal" stuff this morning. He must be wound up about something.

"You know that Worcester fireman who was killed in the line of duty? It was tragic, Claire, tragic, it was."

I'd seen the headlines in *The Boston Globe* but hadn't paid much attention.

"A wife and two kids. They live in Lambs Wood."

Lambs Wood was one town over from Apple Grove, the spot Mangan wanted for his golfers' paradise.

"The widow was the second cousin of my wife's brother-in-law, so of course we went to the wake on Thursday."

"Of course." I was tangled in the web of family relations but I suspected that the real reason why Mangan had shown up was because he wanted to do a little politicking. I could picture him somberly attired, huddled under an awning at the funeral home entrance, catching a smoke but also snagging anyone remotely connected to his agenda.

Mangan was on a roll. I periodically interjected an "Oh," or "Is that so?" or "Well, well" so he knew I was paying attention, but he didn't come up for air.

"And do you know what I found out?" he said, his voice rising with every word. "Mrs. Tannenbaum's daughter has taken on the conservation land cause as a kind of memorial to her mother. She's putting serious money into Whately's re-election campaign with the understanding—the understanding, mind you—that he will support the cause." He practically spit into the receiver. "Isn't that illegal or something?"

I doubted that the quid pro quo was that overt. I was sure that Mangan used the same tactic whenever it was in his interest. I tried to soothe him as if he were a four year old whose brother had seized his favorite dump truck.

"That's useful information, Mr. Mangan. It corresponds with a rumor I'd picked up from one of the committee staff. I don't think there's any reason to panic, though. We knew from the get-go that Representative Whately was a problem."

"A problem? He's downright dangerous."

"Our strategy all along has been to work around him. Even if Whately amasses the biggest campaign war chest on record, he can't compete with the state budget crisis. Remember what I told you? That state budget deficit is our friend. When it comes to funding the purchase of conservation land versus aiding the developmentally disabled, the kids will win hands down every time. Besides, Whately didn't exactly fall in line when the governor was running last term, so the governor's not going to work too hard to help him out."

"I've been thinking."

That didn't sound good.

"I had an idea during the funeral mass. And oh, Claire, it was beautiful, bagpipes playing as they brought the body into Holy Cross Cathedral, firemen in uniform on either side. Even the bishop turned out. They gave him a good send-off."

"It sounds impressive." I picked up a pencil and started doodling pictures of Mangan's nose. They looked like shriveled potatoes.

"What if I were to have a golf outing for key legislators and staff? You would make the selections, of course. You're my gal."

His voice got even louder. I dropped the pencil and moved the phone away from my ear.

"We could bus them to Piney Woods on the South Shore— that's the best example of what I plan to do in Apple Grove. Hand out free golf clubs to all participants—well, maybe not the staffers, they could get a golf towel with the Mangan logo on 'em."

I rolled my eyes. The staff would appreciate a golf club more than their bosses.

"And we could give prizes—lots of prizes."

Mangan had panicked. He should have spent more time praying, less time plotting. I needed to walk him back from the precipice. I picked up my grandmother's paperweight and rubbed the soft surface to calm myself.

"I can see where you're going, Mr. Mangan. We have to be careful, though. We don't want to be too obvious. Besides, there are regulations about that sort of thing—disclosing gifts, amounts, sources, etc."

"But it could be beautiful, Claire, really beautiful."

"I appreciate the team-work we've got going here, Mr. Mangan. Mightn't it be a good idea, though, to save our strongest ammunition until later? We might not even need it."

He was quiet. I had stuck a pin in his balloon. He knew I was right but he didn't like it. He certainly wasn't going to admit it.

"Tell you what," I said. "The House Ways and Means Committee staff is working on next year's budget right now. I'll be sitting down with Craig Adams later today to discuss your situation."

"*Our* situation, Claire, *our* situation."

Why did I keep making that mistake? It only raised Mangan's blood pressure and for no good reason. My forehead began to ache.

"Of course. Our situation. I don't know if you know him. He's the behind-the-scenes chief architect of the House budget." Adams would be able to tell me how far down the list of priorities public funding of conservation land was going to be. Tax revenues were coming in way below projections. After my conversation with Adams, I hoped it might move even farther down the list, if it was there at all.

Mangan puffed into the receiver. The balloon continued to deflate.

"Besides," I said, "I'm still working the other angle—to get our bill buried in an omnibus study."

"All right. You're playing an inside game. That's what I hired you for. But I'm getting impatient, you hear? If you need me to pull the golf clubs out of the bag, you'll tell me, won't you?"

"Of course, Mr. Mangan, of course." I was beginning to sound like him—a troublesome thought.

"I'd need a little time to get it together."

"I really don't think that will be necessary." I felt like I'd walked into a pile of Canada goose poop, and I couldn't remove the stain or the stench.

Chapter 12

The minute hand on my watch crawled toward noon. Maura had set up a meeting with the House Ways and Means Committee budget director for 2:45, which would give me enough time with Barbara before I put my game face back on. When it finally got to be 12:15, I grabbed my purse and headed out the door.

Barbara was standing in the lobby when I walked into the hotel. She rushed over and gave me a hug, then stepped back and studied me.

"The circles under your eyes are darker than usual. I guess we have a lot to talk about."

The diplomatic doorman appeared impassive.

"Why don't we head to the dining room?" I said. Our heels didn't make a sound as I propelled her forward on the plush carpet. "I reserved a table for us by the window so we'll have a view of the harbor."

A uniformed waiter with a toothy grin and a Caribbean accent promptly appeared, filled our glasses with water, and presented us with outsized menus in black leather folders.

"Well?" Barbara said after we'd settled in. "It must be man trouble. Since you've lived like a nun for far too long, that's good news. So what's the problem?"

I stared out the window. A gaggle of passengers was boarding the water taxi for the quick trip across the harbor to Logan Airport. A Lufthansa plane with its bright bluebird logo was sweeping in for a landing. When my grandmother crossed the Atlantic, the trip must have taken days by boat, all in steerage. No upper deck for her.

"Have you ever been to Germany?" I asked.

"Caleb and I took Timmy on a cruise down the Rhine for his fifteenth birthday, remember? Why? Have you fallen in love with a German pilot or something?"

"No, no. You see, I got this box from my Uncle Erich. He's moving into a senior living place and he sent me some things from my grandmother. No jewelry or anything like that. Simple stuff. Crocheted pillowcases, hankies, postcards."

"Postcards?"

"Some with German writing on them."

"I didn't know you spoke German."

"I don't. Richard offered to translate them for me."

"Richard?"

"His name is Richard Truitt."

"Now we're getting somewhere," she said. "Is he good looking?"

Barbara paid attention to the physical attributes of men, although I sometimes questioned her taste. She could swoon over Michael Kitchen on PBS, even though the guy was probably only

5'6" in elevator shoes. I preferred Bill Nighy—tall, slender, angular, with a throaty voice that lured me in.

"He's about six feet tall, almost lanky, with this mass of curly chestnut brown hair. He sails. He runs. He's six years younger than I am."

"You lucky girl."

Barbara's husband was in his late fifties, and she had complained that just as her libido was getting a post-menopausal jolt, his was shrinking.

"He lives in Cambridge."

"I wouldn't hold that against him."

"And he's totally unsuitable."

"Sounds to me like he's exactly what you need. He isn't married, is he? We don't want another Mr. Public Charities on our hands."

Barbara had picked up warning signs that I had failed to see, but when I appeared on her front porch, humiliated and ashamed, she never said "I told you so."

"He's the executive director of the Massachusetts Environmental Coalition."

"Not one of your clients, I take it."

"No," I scanned the room and lowered my voice, "though I agreed to do some work for a developer whose issues are in direct conflict with some of Richard's members."

The waiter, who had been hovering, asked if we were ready to order. I hadn't even looked at the menu but I reverted to custom and ordered a chicken Caesar salad, no anchovies, light on the dressing, coffee later. Barbara decided on an Asian salad with sunflower seeds and slivered almonds, dressing on the side.

"So what does Richard say about this?" she asked.

"We haven't discussed it."

"You'll have to bring it up at some point."

"I called you because I need you to *listen*."

"I was hoping those tired eyes meant you were getting some good sex." She leaned across the table. "You're blushing. You did go to bed with him."

I moved my spoon back and forth across the white tablecloth. "He's a widower."

"Any kids?"

"No."

I already was outside my comfort zone. That would have been a stretch too far. After Barbara and Caleb were married, Caleb had graciously welcomed me into their family circle. When Timmy was born, they declared me a surrogate aunt and let me lavish him with attention whenever I wanted. At my age, that was the closest I'd ever get. I could swoop into his life for special treats without the responsibilities of parenthood.

"His wife died about two years ago. He's still recovering. More than I realized."

"I would hope so. If I passed away, I'd like to think Caleb would mourn for at least a couple years before he hopped in the sack with somebody else. Although these days, I wonder if he might just become a celibate monk."

Some men couldn't function without a woman for more than sixty days, which made me wonder what else was going on with Caleb. Barbara, God bless her, had held up her end of the bargain with panache. Caleb didn't have to worry about anything. She was a Martha Stewart without the cunning.

"Barbara! You must be reading women's magazines when you go to the hairdresser."

"Don't knock it. You can get a lot of good info out of them."

"The venue was less than perfect. We were at the duplex where he and his wife lived. We ended up in his—in their—old bedroom. Their old bed, for heaven's sake. Laura loomed over us the whole time. He got spooked. It was humiliating."

"What on earth was he thinking?"

"I don't think he *was* thinking. Neither was I, though I should have been. We hopped into bed, made love, and then remorse swept through the room like a dense fog over the Outer Banks. But it's a risky alliance, anyway."

The waiter appeared with our salads. We waved him away before he had a chance to ask if we wanted any fresh ground pepper.

"I need to bury it," I said.

"Sounds to me like your relationship has just been born. Give it a chance to breathe before you suffocate it."

Her imagery was cringe-inducing. I had this vision of an adult me straddling an infant Richard, shoving a pillow over his head while his little arms thrashed through the air in protest.

"He still has my postcards. I forgot to take them when I left."

"Maybe your subconscious was trying to protect you from a hasty retreat."

"He sent flowers."

"At least he recognizes that a serious apology is in order."

"I feel like my life is out of control. I lost my biggest client to a big Texas firm that handles its governmental affairs in house. I've taken on one who's more trouble than he's worth, and that's saying a lot. I stare at my grandmother's paperweight when I should be making phone calls. And I end up in bed with a grieving widower."

"You forgot to mention the part about where you and Richard represent folks whose interests diverge."

"That too."

"I hope you don't have a lot scheduled for this afternoon." She pushed up the sleeves on her cashmere sweater. "We're going to be here for quite a while."

I looked at my watch. "Actually, I have to hike over to the State House to see if I can get some information that will calm the client I mentioned."

"Then we don't have a lot of time. Face it. One way or another you're going to have to talk with him. Did he include a card with the flowers?"

"Yes."

"What did it say?"

"All it said was 'Forgiven? Richard.'"

"Why don't you send him an email. Just say 'Yes.' Then see what he does next."

"That puts the ball back in his court."

"It wouldn't hurt you to cede a little control in this situation."

"You know me too well."

"Listen," Barbara said. "He could be the kind of guy who makes a shrine to his dead wife and stays stuck in his grief. If that's the case, he's not your responsibility. Or…" she leaned across the table "or, he could be ready to burst out of the mausoleum and make a new life for himself. Inexpertly, I'll admit, but still, he tried. In which case, you appear to be the woman of choice—at least for now."

"For now. That's another reason to put an end to this. I don't need any more hurt."

"In light of your recent experience…"

"It wasn't that recent."

"In light of past experience," she said, "you are right to approach the situation with caution, but that doesn't mean you have to slam on the brakes. You still don't have enough information to know if he's someone you want to get in bed with."

"I already have."

"That's not what I meant. You should be asking if he's worthy of your trust, your affection, your love, your commitment."

"I don't even know what he sees in me."

"You sell yourself short. You always have when it comes to men."

The waiter reappeared with a dessert tray laden with cream-filled confections. We ordered coffee, no dessert.

"Lighten up a bit," she said. "Don't be afraid to take a bite of that Boston cream pie. He'd certainly add a little zip to your weekends. That's an appealing prospect."

"This is a side of you I haven't seen before."

"Chalk it up to mid-life rumination. Maybe even envy."

In the ensuing silence, I became aware of how quiet the room was. We were the only diners left.

"Why don't you suggest that the two of you get together over a meal away from either one of your bedrooms," she said, "and see where the conversation goes. After all, he still has your postcards."

Barbara made it sound easy.

"What would I do without you?" It felt so good to have a friend who really knew me. Sometimes I thought she knew me better than I knew myself.

She laughed. "I don't know."

I realized all our conversation had been about me. While I paid the bill (the Jamaican got a hefty tip for staying out of the way), I asked her how she and Caleb were doing.

"Nothing much has changed. Right now I'm more worried about Timmy. He came home exhausted after his finals. He falls into bed by ten and wakes up around nine the next morning."

"That doesn't sound unusual. If I could have, I would have slept until eleven when I was on summer break, but that was not an option. I was elbowing my way onto the MTA by eight so I could walk into the Speaker's office by nine."

"I'm worried about him. He's supposed to begin an internship in a pharmaceutical lab in mid-June, but I wonder if he should take the summer to rest before his senior year."

"I don't think that's a good idea. Even though Timmy doesn't need to worry about financing his education, lucky boy, the experiences he'll get in that environment could help him in medical school. Don't be overly protective. Timmy's a smart young man. He'll make a good decision."

Chapter 13

To avoid further queries from Maura, when I left the Harbor Hotel, I walked straight to the State House. I should have been focused on work. Instead, I thought about Richard.

"Why don't you get together over a meal and see where the conversation goes," Barbara had said. In theory, that sounded good, but I wasn't sure. Worst case scenario, Richard could meet me, return the postcards, apologize, and say he hadn't realized he needed more time to grieve. No harm no foul there, I guess. Or he could say "The first time didn't work so well. Why don't we try again after dinner? Your place this time?" That would be a non-starter. I could say, "Why don't we take our time and get to know each other better? Shelve the sex for a while." After all, our relationship had begun in friendship—a dubious friendship, since we were at odds in our professional lives. I was drawn to that scenario, sort of, except my recent romantic encounter was like a sugar high after years of dieting. You eat the sweet, you get a rush, you crash, you want more.

Next thing I knew I was trudging up Park Street, the Golden Dome of the State House before me, shining in the sun.

I ducked into an empty committee room to plan my approach with Adams. I liked Craig. He was embedded in the system. He had worked as a legislative aide right out of community college, rose up through the ranks, was invaluable because he had been through so many budgetary cycles, and took pride in that knowledge. Straightforward would be best. Otherwise he would sense it. Besides, my credibility was at stake. I would need him in the future on issues that had nothing to do with Mangan.

Mangan. He was like those Lyme-bearing ticks that plague New Englanders every summer. I could get bitten if I didn't act fast.

When I opened the door to the outer office of the House Ways and Means Committee, I greeted the receptionist, who knew me from countless previous visits, told her I had an appointment, and asked if Adams could spare a few minutes. She dialed his extension, said he'd be with me shortly. I helped myself to a drink from their water cooler, tossed the paper cup in a nearby gray metal trash can already half filled with them, and stared vaguely at some notices on a bulletin board until Adams ushered me into his office.

His cubicle was covered with stacks of bills, reports, and memoranda on every available surface. The one perk that came with his position was a window. The glass was dirty, an air conditioning unit blocked half the space, nevertheless, he ranked a window. He took a pile of papers off a grimy wooden straight-backed office chair and waved me into it. His jaw was in perpetual motion. Adams was a relentless gum chewer--the result of having stopped smoking several years ago.

A picture of his daughter was on the corner of his desk. She looked just like Craig--the same square face and prominent jaw. An inexperienced driver, she had been coming home on a wintry Saturday night when freezing rain turned into black ice. She'd totaled the car, crushed both bones in her left leg, had multiple surgeries. I'd helped organize a fund raiser to pay for their gargantuan medical bills.

I asked how she was doing. Craig said although she walked with a slight limp, she now had recovered, thank God. She'd been given a scholarship to Brown, based in part on the essay she'd written about what she had learned about herself after the accident. She would begin in September. I thought that was a singular accomplishment. I told him so, and I meant it.

Then I eased into the reason for my visit.

"One of my clients is interested in acquiring some distressed farmland north of Worcester to develop fifty-five and over housing and amenities. Studies have shown that, with baby boomers nearing retirement, the need for that sort of development is growing. I've heard rumors about appropriating some state money that, coupled with private financing, would convert the property into conservation land. That would preclude commercial development."

He didn't say anything.

"So on behalf of my client, I'm trying to figure out what's happening with the House budget."

Adams tip-tapped the eraser end of a pencil on his desk while I spoke. Was he impatient, or was he still missing his cigarettes?

"I've been approached by a couple of members about this issue," he said (not a good sign), "one of whom is focused on re-election." (That probably was Whately). "The Chair of House Ways and Means recognizes his dilemma, but we're also facing pressure from human services groups who want more funding for home health aides, disabled kids, social workers mandated with protecting children from abuse and neglect, etc. There's not enough money to go around. What else is new?"

I gave what I hoped was a knowing smile. "I'm aware," I said, "that the Department of Human Services is under fierce attack."

A number of children had been placed in inappropriate foster care settings, with disastrous results. It was a top of the fold front page headline in *The Boston Globe* for three days.

"You've got that right. Only last week some demonstrators camped outside our office shouting 'Do the right thing. Save our kids.' It was impossible to work."

The organizers of the demonstration were part of a shoe-string non-profit interfaith religious coalition. Frustrated by inadequate attention to the problem, they decided to increase the volume, both figuratively and literally. The marble floors amplified the din. I admired their chutzpah. Some days, I wished they were my clients. Instead of protecting the interests of energy gluttons I could help folks who really needed it. I would feel cleaner. Poorer, but cleaner.

I nodded in sympathy. "I was here," I said. "They blocked the hallway."

"The Capitol police finally came and ushered them out of the building."

The pencil tapped an off-beat rhythm. "I can't promise anything," he said. "You never know what might surface before the ink is dry."

Had Richard and some of his environmental zealots met with Adams?

"I understand." Come on, Craig, give me a little more.

"But at least for now, although a line item for conservation land might be in the budget, the money will be allocated to other districts—the Berkshires chief among them."

He smiled. I smiled. That was encouraging news.

He unwrapped two more sticks of gum. "However, you re-member when Representative Harris tried to outflank my boss after Representative Tocco died?"

On alert, I leaned forward in my chair. "I remember it well." The Ways and Means Committee chairmanship was a prized plum, offering increased status, staff, influence, and pay.

"She hadn't paid her dues, but she thought she could waltz in and get the job."

"She didn't understand the system." She apparently hadn't had a mentor to help her decipher the unwritten rules. Thank heavens for Big Tom Callahan. I wouldn't be where I was without him.

"Representative Whately supported my boss during that battle. You know how the system works," he said, cracking his knuckles.

I hated that sound but kept a neutral visage.

"That makes him more inclined to help Representative Whate-ly," he said. "So that's all I can tell you for the time being."

Meeting over. My time was up. In fact, he told me what I need-ed to know. Translation: anything could happen, so you'd better devise a back-up plan.

"Feel free to stop back in a couple weeks after things are closer to being finalized," he said. "It's always good to see you. We go back a long way."

I thanked him profusely, and told him that our conversation, as always, had been extremely helpful; that I hoped he knew what an essential figure he was on the Hill, and that I deeply appreciated our collegial relationship. I may have laid it on a bit thick, but he probably received little acknowledgement for his work. Affirma-tion happens infrequently, so when it is doled out, the effect gets magnified. Besides, I didn't say anything that I didn't believe.

I was disappointed. What could have been relatively straightforward was going to take more work. I would need to begin a round of meetings with select legislators and talk with the Senate Ways and Means committee staffer. I would ask Maura to prepare a report on any bills related to state-funding of conservation land, make a list of legislative co-sponsors, and dig up any news clippings on the subject. With that information in hand, I could develop a list of reasons why those matters deserved further consideration in an omnibus study, thus delaying any legislative action until after Mangan got his farmland. In my line of work, nothing ever was easy or straightforward, but this was one of those times that I wanted it to be.

When I got back to my office, I took Barbara's advice and called Richard.

"I was hoping to hear from you," he said. "Let me close the office door."

"Would it be better if we talked this evening?"

"No. I have some things I need to say, and the sooner, the better."

I heard him take a deep breath.

"First," he said, "I'm sorry."

He'd already communicated that, but I was glad to hear him say it. "The flowers were sweet. And very generous. You didn't need to send them, but I do love flowers, and they are beautiful, so thank you." Would Barbara approve of that opening?

"Something was called for under the circumstances."

It certainly was.

"The answer to your question is, 'yes,' you're forgiven, though I need to hear more about where you think you are right now." Forgiven? Maybe. But I wouldn't forget.

"I thought I was ready to begin a new chapter in my life. I guess I'm less ready than I thought. And the location didn't help."

"You've got that right."

"You're angry." Richard made it sound like a statement and a question at the same time.

"No." I straightened a piece of greenery in the flower arrangement.

"Well, probably a little. Angry with the situation. Life is filled with so damned many complications. I deal with them all the time in my work but I'd like to keep them to a minimum in my personal life."

"So what are you saying?"

"I guess what I'm saying is…well, I don't know what I'm saying." I turned around in my swivel chair and looked out the window at anchored sailboats twisting in the wind.

"I'd like to see you again," he said.

I remembered his fingers brushing against my cheek—soft, ever so soft.

"Oh, Richard."

"Could we start over? Besides, I still have your grandmother's postcards."

"Yes, the postcards." I massaged Grandma's paperweight and took a deep breath. "Why don't we work on our friendship. Get to know each other better. Keep things out of the bedroom for a while." Straight out of Barbara's playbook.

"That makes sense," he said, "though I don't know how long I'll be able keep that commitment."

So Richard felt it, too. What would my grandmother say if she knew why her paperweight was moist?

"How about next Saturday?" he said. "Maybe take in a movie at Kendall Square, have supper afterwards? Would that work for you?"

The last thing I needed was some romantic movie with a lot of explicit sex scenes, but as my Dad used to say, in for a penny, in for a pound. "Yes, that would work."

"I'll see what's playing and be back in touch."

"Sounds good." Did it?

"And thanks." he said. "For giving me another chance, I mean."

"See you Saturday."

I called Barbara. I wanted to hear her say "Way to go!" but she wasn't home, so I left a message. Then I walked over to Beacon Hill Readers, found the travel section, and bought some books about Germany--German history and culture, German customs, and a Michelin guidebook. The guidebook was an afterthought.

When I got home, I turned on the fire in my gas-lit fireplace, curled up on the sofa, and opened the book about German Christmas traditions. It had glossy photographs of fir trees which looked like they had come straight from the Black Forest, with delicate glass ornaments and glowing candles (a fire hazard, for sure; if anyone in my condo was caught hauling in a real tree, they were fined a thousand dollars).

Before Daddy died, Christmas mornings were a blow-out. The artificial tree (pine scent optional) was so tall that it almost touched the ceiling. Decked with white lights, white ribbons, and white ornaments straight from Bloomingdales, the only color was from presents that spilled out in all directions below the lowest boughs.

On Christmas Eve, we dressed up and walked to the neighborhood Congregational church, a gray stone edifice with stained glass windows glowing in the dark. One year when the congregation started to sing *Silent Night*, Daddy fished a handkerchief out of his pants pocket and blew his nose. He said he was coming down with something, but he wiped his eyes, as well. Did he know what was ahead? Did Mother suspect?

Germans, the author wrote, still treated the Christmas season as an opportunity for reflection, celebration, and time with family and friends. With no family of my own, the holiday was a time to be endured rather than celebrated. I usually spent Christmas Eve with Barbara, Caleb, and Timmy. They navigated Christmas day between Caleb and Barbara's parents and siblings. Barbara tried to make me feel like one of the family, but I was an outsider. There was no point in pretending otherwise.

I decided to find some pictures of my grandmother, and located an old family photo album, stuffed behind a jumble of miscellany on the top shelf of my bedroom closet, covered in thick, waxy dust. I cleaned both it and my hands before opening it.

Grandma Petersen was on the first page in a head and shoulders pose next to my grandfather. Her face was bathed in light that played up the sheen of thick dark hair piled on top of her head. (Was that where mine came from?) She had well-defined eyebrows, apple cheeks, and a closed-lipped smile. The neckline of her lace-trimmed dress reached from under her chin all the way to her earlobes.

On the next page, she stood behind Uncle Erich and my father, one hand on each shoulder. Uncle Erich was a foot taller than my dad. When was that picture taken? Grandma must have been younger than I was now.

How different from the way I remembered her—stooped over with a bulge in her spine, the result (so my mother told me) of a disastrous fall on an icy sidewalk; wrinkles that circled her neck and ran up the sides of her face; thinning white hair, usually pressed down by a hairnet; faint eyebrows with glasses that slid half-way down her prominent nose. But her smile was the same, the corners of her mouth always turned up. She gave good hugs. She made me smile. She always did.

Grandma's spirit was tugging at my soul.

Uncle Erich hadn't returned the postcard I'd enclosed with my thank you letter. He probably was so busy with the move that he had forgotten. Or maybe he was sick. If he went, all hope of finding out more about my family would get buried with him.

I dashed into my bedroom and pulled my old black address book out of my desk. I had no phone number. I called information. Did they have a listing for Erich Petersen at 226 Fourth Street in Oretown? That number was disconnected. Did they have a new number? The operator apologized. Nothing. I was stuck.

Chapter 14

When I got into the office on Tuesday, Maura was sitting at her desk, organizing the mail. I told her about the postcards, the peppermint candies, and my unsuccessful effort to reach Uncle Erich.

"Would you like me to try?"

"I already called information. They had no listing for him."

"Give me whatever you have. Complete name. Old address." She was using her clipped, Ms. Efficiency voice. "You say he's moved into a retirement home?"

"That's what he wrote. I haven't heard from him since he sent the box. Who knows what's happened to him."

"Let's not get ahead of ourselves. Give me the address and get on with your work."

Sometimes the lines between employer and employee got blurred. That was one of those times, and I loved her for it.

I fortified myself with a mug of strong coffee, then called Piper

Mangan. I said budgetary constraints were in his favor, then eased into the bad news. Did he remember when the House Ways and Means Committee chairmanship was up for grabs? Unfortunately, from our perspective, it was Rep. Whately who helped the chairman get his new position. For that reason, as often was the case in these matters, it was possible, just possible, based on the theory of "I'll scratch your back, you scratch mine," that the conservation line item could appear in the House Ways and Means budget. Not to worry, though, I said, because even if the House budget caused us problems, we probably could avoid them in the Senate. If that wasn't successful, when the two committees met to work out their differences, we'd have another chance to take care of the issue.

In the meantime, I told him, I was working on our second strategy (I was careful to say "our")—namely, to get any relevant land-use legislation bundled into an omnibus study, not to be contemplated (if even begun) until after the November election. We would know more in a couple of weeks.

Mangan was uncharacteristically silent as I spun out these tactics. When he did talk, the volume and speed of his words were on an escalating trajectory.

"You sound like one of my contractors. He says he'll get the job done in a month, but when he uses words like 'possible' and 'probable' I know it'll be three months, at least. I may look like a Polish plumber but I wasn't born yesterday. Damn that Whately, I knew I should have offered him free membership in one of my country clubs."

"I don't think that would have helped, Mr. Mangan." The faster Mangan talked, the slower I spoke. "As a matter of fact, it would be illegal. The state has clear restrictions on the cost of gifts to legislators and other government officials. That definitely would be over the threshold."

"I took the wife on a drive out to Apple Grove last Sunday. We stopped in the village. The general store makes the best apple cider and sugared donuts anywhere, but the label on the jug said it was from New Hampshire. So I said, 'You're promoting New Hampshire cider now?' And the gal behind the counter said, 'Yah, last fall's apple crop around here went bust. The trees have a parasite or something. Don't know if they'll recover.'"

"That's very useful information." I wasn't sure where this was leading, but I doubted it was good.

"So I did a little poking around. The apple trees have fire blight. Ever heard of it?"

"I can't say that I have. When I buy an apple, it comes prewashed with a little sticker on it. A Janey Appleseed I am not."

He didn't get the joke.

"It was news to me," he said. "Some sort of thing that can mess up the whole shebang—blossoms, fruit, limbs, trunks. I drove out again yesterday and looked at the trees. They're a sorry sight, Claire, a sorry sight. No wonder the farmers want to sell. And in their situation" (this sounded like "sit-chee-ashun"), it should be for a reasonable price. A very reasonable price."

What Mangan really meant was that he could acquire the land below market value, but that cut two ways. If Mangan could get the land on the cheap, so could the environmentalists.

I needed to fortify myself with more coffee, but the mug was empty.

Then he raised the specter of the golf outing again. He said he'd ordered some embroidered golf towels that said "I share Piper's dream."

"Get it? Piper's dream?"

I grimaced. Pipe dreams implied wishful thinking. And maybe that's exactly where this was heading but I wasn't about to tell him that. Thank goodness he couldn't see my face.

"I still think we should hold off, Mr. Mangan. You might risk compromising them and yourself. I'm sure that's not what you want." How was that for bullshit? I could sling it with the best of them.

"Well I know one thing for sure. If necessary, I'm going to give, and give generously, to Whately's opponent."

"The source of substantial gifts also has to be declared," I said.

"Can't a guy get a break around here?"

"Take it easy, Mr. Mangan. We've got a lot of arrows in our quiver. I'll call you after I meet with the Senate Ways and Means budget staffer. In the meantime, it's a beautiful day. Go play a round of golf on one of your courses. It will take your mind off things."

My hand was cramped from clutching the phone. My neck ached. I rummaged around in my desk and found a small tin of aspirin. As Mangan had pointed out to me, he was no dummy. He was well aware of the state ethics laws, he just didn't like them. If he could find a way to skirt them to get what he wanted, I had no doubt that he would. Mangan was beginning to remind me of my father, without the polish.

The photo gallery in the office of the Senate Ways and Means Committee budget director had a single purpose--to impress. Framed pictures lined the wall behind his desk—of him shaking hands with the Governor, the Senate President, the Senate Ways and Means Committee Chair, the chair of the Democratic state party, etc. They were like wallpaper.

While I waited for him to get off the phone, I noticed one in particular. Eyes shaded by a red hat with the Marine logo Semper

Fi on the brim, big grin on an oddly boyish fifty-year old face, he and three other men stood in front of a golf cart, hands clasping a gigantic silver trophy. So when I told him that my client was interested in acquiring some farmland north of Worcester to develop fifty-five and over housing and amenities, I didn't hesitate to mention that he was a respected developer of pro-designed golf courses, including one geared to the special needs of disabled veterans. (That was stretching things a bit, but I assumed that Mangan would have to comply with ADA standards like everyone else.) I suggested that as baby boomers (a cohort noted for high voter turn-out) reached retirement, they would be in need of new recreational opportunities and low-maintenance living arrangements such as those my client had in mind for Apple Grove.

I gave him my best pitch. He was non-committal. I couldn't tell if that was discretion based on years of experience, or if something more complicated was going on. It made me nervous.

After that meeting I went to the State House library to begin research into a comparison of Worcester County demographics twenty years ago and present, with particular attention to increased numbers of people fifty and over, their economic circumstances, educational attainment, and recreational habits. It might take some digging, but I hoped the information would be persuasive.

My next step would be to sit down with each member of the Joint Committee on Environment, Natural Resources, and Agriculture. I intended to press for a hold on all bills relating to state funding for land purchases until a legislative study could be completed in light of changing demographics. That might take a couple of years. By then Mangan could make an offer the beleaguered apple farmers couldn't refuse, buy the land, and be well on his way to those eighteen holes. At least that was my hope.

I called Mangan and gave him a report. I kept it short, upbeat, and to the point. I didn't want to get into any more rambling conversations about dead firefighters, diseased apples, and Piper's Dream.

It was late afternoon when Maura sashayed into my office with a big grin on her face and a little piece of paper in her hand.

"I found him!"

"You what?"

"Yep. It took a few phone calls," she said, "but I found him." She wove one foot around the other in a little dance step.

"However did you manage it?"

"I know a thing or two about senior living communities. I'm scared to death that I'll have to put Mother in one of them if her memory gets worse. Thank God for Medicaid, because they cost a bundle, though Ohio prices may be better than Massachusetts."

"I didn't realize..."

"We're holding our own. She forgot to turn off the gas burner on the stove the other day, but it was on low, and I've done that myself. The flame is hardly visible."

"If I can do anything to help, you'll let me know, won't you?" Even as I said it, I wasn't sure what I could do beyond make certain that Maura kept her job.

"I did a search for senior living communities around Oretown," she said. "There must be a lot of retirees in northern Ohio, that region alone has five. So I started calling and asking for Erich Petersen. When I got to number four, I hit the jackpot."

"You are amazing."

"Don't I know it!" She presented the paper with a flourish.

"Did you speak to him?"

"I disconnected when the phone started to ring. Yours should be the voice he hears, not mine."

"You're an angel."

"Consider it payback for that gift certificate you gave me for dinner at the North End. Mother said it was the best Italian food she's ever eaten."

Judging by her mother's dress size, she'd had more than her share of pasta.

"I forgot all about it," I said.

"By the way, have you had any lunch yet?" she asked. "I've got to pick up some stuff at Staples and there's a deli around the corner. I could get you a salad or a sandwich or something."

"Thanks, but I'm fine. You've done your good deed."

She gave me a "forget about it" wave as she walked out.

I didn't think it would be possible to locate him, certainly not so quickly.

My mouth felt dry. I grabbed a bottle of water from the office mini-bar. It didn't help. I'd been to the bathroom a half hour before but I had the urge to pee again. I paced around the room. Finally I picked up the phone and punched in the numbers. He answered on the third ring.

"Uncle Erich? It's Claire. Your niece." Of course he knew who I was. Why did I say that?

"I just moved in a couple weeks ago. How did you find me?"

"Just a lucky guess. You said you were moving into a retirement facility. There aren't that many around Oretown."

"I'm still getting settled."

"How do you like it so far?"

"Well, the food's good, I'll say that for 'em. And I never did much cooking. Peanut butter's a great source of protein."

"Don't I know it." His voice was like an old eiderdown

wrapped around my shoulders.

"Now I get one hot meal a day whether I want it or not. I get a choice, lunch or supper. It's up to me."

"That sounds pretty good. I don't spend much time in the kitchen either."

I waited for him to say something, but the only sound on the other end of the line was labored breathing.

"How's your health? Are you OK?"

"I'm getting up there. I was ninety on my last birthday."

I was embarrassed. I had been so preoccupied with work that I'd forgotten to send a card.

"My joints are a bit stiff now," he said. "I'm s'posed to use a cane or a walker. They've got me in physical therapy. If you ask me, it's a waste o' time. But somebody comes to get me and take me to the gym, so I guess I don't have much choice."

"It was so nice of you to send the things from Grandma."

"It seemed a shame to throw them out."

"I've got her paperweight on my desk." I polished the smooth surface with my thumb.

"Oh, yah, that paperweight. I brought it back from Germany after the war, gave it to her."

"That's funny. I thought it was made in China."

"Pro'bly was. I kind'a liked the look of it. People were selling anything and everything just to get a pack of cigarettes. And the kid who sold it was so scrawny."

"Cigarettes?"

"They used 'em like money. Traded 'em for food. I gave her a candy bar, too, and some gum. She sure liked that gum."

"I bought some books about Germany the other day. I know so little..."

"Some things you don't want to know."

"Uncle Erich, could I come and see you some time?" I blurted out the question without thinking.

"I'd like that," he hesitated, "but I don't have any place to put you up."

"I'm sure I could find a motel. There's so much I'd like to know about our family. My father never talked about it."

"I don't know how much I remember, but it sure would be good to see you. You probably shouldn't wait too long, though. I'm here now, but at my age, I've got one foot in the grave and another on a banana peel." He gave a wheezy chuckle.

"I promise. I'll do it real soon."

"It sure would be good to see you."

"Thanks so much. Thanks for everything."

"You're family. That counts for a lot."

I swallowed hard. "I'll be back in touch and we can set up a time that works."

"You do that, Claire. You do that."

"Well, bye for now."

"Thanks for calling. You made my day."

Chapter 15

Richard phoned on Thursday with a list of potential films. I couldn't remember the last time I'd been to the movies. I never read newspaper reviews, so I asked him to choose something that was (a) not violent (I couldn't stand to see two kids in a fistfight on the playground, let alone watch a movie with mass slaughter); (b) not romantic (that could make for an uncomfortable after-film conversation); or (c) too angst-ridden (why pay to weep when you could do it for free?).

He said my guidelines had presented a challenge, but at the theater near Kendall Square, which often aired documentaries, it was less of an obstacle.

We sank into plush chairs in the darkened hall and snacked on buttered popcorn from the same bag. About a half hour into the movie, popcorn dispensed with, Richard's arm moved to the back of my seat and rested on my shoulder. It stayed there for the duration. I made no effort to remove it.

He reached for my hand as we walked to a restaurant near Inman Square. Was this what Barbara had in mind? Ease into things? See how it feels? I must admit, it felt good.

The movie evoked a discussion about safe subjects (cinematography, quality of the script), all while we drank beer and consumed a pile of barbecued chicken wings. A waitress appeared, brought fresh napkins, removed the detritus, and took our orders for the main course.

"I brought your postcards," Richard said, "but I don't want to touch them until I wash up."

I looked at my hands. The cuticles had a pink tinge from barbecue sauce. "Good idea," I said. "See you in a minute."

When we'd settled back into our booth, Richard pulled the postcards out of a small backpack, checked to be sure the table was dry, and lined them up. He had applied a sticky note to each one with the translation written in small, neat block letters. One by one, he explained what they said. Other than the two from her sister, the rest were brief explanations of locations without more information. Were they places my grandmother had visited before she left Germany?

"I checked," he said. "All of them are from Saxony, around where you said your grandmother grew up."

"You spent a lot of time on this."

"It made me want to brush up on my German."

"I found a picture of my grandmother when she must have been in her late teens. She and another woman were in the same outfits, like household help, with a baby in a carriage."

"Could it have been her sister? The one from Grimma?"

"I don't know. There's so much I don't know. I should have been working the other day. Instead I went over to Beacon Hill

Readers and bought a bunch of books about Germany."

"I think there's a trip to Deutschland in your future."

"I haven't taken a vacation in years—at least, not a long one."

"Maybe it's time to start," he said.

"I'll tell you what may be in my future. A trip to Ohio. I called Uncle Erich."

"That was nice."

"You don't understand. I haven't seen him in years."

Richard put his elbows on the table, his clasped hands under his chin. Was his look one of empathy or judgment?

"One of the things in the box was a paperweight. I was fascinated by it when I was a kid. I mentioned it to Uncle Erich. He said he got it during the war."

I wiped a ring of sweat from my glass off the table. "Uncle Erich played poker when he was in the Army."

"That was one way to pass the time."

"Unfortunately for us, when he came home he taught the finer points to my father."

Just then the waitress arrived with our burgers and fries. I busied myself with food—ketchup on the plate, mustard on the burger, pickles banished to the side.

"From the look on your face, I take it there's more to the story."

I took a swig of beer. Dutch courage, I think they call it. I'd kept that part of my life sealed off, closed up tight. Barbara said I was repressed. I told her it was a useful coping mechanism which had served me well for decades.

I twirled a French fry through the ketchup. How much could I tell him without slobbering all over my hamburger?

"I told you my father died when I was thirteen."

"Not an easy age in the best of times," he said. "You must have been devastated."

"You got that right. What I didn't tell you…" I lowered my voice, "what I didn't tell you was, he was a problem gambler. He'd gotten in over his head with high stakes poker. I didn't find out until after he died. If Mother knew, she'd been in denial. He left her with massive debts."

He reached across the table and covered my hand with his. "I don't understand how a man could put his family at risk like that. It's so irresponsible."

"We'd lived in this big Victorian show-place in Newton Highlands. Mother sold it to help cover the debts and we moved into this dinky little apartment in another part of Newton. She was determined to keep me in the school system. Said she wanted me to get a good education. My girlfriends—well, former girlfriends except for my friend Barbara, the others dropped me when I fell out of their social class—they all went off to Europe or took horseback riding lessons on their summer vacations. Not me. When I turned sixteen I got a summer job in a pizza place in West Newton. When the girls came in on Saturday evenings, they joked about my apron, which said 'Heaven is where all pizza makers are Italian.' I was so embarrassed. I swore I'd never wear an apron again. And I haven't."

I pulled a toothpick out of my hamburger and made a jagged design in the ketchup.

"I get the embarrassment. On two teachers' salaries, we only could get to Cape Cod for a week, while some of my classmates— sons of Harvard professors—were off to Oxford or Cambridge while their dads were doing some research project."

"Mom found work in a candy shop. That's how I became a lobbyist. She knew Speaker Dunleavy. He used to come into the store. She wrangled me a summer job in his office. After I graduated from U Mass, I went to work for Big Tom Callahan. So that's my story."

I'd given him the expurgated version. That was hard enough. Why I'd decided to do it, I didn't know. All the while, I studied those eyes to see if the crinkles had shifted. They hadn't.

"What I see is a woman who was tempered by that experience and came out stronger as a result. Now I understand where all that focused drive comes from. I've watched you at the State House. When you buttonhole a legislator, he doesn't stand a chance."

"I hope so." I was worried about whether I could get Mangan to goal without compromising my sense of right and wrong.

"If this table weren't in the way," I said, "I'd reach over and kiss you."

"I'll take a rain check. In the meantime, eat. Your food's getting cold."

"So am I. It must be the air conditioning." I put on my sweater. The decibel level in the restaurant had increased.

Richard downed the rest of his beer, then leaned across the table. "Have you ever gone birding?"

"I've seen an exhibition of Audubon prints at the Museum of Fine Arts." I'd gone to one of the wine and cheese galas sponsored by a client, but that was as close as I'd come to the real thing.

"I guess not," he said. "Laura and I shared most things, but she was more inclined to concerts, less to nature. So I went on my own."

Relating to Richard was like opening a Russian nesting doll. You thought you'd reached the last, and then another, smaller one popped up. How many had Laura's face on them?

"Would you like to try?"

I didn't want to get into a competition with a dead wife.

"This might be a challenge. I'm not the patient sort. Is it hard? I'll bet they move around a lot."

"It's relaxing. You take a walk through the woods or by a salt

marsh or the ocean, binoculars around your neck, and pay attention. See what kind of birds you can spot."

"Are there bugs?"

"Bug spray, but only if necessary."

Not my idea of perfume.

"I assume you don't have binoculars," he said.

"You guessed right."

"I think I've got an old pair of my Mom's lying around somewhere."

If they'd been Laura's, that would have scotched any environmental forays. His mother's, I could handle.

"If you get appropriately outfitted," he said, "and by that I
mean jeans and such, I'll supply the equipment."

"All right. I'm game." At least I could give it a try.

"Great. Let's plan on it. Are you free tomorrow? I could pick
you up at nine, take you out to Great Meadows in Concord. It's a
pretty place this time of year."

"Sounds interesting." I liked the idea of seeing Richard in his
"natural habitat."

When we finished our meal, we meandered through the MIT
campus. It was a mild evening. The new-mown grass smelled
sweet. Music blared through open dormitory windows. Students
sat on stone steps, drank beer and talked loudly. Just before we
crossed Massachusetts Avenue, Richard pulled me under a leafy
maple, pressed me close, and kissed me. The second kiss was more
insistent than the first. I felt like I was in college again, except when
I'd been in college, I hadn't had time for such dalliances. My body
melted into his.

As I climbed into the back of a cab, it was my turn to seize the
initiative. I kissed him one last time. "That was a perfect evening."

"To be continued," he said.

Chapter 16

We eased into what soon became weekly outings. I would put on my new hiking boots, designer jeans, and a fleece I'd bought at LL Bean (the latter a life-style concession). Richard would pick me up in his "old but serviceable" Honda Civic promptly at 9:00 on Saturday mornings (he was a stickler for being on time), thermos bottles of hot coffee and a bag of donuts on the front seat, Hillbilly at Harvard on the radio, and take me to one of the nearby Audubon sanctuaries. Each one was a revelation. He knew them all.

Richard explained that serious birders arrived at dawn, when birds were having their breakfasts and were easier to spot, but he had taken pity on me and recalibrated our starting time. So many cars typically were in the parking lots, triangular blue Audubon stickers pasted on their back windows, that they spilled into adjoining neighborhoods. I was amazed. Who thought that birds would be such a draw?

Because Richard was a bit younger, I was particularly sensitive about how I looked. Before I dressed for our first Saturday outing, I had scrutinized my body in the full-length bathroom mirror. The results at age forty-nine were more than acceptable. Not an ounce of fat on my belly, neck still as God intended, beginning crows-feet, but they accented my eyes when I smiled. Thus far the difference in our birthdays hadn't seemed to matter.

Barbara teased me about the transformation—I, who resisted dining al fresco to avoid mosquitoes. She knew me too well. And those walks rounded out the picture of who this man was—an idealist with simple tastes and a nature-based spirituality who had managed to penetrate, ever so slightly, the protective sheath that encompassed my heart. I began to see why Richard's members were so zealous about protecting the environment.

On the first walk we held hands. We kissed. We probably scared away more birds than we spotted. It took only two more Saturdays before Richard didn't need to pick me up. We arose together at my place. Richard said we were in keeping with the behavior of birds right after spring migration. They'd arrived, they were hungry, they were horny. So were we.

I liked his sense of humor.

Before Richard, I had felt no need to venture beyond the two square miles radiating out from the Boston Common. These encompassed my favorite restaurants and clothing stores— boutique shops along Boylston Street (conveniently located near the Four Seasons) and Newbury Street (near the old Ritz). Now I was in a parallel universe--dense woods, rock strewn paths, wildflowers, and poison ivy, resulting in a curious patch of itchy bumps on the back of my left hand. My heels were sore from blisters I'd developed from the new hiking boots. Barbara told me to apply moleskin to the blisters, calamine lotion to my hand, and deep breathing to relax. She said the blisters just as easily could have been hives brought on by the new emotional terrain I was exploring.

Richard may have been at the university level of emotional intelligence, but I still was in grade school. The more time I spent with him, the more schizophrenic I felt. Who was the real Claire Petersen? The hiking boot clad Saturday morning birding neophyte, or the sophisticated, pragmatic, focused St. John suited lobbyist?

I was skittish. "He let me down once," I said to Barbara. "Can I trust him not to do it again?"

"You've given it time, but it's not finished between you. You'll have to talk with him about it."

"I don't know how."

"You'll find a way."

Then one Saturday afternoon we stopped off at his duplex so he could pick up a change of clothes. I went into the bathroom to de-tank. On impulse, I opened a drawer beside the sink. It was filled with Laura's cosmetics.

I stormed into the living room.

"What's this all about?" I said, clutching a bottle of perfume in my hand.

He focused first on the piano, then a hole in the rug—on anything but me.

"It's her scent," he said, his cheeks coloring. "I haven't been able to clean out that drawer. It smells like lilacs, and it's the only thing left. When that goes, she's gone."

I was tempted to walk out again, but I could hear Barbara urging me to stay and work it out—at least try.

I put the perfume bottle on the coffee table. Richard was on one side, I on the other. Somewhere in the dining room, a clock clicked, marking the seconds.

"I'm not asking you to forget her. She was an integral part of your life. She helped shape who you are." I closed my eyes and took a deep breath. "What I need to know, do you have enough room in your heart for me without her shadow?"

Richard started to speak, but I raised my hand to stop him.

"Don't answer right away," said. "Think about it. I'm going back home. This is too important to gloss over."

That's where we left it. I took a cab back to Boston.

It was a long week, but when I told Barbara what had happened, she commended my courage and urged me not to be disheartened. "He'll come around," she said. "He just needed a little extra push."

I wasn't so sure, but she calmed me down.

Richard called on Wednesday to ask if I still wanted to go birding the next Saturday. I took that as an encouraging sign and said yes. On the way back from the Belmont Wildlife Sanctuary we stopped at his place. I went into the bathroom again, and it wasn't only because I'd had a thermos full of coffee. My hands were moist as I opened the drawer beside the sink. It was empty.

My heart was full.

When I asked him about it, he said that he never would stop loving Laura, but he was learning that love wasn't restrictive. It was expansive.

Not long afterwards, Barbara and Caleb invited us for Saturday night dinner. "Enough of this secondhand information," she'd said. "I want to see him for myself." Afterwards she'd pronounced him "very promising."

And thanks to birds, we hiked our way out of Richard's deceased marriage. The time during which I coasted along in that generous space ended, however, when he stopped in mid-trek and said "We've got to talk."

Now what?

Richard had been more silent than usual. I sensed he'd been wrestling with something. I may have been a poor judge of men, but my antennae were finely honed after years of intuiting my father's moods at the breakfast table. Ebullient? Then he was a playful tease and I would dissolve into giggles. Sullen? What had I done wrong?

"About what?" I said.

"We're together in our personal life and at odds our professional. We need to square the circle."

I kicked at a tree root. "I know we need to have this conversation. Do we need to have it now? Things have been so great."

He pushed some stray leaves aside with his foot. "We can't go on like this forever. There are principles at stake."

Piper Mangan was slithering into our bedroom like the black snake I'd spotted beneath a rock the previous Saturday. Richard had assured me it was harmless but I wasn't convinced.

"I know your clients are big business types," he said. "I hoped that spending time with me in the woods might give you a different perspective about open spaces."

"Well, maybe it has, a little." Less than he'd hoped, more than I'd expected. I adjusted my binoculars. The plastic strap was digging into my neck. "Most of my clients are for responsible regulation. They see which way things are going. I've advised them to get out front, show that they care about the environment. I think they do. And I've told them it's a smart business strategy." I looked at him for confirmation.

"Not likely where their bottom line's concerned."

A birder appeared on the path behind us, a navy cap with a Boston Red Sox logo on her head. When I thought she was out of earshot, I turned to Richard.

"This is all theoretical," I said. At least I hoped it was. "For now, can you and I come to an understanding about how we'll navigate issues if they arise?" I'd given this some thought. I wasn't sure it would work, but I wanted it to.

"That already are arising." Richard put his hands in his pants pockets.

"Piper Mangan."

"The one and only."

There it was, no longer avoidable. "Maybe I've misunderstood. Do these birding expeditions have a subtext?" I said. "Are you trying to get me to drop the Mangan account?"

"Let's sit down." Richard motioned to a nearby boulder big enough to accommodate us both. While I moved my rear around in search of a comfortable position, he hefted his binoculars and trained them on dense foliage where a bird was emitting tantalizing chirps.

When he put them down he said "I wonder if you fully understand Mangan's reputation. I've seen his kind before. In fact, I had to deal with one of them when I was working with that Cambridge consulting firm. He was trying to skew some reports about the environmental impact of what, clearly, was a noxious substance. He was unscrupulous, ruthless, heartless. I almost got burned on that job. I'll never make that mistake again. Some bright red lines I will not cross."

I untied my hiking boots, slipped them off, and rubbed my sore heels through thick socks. Though the blisters had disappeared, my hand still itched.

"I still don't get why you agreed to take Mangan on," he said. "He's scarred the land with his bloody golf courses."

"I know. He's not even a diamond in the rough. More like anthracite coal."

So much for my attempt at humor.

"Explain it to me," he said.

"I think his plan to create more middle-income housing for retirees has some redeeming value. Worcester County really needs it." I half believed what I was saying. They needed the housing. Not the golf course.

"Maybe in the hands of some other developer, but not Mangan."

"I'm giving him the benefit of the doubt."

"And bulking up your bottom line."

His voice had a hard edge. I sensed an unforgiving streak that I hadn't seen before. Had I miscalculated yet again?

"Damn it, Richard." I heaved a stone at an innocent squirrel. "He walked into my office after my biggest client disappeared, gobbled up by an out of state firm. The decree came down, and just like that, twenty percent of our revenue vanished."

Richard gestured with his thermos, offering me a drink of water. "Why didn't you tell me? I didn't know."

"Nobody knows, only Maura. I trust you to keep it that way. Perception is eighty percent of reality. But my costs keep rising, and I'm feeling the pressure."

The wind was picking up. My lips were dry. I moistened them with my tongue.

"Did Mangan know?"

That had not occurred to me before.

"Look," I said as I zipped up my fleece, "you and I talk the same language. We're just on different teams."

"I'll admit it—only to you, and only where I won't be overheard—some of the folks I have to deal with are a little, well, shall we say, lacking in perspective. They want to protect chickens so they can roam free, but when it comes to the human species, they aren't always so compassionate."

"I've noticed." Was Richard one of them?

I hoped he wanted to walk this back as much as I did. I slapped at a bug that was buzzing around my neck.

"Here's what I've been thinking," he said. "As long as we play it straight, keep confidential information confidential, make the best case we can where it counts, treat each other and our clients with respect, and avoid shop talk in the bedroom" (he nudged my arm as he emphasized this last point), "we should be able to make this work." The sentence ended with a question.

A mother duck and her babies had moved from the underbrush into a nearby pond. The only sound was their quacking. A swarm of gnats moved in sync through a shaft of sunlight. The silence stretched uncomfortably.

"You paint an ideal scenario," I said.

"Can you keep Mangan in line? He's not like the rest of your clients. They may fight hard, but they play by the rules. I'm not so sure about Mangan."

I was growing less sure with every phone conversation, but I wasn't about to cede the point. I felt like I'd been holding my breath for the past ten minutes. I rubbed my hands back and forth on my thighs. "Well, let's give it a try. So far, we've been doing pretty well. At least I think so."

"Nothing critical has happened yet."

"Do you know something you're not telling me?"

"No, nothing like that. Just based on his reputation. He could take you for a ride before you even knew you were in the car."

Everything that could be said, had been. I was eager to shift the mood, bring us back to bird-land without the gnats. "Can we jump over that stream when we come to it?"

"I guess we'll have to."

I laced up my boots. "And in the meantime, my tush is getting sore from sitting on this rock."

"Want me to rub it?"

"Are you offering to give me a massage?"

"Let's go back to your place and seal the deal with a kiss," he said.

"And just where do you intend to plant it?"

Chapter 17

Richard and I were sipping coffee and eating French crullers at a café on Charles Street on a Sunday morning when he said "Have you booked your flight?"

"To where?"

"Ohio."

"Not yet."

"It sounds like you shouldn't wait too long."

"That's what Uncle Erich said."

"Besides, maybe there's more to the story about your father."

"You mean it could be even worse? I'll never forgive him for what he put us through."

"Calm down. Don't stab me with your donut. I just mean maybe the picture's more nuanced. It's a possibility. You won't know unless you talk with him."

I brushed some crumbs off the table and onto my saucer. "If

I see my uncle, it's to find out more about my grandmother. That's all."

"OK. I get it." He finished his coffee. "The legislature will be out of session on Memorial Day weekend. Why don't you go then? I'd love to take you to Vermont, but it can wait."

So that's how I decided to visit Uncle Erich.

When I called to see if it would be convenient to visit, Uncle Erich sounded hesitant. First he asked if I knew how to get from the airport to Oretown. I assured him that I'd made many business trips where I'd had to rent a car and find my way into unfamiliar territory. Still he wanted to tell me, in great detail, about landmarks I should look for as I neared the Lakeside Retirement Community on Elm Street—Matt's soft-serve ice cream stand, a Salvation Army thrift store, a food mart and gas station, and Our Lady Help of Christians Catholic Church. Except for Our Lady, it sounded like he was intimately familiar with these locations. No Brooks Brothers in sight. I wasn't surprised that Daddy didn't go back home.

Then he worried about where I would stay. "I can't put you up here," he'd said. "The place suits me fine, but it's not geared for company. It's just a bunch of old folks."

Did he ever have visitors at Grandma's old house? Did he want them? Had I made a mistake?

"Don't worry about that," I said. "I've found a motel about a mile away." It was one of those ubiquitous chains that served a "continental breakfast" in the lobby from 6 to 9—my idea of camping out. "It'll be convenient," I said. "And I'd really like to see you."

Once we'd clarified those details, he warmed up to the idea.

"When I was cleaning out the house," he said, "I found an old album of your Grandma's I can show you."

"I'd like that. Say, if you feel like it, I can take you out for lunch or dinner."

"What I'd really like is one of Matt's hot fudge sundaes with lots of whipped cream. I haven't had one o' those in a long time." I was a Häagen Dazs fan, but I could adjust.

"That sounds perfect. I should arrive sometime on Saturday in late morning."

"I usually take a nap after lunch, but I'll be sure to be awake by 2:30."

And that was how we left it.

Lakeside Retirement Community encompassed several buildings haphazardly linked together by enclosed walkways. They looked like they had been joined by necessity rather than design. The complex was surrounded by a macadam parking lot and occasional bits of grass. If Elm Street had been tree-lined at one point, the trees had disappeared long ago. The "Garden City" of Newton it was not.

In recognition of Memorial Day, an American flag had been draped above the high canopied entryway. It billowed whenever the sliding glass doors opened. Two women were seated on a bench, walkers parked in front of them. They ceased their conversation long enough to study me as I made my way to the entrance.

"Nice day," one of them said to me. I stopped in mid-stride. I wasn't used to being spoken to by strangers. It wasn't done in Boston.

"Yes," I said, "now that you mention it, it is, isn't it?" The dashboard thermometer said that the temperature was seventy-five degrees.

"Are you here to visit?" the one with spindly legs and spectacles on a chain around her neck asked me.

"Of course she's here to visit, Helene," said her companion. She clutched the arms of her walker with bulging purple veined hands. "She's got a lot of years ahead of her before she comes here."

I struggled to keep my face neutral.

"We're like professional greeters," the first one said.

The sliding glass doors continued to open and close as I stood at the threshold.

"Well, I think you should get paid," I said. "You're very good at it."

"They couldn't afford us," Helene said.

They giggled as I walked inside.

A long bench with scuffed legs and faded seat was pushed against the wall of a short entryway. A woman with tightly permed gray hair—another retiree?—sat behind the front desk in the reception area, watching television. The station, tuned to Fox News, was placed on mute, words scrolling along the bottom of the screen— another reminder that I wasn't in Massachusetts anymore. Just then an elevator door opened and out came a uniformed aide pushing a woman in a wheelchair, her head lolled toward her shoulder.

"Can I help you?" the receptionist asked me. Then she turned toward the elevator and said, "Good afternoon, Mrs. Montgomery. Glad to see you out and about."

The wheelchair occupant smiled with one side of her mouth and managed a wave as she was wheeled down the hall.

I had been insulated from the assaults of old age. Here mortality and all its precursors—deteriorating bodies, diminished capacities, loss of independence—were in my face. I could see how space became available. The death rate must be substantial. I wanted to turn around and take the next flight back to Boston.

"Can I help you, dear?" the receptionist asked again.

"Oh, thanks. I'm here to see my uncle, Erich Petersen."

"Yes, he's one of our new residents. Let me tell him you're here. What's your name?"

"Claire Petersen."

"Are you from around here? I don't think we've seen you before."

"No, I flew in from Boston this morning."

"My, my, that's a long way. Your uncle is a lucky man. Well, welcome to Oretown. Be sure to look at the lake while you're here. The view at sunset is spectacular." She spoke with civic pride.

She called my uncle. "He says you can go on up. Take the elevator to the third floor, turn left, go through the first hallway, make another left, and his door will be on the right. Number three-two-seven B. Enjoy your visit."

"Is there a water fountain nearby? I could use a drink."

"Sure, dear. Just down that hall. Or if you want some pop, go a little farther and you'll see the convenience shop. They should be open now."

So far I'd seen only old women. At age 90 with most of his faculties (at least as far as I knew), if Uncle Erich sent the right signals, he could have a fresh batch of cookies at his door every afternoon. How could he stand it?

Chapter 18

When I saw Uncle Erich standing outside his door, leaning on a cane, my heart raced and my eyes moistened, reactions for which I wasn't prepared.

I hugged him. Despite being bent over, he still was a few inches taller than I. He was so thin that I could feel ribs through his flannel shirt.

"You found me all right," he said.

"Your directions were perfect."

"Come on in and set a spell. You must be tired after that long trip."

Actually, I felt like I'd consumed four cups of coffee. The last time I had seen him I was in my teens. Now I was encountering him from the perspective that comes with age, both his and mine.

He eased into a brown fabric recliner, raised the footrest, and propped up his slippered feet. He wore no socks. His ankles were swollen. Pink and purple blotches circled the tight, puffy skin.

I sat across from him on a threadbare sofa, a reject even by Salvation Army standards.

"How about you?" I said. "Are you exhausted after your move?"

"Took me a couple weeks to catch up—as much as I'm going to these days. Expecting you perked me up real good."

I wasn't sure what to say next. I reached into my purse and pulled out a gift-wrapped box of Godiva chocolates I'd purchased at the airport at the last minute. I was ashamed that I hadn't given it more thought.

"You didn't have to go and do that." When he smiled, his lips stayed together and turned down a bit at the corners, just like my father's. He carefully unwrapped the box, smoothed out the paper, and set it on a table next to his chair. "But I'm glad you did. Dark chocolates! I love 'em. Here, you should have the first piece."

"They're for you, Uncle Erich. I'm glad you like them."

As I watched him eat one, then another, it struck me that I probably was seeing an older version of what my father would have looked like had he lived into old age. If he'd taken better care of himself, I would have had the chance to find out.

Uncle Erich had generous features—long straight nose, wide mouth with thin lips, ears that stuck out a bit, glasses that magnified his blue eyes. His voice was a soft baritone. There the similarities ended. As far as I knew, Uncle Erich had stayed close to home and kept to himself most of his adult life. When my father got out of college, he'd hopped on a bus bound for Boston before the ink was dry on his diploma.

A crocheted throw was draped over the back of the sofa. I swept my hand over the soft, multi-colored squares of yarn, "waste not, want not" leftovers with no particular design. "Did Grandma make this?"

"Yep. She was always busy workin' on somethin'. It's real comfy when I stretch out. I had to get rid of most of the furniture when I moved here." He waved his arm around the small living room. "Not that there was a lot, but I kept a few things."

The place looked like a combination of early attic and late basement.

"How are you settling in?"

"I've got a nice view of the lake from my bedroom window. Go on in and take a look."

I walked through a narrow kitchenette—small stove, sink with dishes stacked neatly in the drain, apartment sized refrigerator, a few cabinets—and into his bedroom. Outfitted with monastic simplicity, it contained a dresser, chest of drawers, twin bed, and closet. The bed was covered with a faded duvet, the nightstand laden with books. On top was a Bible, a rubber band around the dirty white leather cover to keep the binding from falling off. A small bathroom with shower stall was across from the bed. Emergency pull chains were strategically located in each room.

The space felt cramped. I knew what it was like to live in tight quarters. My mother and I had done that once. I would never want to do it again. My living room was bigger than his whole apartment.

"Great view, huh?" Uncle Erich yelled.

I was barely able to glimpse the lake through a mass of buildings.

"I was real lucky to get this unit," he said. "Folks on lower floors can't see spit."

I returned to the living room sofa.

"Thanks again for sending me that box," I said.

"Petersen and Associates. Sounds important."

"I deal with state tax policies that affect utilities--oil, gas, and electric, that sort of thing. Mom paved the way for the job right out of college, and I've been doing it ever since. Sometimes it's just exasperating, but I'm pretty good at it."

"I'll bet you are. Like your Dad."

I hoped not. He lived close to the edge, then tumbled over with no thought for the damage he left behind.

"When did you retire, Uncle Erich? I've been so occupied with my own work that I kind of lost track." I wanted to apologize for neglecting him for so many years, but I didn't know how.

"I was seventy-eight. At the old A&P on Main Street. Started when I got out of the Army, worked my way up. That's before it was sold to one of those big overseas grocery outfits. Things changed a lot afterwards, but I hung in there."

"Good heavens! You must have been there over fifty years." I couldn't picture trudging up and down the State House steps for five decades. Some days, it was hard to contemplate five more months. Then again, I couldn't imagine anything else.

"Fifty-one." He straightened in his recliner and pointed to a small plaque. "They gave it to me when I left. The manager wrote me a real nice letter. I pasted it on the back. Take a look."

Uncle Erich was acknowledged for being "honest and loyal; a man of integrity who knew his job; and a kindly mentor to new employees."

If somebody gave me a plaque, what would it say? "With her elbows out and her knees together, she kept our taxes low."

I brushed off the dust and put it back on the shelf.

"Jobs were scarce after the war," he said. "I was lucky to get it. The manager was a member of our church. He knew me from when we were boys in Sunday School. That helped. I was in charge of produce, don't cha know. We were always understaffed. Every time I turned around I was training some new kid who only stayed for a coupl'a years. But I knew the business. They couldn't get rid of me."

I couldn't picture Daddy in an apron with his elbows in lettuce and spinach eight to ten hours a day.

"So how did the move go? I'm sorry I couldn't have been here to help." The thought had never occurred to me, but now that I saw him, I wished it had.

"The old neighborhood changed a lot over the years. When your Dad and I were growing up it was filled with Germans, but by the time I left, most of them had moved out."

I envied being able to live in the same home for decades, swaddled by memories. At least if they were good ones. Memories were tricky.

"I couldn't keep up with it anymore. Arthritis, bum knees, gout. Sometimes it hurts like the devil." He shifted in his chair. "Hired the neighbor kids to mow the lawn and shovel the walks in the winter. When it came time to move, I gave my old tools to the fella next door, passed some furniture along to the couple across the street. They came over and helped me pack."

What little he had, and he still was giving.

"Can I get you anything, Uncle Erich? A glass of water? A cup of coffee or something?"

"That would be real nice. Tap water. No ice. Hurts my teeth."

I patted his shoulder as I walked by. He reached for my hand and held it. Just held it.

"I'm glad you're here," he said.

"So am I." And to my surprise, I was.

"Make yourself at home in the kitchen, but dinner's early. We should be heading downstairs around five, otherwise the salad bar will be picked over."

I gave him his water, then leafed through a photo album he had placed on the coffee table. The first picture was of two women dressed in identical outfits in front of a country house surrounded by woodlands.

"Is one of these women Grandma?"

"Yep. Your Grandma was a cook in a big house in Chemnitz. Three families and all the kids. She fed 'em all."

"Good heavens!"

"Earned thirty marks a month, about seven and a half dollars. Said that was good wages then. Every other Sunday off."

I worked hard, too, but I wasn't standing on my feet over a hot stove all day. And I made sure I got paid well for it.

"How did she learn to cook?"

"I guess just by doing. There were twelve kids in her family. They had big families in those days."

"How could they all fit around the kitchen table? Her poor mother must have been a wreck."

He fumbled with an arm cover on the recliner. "She helped her mum. Started work when she was sixteen."

With all those siblings, she might have wanted to get out of the house.

"Got hired by a family in Leipzig," he said, "graduated to the big house, then worked in a castle."

"No wonder she was such a good baker." And no wonder she wanted to come to America. But her life ended up being just as hard, if not harder, than it had been in Germany.

"She sent us a stollen every Christmas."

"I know. I wrapped it up real good, took it to the post office for her."

The phone rang. The ringer was loud.

"Hello," he said, bellowing into the receiver. "Well, isn't that nice. Yep, I'm settling in fine."

I could hear a woman's voice.

"I'm glad you can use 'em. No room for 'em here." He held the phone close to his ear. "Not this weekend. My niece is here, all the way from Boston." He looked over at me and winked. "Next weekend? Well sure, I'm not goin' anywhere." He chuckled. "Least as not above ground. No need to call. Just come on over any time after 2:30. Bring the kids."

"That was Mrs. Martinez," he said. "The family that lives across the street. Nice couple." He looked at his watch. "It's 4:45, we'd better get a move on."

Apparently we were on EST—elder standard time. He pushed the lever to his recliner and eased his way out of the chair.

"As much a move as I get on these days. Think I'll use the facility before we go. Make my bladder gladder."

Chapter 19

He used his walker to slowly maneuver the hallways. Every time he picked it up and set it down it made a soft metallic click that, for some reason, irritated me. Then I was annoyed by my impatience.

The dining room, a scene of thinning hair, sagging skin, and shuffling feet, was like being in a 'fun house' with distorted mirrors. I might spend hundreds of dollars on anti-aging creams, but was this my future?

It was 5:00 and the place was bustling, as much as octogenarians bustle anywhere. Walkers were parked along the walls. Wheelchairs were everywhere. Aides helped with trays for those too palsied to carry them. The salad bar, in a station at the center of the cavernous room, was a big attraction. Lines snaked along both sides. Uncle Erich was right about its popularity. I expected an altercation to break out any minute over the olive tray.

He spotted a table for two in one corner. The tablecloth had been wiped free of crumbs from previous diners. A bubbly teenager in maroon slacks and shirt with white apron arrived and said "Hello, Mr. Petersen. You've got company today."

"Yep." He beamed. "This is my niece—Claire Petersen. My brother's girl. She flew in from Boston this morning."

"All the way from Boston," she said. "I'd like to go there. See the Mayflower and stuff."

"Zofia's finishing high school in June," Uncle Erich said. "Starting nursing school in the fall, aren't cha?"

"Mr. Petersen's real nice. He always thanks me when I help him with his tray."

"I never got waited on, Zofia. Always took care of myself. A man could get used to this."

She giggled.

Was Uncle Erich less reclusive than I thought? Perhaps years working in the grocery store had fostered his ease with the public. I flashed back to Richard's banter with May in the Thai restaurant. They both wrapped their words in warmth, and people responded in kind.

Ice cubes clinked against a metal pitcher as Zofia poured our water. "I remember," she said. "No ice for you."

We made our way to the buffet. I took two trays—one for Uncle Erich. In addition to the salad bar, the main offerings included lentil soup (easy on dentures, I supposed), chicken and fish in non-descript sauces, mashed potatoes, overcooked green beans, and macaroni and cheese. The Four Seasons it was not.

When we returned to our table, Uncle Erich tucked his napkin into his shirt, then launched into the mac and cheese.

"Tell me about Grandma's postcards," I said. "Some are pictures of German countryside, and a few have writing on them. I don't speak German but a friend of mine offered to translate them for me." It was because of Richard that I was in Ohio. If he hadn't prodded me, would I have come?

Uncle Erich leaned forward and cupped a hand to his ear. With the cacophony of voices around the room it was difficult to hear, but I wondered if he needed to get hearing aids. Maybe I could broach the subject before I left, arrange for him to get his hearing tested. If he needed a device, I'd gladly pay for it.

I projected my voice. "I said, one is of a huge manor with a gatehouse."

"That was the castle she worked in."

"I wonder if it's still there."

"Nope. Got bombed during the war." He rubbed his thigh, took a drink of water, looked around for Zofia, pointed to our glasses. "Like everything else around there."

He stared out the window. I waited for more information, but none was forthcoming. Maybe tomorrow.

"See them roses," he said. "One of the residents decided we needed a bit of color. They like it there. Your grandma had some in the backyard, remember? Said they reminded her of where she grew up."

"What was Christmas like when you were a kid?" I hoped that would be a safer subject. "I bought a book about German traditions, and one whole section was about Christmas."

"We didn't have much money during the Depression. Nobody did. At least we had a roof over our heads and clothes on our backs, even if Papa re-soled our shoes with old rubber tire tread."

"That was inventive."

No wonder my father liked expensive shoes, a penchant I had inherited. I shuddered to think of him plodding around on that thick black rubber. Did he hide his feet under the desk at school to avoid getting teased?

"Once things were so tight that we didn't have a tree. Papa made a chandelier-type contraption out of tin cans, put little oil lamps on it, and it made angel shapes on the ceiling when it turned. He was good with his hands."

Something got lost when the gene pool was passed along. Daddy couldn't pound a nail without whacking his thumb.

"When Christmas came," he said, "our mum would string a big white sheet across the entrance to the living room. We weren't allowed to go in there until Christmas morning. Your dad used to get down on his knees and blow the sheet so it'd move and he could get a peek at presents under the tree. We mostly got clothes, but Papa was real good at whittling whistles and cars out of wood."

I'd always thought the Christmas hoopla at our house was my mother's doing. She practically lived at Bloomingdales. Maybe it had been my father's idea. He liked being the big shot, strolling around with a wad of bills in his pocket. Or maybe mother did it because she knew he liked it. I didn't know anymore.

"Things were hard enough before Papa got sick," Uncle Erich said, "but after was bad. Your Grandma took in other people's laundry, baked kuchen that we boys sold in the neighborhood. I was older. I got a job at a bakery to help pay the bills. It was harder on your dad. He just kind'a got lost."

"He never talked about any of this."

"What you don't talk about you don't have to think about. Least that might'a been his idea. He'd been smarter than me at school, but after Papa died, his grades went down. He started playing hooky. Smoked behind the garage."

Started young, never stopped, probably killed him.

I knew what it was like to lose your father at a young age. My experience paralleled my father's in a way I hadn't considered. What would have happened if he hadn't dropped dead when he did?

"Where did he get the money for cigarettes?" I asked.

"Shooting craps. Picked up loaded dice somewhere. Kids suspected it but they could never prove it. He'd switch 'em with regular dice to keep em' guessing."

My jaw tightened. A con artist at eleven. I thought Dad's taste for gambling came from Uncle Erich. It turned out he'd learned much earlier.

How could he get up every Sunday morning after having played poker with the boys on Saturday night, look us in the face over the breakfast orange juice, and live with himself? I guess he couldn't. And because we only found out about the extent of his problem after he died, I couldn't confront him. I probably took it out on my mother more than she deserved. No wonder I was confused.

"I'm sorry. What did you say?" My ears were ringing. The story was more nuanced than the one Mom had told me.

"That's why I taught him poker when I got back from the war. At least it was a game of skill. He was smart, learned real fast, beat me every time. But we only played for pennies. I didn't know it would get him into trouble."

I pushed away my plate. I'd lost my appetite. How could I have blamed this dear old man?

"Mom said she didn't realize he had a problem. He was good at hiding it. We didn't find out about his gambling debts until after he died."

Uncle Erich rubbed his forehead. "I'm sorry. I guess it was a mistake. Your Grandma and I suspected that something was wrong. I wish we could have helped."

"Mom said, 'when bad things happen, you just have to buck up.' And that's what she did." She hunkered down, shut out distractions, pressed on, dragged me along with her.

"I s'pose that's true. Takes a lot of energy. Took me a long time to figure that out. If you don't mourn right, you can't live right. You just kind'a close down. I learned the hard way."

My head ached. I reached in my purse and dug out two aspirin, snuck them into my mouth when Uncle Erich wasn't looking.

He lifted a bony hand and waved to Zofia.

"Had all you want, Mr. Petersen?" Zofia said.

"Yep. Sure was tasty. Now how about a piece o' that chocolate cream pie. You want one too, don't cha, Claire?" He rubbed his hands together in anticipation.

I really didn't, but I agreed to please him. He wolfed down his pie, threw his napkin on the table, and wrapped his hands around the arms of the chair to propel himself up. It took him two tries. I reached out to help but he waved me away.

"Let me get the walker, Uncle Erich."

"That'd be real nice. It's good to have you here, but I'm afraid I'm all tired out now. Can we call it a night?"

It was 6:15.

"Of course."

"You're coming back tomorrow though, aren't cha?"

"I wouldn't miss it for the world. When do you want me to be here?"

"I'm not makin' it to church much these days, so any time after 9:30. I'll be breakfasted and rarin' to go by then." He chuckled. "As rarin' as I get at my age."

We made our way down the hallway toward the elevator and the front entrance. I gave him a hug and a kiss. The stubble on his chin rubbed against my cheek.

"Now that's bound to give me a good night. You get some sleep now, ya hear? You've had a long day."

Chapter 20

I opened the door to my motel room, kicked off my shoes and fell on the bed. The walls were beige, the woodwork was dung brown, the bedspread was "earth tones." A generic pastoral scene in plastic frame hung on the wall above a dresser. The bathroom emitted a faint scent of bug spray.

I kept thinking about my Dad. Mother was all business, but Dad could be playful. When I was little, he'd make up silly songs that sent me running around the room in giggles. I would put my head in his lap, he'd stroke my hair, call me his "little chickadee." Those were the good days.

Other times he was withdrawn and I wondered what I'd done to disappoint him. I tried to be his good girl. I would show him my school papers with five gold stars, hide love notes in his pockets where he would find them on his way to the office, put the morning newspaper on the breakfast table next to his chair, but I couldn't touch him. Not then.

Uncle Erich had offered fresh details that made me see both brothers in a different light. Seared by the Depression, Uncle Erich coped in one way, Dad in another. He was in a relentless pursuit of status that had eluded him as a child. It must have exhausted him.

And what drove me? A win for a client at the State House? A new pair of Jimmy Choo shoes to celebrate? Breakfast with Barbara at The Four Seasons?

It was only 6:45 and I didn't know what to do with myself. I tried to read a *New Yorker* I'd stuffed in my bag, but I couldn't concentrate.

I phoned Richard.

"I was hoping you'd call."

"I'm not interrupting your dinner, am I?"

"I had leftover Thai tonight. Just finished."

"Talk about the rust belt," I said. "This motel I'm in. I feel like I'm camping out." I described the decor. "Oretown—at least what I've seen of it—looks like parts of South Boston before urban renewal."

"It's definitely not up to your standards."

Richard would have been comfortable in a tent with a sleeping bag and a campfire. So, I suspected, would Uncle Erich.

"But the motel is close to Matt's ice cream stand. I promised Uncle Erich I'd take him there."

He laughed. "It doesn't take much to make him happy."

That was part of Uncle Erich's allure. Richard's, too, I was beginning to realize.

"Gosh," I said. "if I don't do it tomorrow, it won't happen."

"Is everything all right?" he said. "It's a bit early."

"I guess old folks are on a different schedule. Uncle Erich and I were in the dining room by five. He wanted to be sure to get there before the salad bar was picked over."

"If he eats supper at five, you'd better get ice cream right after lunch."

"He takes an afternoon nap."

"I'm sure you'll work it out."

"I'd better. I don't want to disappoint the old guy."

"So how's it going?" Silence. "Are you there?"

"I don't know how to answer that." I massaged an insole. "I mean, he seems really pleased to see me. Thank you for giving me that little push."

"It didn't take much prompting. You were ready."

"I came to Oretown to learn about my Grandma. I hadn't anticipated how it would feel to see Uncle Erich. Oh, Richard, I feel like death is stalking me around every corner. And believe me, there are a lot of corners in those buildings." I picked at a loose thread in the bedspread. "Uncle Erich is my last link with any kind of family, and he's ninety years old. He's so frail. I wish I hadn't waited so long."

"That's one reason I don't take any day for granted. I want to suck every bit of juice out of the mango, and so should you."

There was Laura, hovering again. "I'm sorry, Richard."

"No need to apologize. It's my new mantra. I'm still a neo-phyte, but I'm working on it."

"He's in this tiny little apartment—smaller than the place that he and Grandma lived in, and that was like a doll house, but he doesn't seem to mind. He had a very ordinary job, in charge of pro-duce in a grocery store, yet he's proud of what he did. He started working there right after the war, stayed until he retired, well into his seventies. Daddy would never do something like that."

"Does it matter?"

Did it?

"And I discovered something else. The family story about Uncle Erich being a recluse? Bunk. He's not shy. The neighbors across the street called. They plan to visit him next weekend. The people in the retirement home know him already. He's charmed the young girl who waited on us in the dining room."

"That Petersen touch."

"What do you mean?"

"Don't you know? You do that, too. Pay attention to people who often get ignored. They notice."

I plumped up two pillows, put them against the headboard, and leaned back.

"What are you doing while I'm holed up in this dump?"

"I was going to read *The Times*. And I have one of those German beers you brought me."

"I'm stretched out on the bed, too. If I wanted to get a *Times*, I'd have to drive back to the airport."

"Did you find out anything about the postcards?" he asked.

"The big residence with the gatehouse we looked at? Grandma was the cook there. Uncle Erich said it was bombed during the war. I wanted to ask how he knew, but he changed the subject."

"I wondered about that. German cities were pulverized by Allied bombs."

I had skirted around the big reveal. "The stories about my father feel more complicated than my mother's version."

"Do you have the hiccups? Get a glass of water. I'll wait."

"I'm OK. Just trying to process everything, and I don't know what to do with any of it."

"If you want to talk about it…"

"It's all too much."

When Timmy was two, he had a little red box with various shaped holes in the yellow top. He was supposed to fit the right shapes—stars, squares, circles, oblongs, triangles—into the right holes. I felt like I was trying to fit square blocks into round holes.

"You don't have to be strong all the time. You can lean into me once in a while."

Could I? Richard might be sucking juice out of mangoes, while my mantra had been "You'd better take care of yourself, because if you don't, no one else is going to do it for you."

"Call me tomorrow?" he said.

"I will. For sure. And thanks."

"For what?"

"For listening."

I spent the rest of the evening channel surfing. When I couldn't stand it anymore, I turned out the light. Instead of counting sheep, I thought about running my fingers over Richard's body—a body with which I was becoming increasingly familiar. The result was anything but sleep-inducing.

Chapter 21

The hallway to Uncle Erich's apartment was deserted. Potted geraniums on a table by a window gave the area a musty smell. Sounds from televisions filtered through doorways.

I rapped on Uncle Erich's door, waited, knocked harder, and was relieved to hear movement inside.

"Am I too early?" I said when he opened the door.

"No, you're right on time, gal."

I kissed him. Gray stubble scratched my cheek.

"These old bones are pretty stiff in the morning. Come on in." He hobbled across the living room, fell into his recliner and rubbed his hands back and forth across his thighs.

"Do you take any medication for your arthritis? Can I get you something?"

"Already did. Takes a while for it to kick in. Another cup a 'joe' would be nice. I usually just have one, but I think I'll cheat this morning. Live it up while you're here."

"Coming right up. How do you take it?"

"Black. Nothin' in it. Coffee's above the sink." That was how my father liked it, too, but mother brewed his in a French press. No instant for him.

"So how did you sleep?" I asked as I busied myself in the narrow kitchenette.

"Like a baby. 'Cept I didn't cry. How 'bout you?"

"Fine, thanks."

I hadn't, really. I had dreamt that a miniaturized version of my uncle, who morphed into my father, was crouched in the corner of a dark, coal-blackened basement that smelled of pickles. He was sobbing and wiping the snot into his sleeve. I wanted to comfort him, but I couldn't reach him. I was stuck on basement stairs that ended in mid-air. The floor was fathoms below. I was afraid to jump, paralyzed on the last step. I awoke exhausted.

The coffee mugs looked like they could use an extra wash. I found some detergent next to the sink.

"Do you still want to go to Matt's for ice cream? We could go out for lunch, finish up there for dessert."

"That sounds real nice. As long as it's my treat."

"Oh, let me do that for you."

"I haven't been there in a long time. Used to take your Grandma. She liked their chocolate dipped cones."

"Good. We have a plan."

I put the coffee on the table next to his lounger and returned to the sofa across from his chair. He inhaled the aroma, then slurped contentedly, reminding me of construction workers at the donut shop on Washington Street before their morning shift.

"Ah, that's good," he said. "Thanks. Not used to being pampered."

And I wasn't used to doing the pampering.

"I'm yours as long as I'm here. If I can do anything for you, I want to."

"You're here. That's what counts."

And to think I might not have come. I couldn't make up for all those lost years, but I was going to savor every minute I had with Uncle Erich, then see him regularly in the future. If I had to skip out of the office on Fridays once in a while, I would do it. The legislature never was in session then, anyway.

"Whenever I smell coffee I think o' your Grandma," he said. "She used to like a cup with her morning Kuchen. She got up to make breakfast before I left for work, and I went real early. Got all those vegetables lookin' real perky, picked out the spoilt ones before the customers came in at eight. We'd sit at the kitchen table together. It was a good way to start the day."

At Richard's urging, he and I had begun to share some weekends, but it still was a novelty. I wasn't sure I would like it as an everyday occurrence.

"I'll bet she liked it, too," I said.

He looked toward the window. "I still miss her."

"I do, too." I missed the whole lot of them, or what could have been but never was.

"Tell me more about the things in the box you sent," I said. "The German books with pictures of kids on the covers are children's books, right?"

"Your Grandma read 'em to us when we were young'uns."

"In German?"

"Yup. That's what we spoke round the house, least 'til we started school. Probably wasn't a good idea. Folks were suspicious of Germans back then. Memories of the first war and all. The Italian kids teased your Dad about his accent. Called him a dirty Hun.

He didn't know how to handle it. Being an older brother, I settled things. After that we didn't have any more problems."

"Did my father help?" My Dad didn't strike me as the pugilistic type.

"Aw, hon, he couldn't fight his way out of a paper sack. Wasn't his way. He was more clever with his mind. Could think of ways to get at 'em more subtle-like."

"Sometimes he was too clever for his own good."

"Don't know about that. We didn't hear much after he moved East. Wished we had. Yer Grandma would have liked it."

My lips felt dry. I worried a piece of skin in one corner until it bled.

"He didn't talk about his family," I said, "and I never understood why." If he had opened up, even a little, maybe some of my resentment would have dissolved.

"Can't rightly say. Guess I was too caught up in my own stuff to think much about it."

My Dad had glided his way along the surface—at least that was the impression he left. When he graduated from high school he joined the Army. On the rare occasions that he mentioned it, he talked about going to dance halls with the boys on Saturday evenings. He used the GI bill to finance his way through Ohio State. After he graduated, a fraternity brother's father offered him a job in Massachusetts at an advertising firm, and he never looked back.

"Made a good life for himself, I guess," he said.

"It was more complicated than that."

"Your Mom told me some after your Grandma died. Sounded hard on you two. But look how you turned out. She was real proud of you. Your Dad would be, too."

He rearranged some newspapers on the table next to his recliner.

"Had a girlfriend before I enlisted."

I had wondered. A single man all his life, living with his mother until she died...

"Thought about asking her to marry me," he said, "but it didn't seem like the right thing to do with the war and all. She wrote for a while. Then the letters slowed down. At first I thought it was because of the mail. Not easy to get letters. Eventually they just stopped."

"Did you ever find out what happened?"

"Your Grandma wrote me, broke the news, said the girl'd married some fella working in the steel plant. Years later she came into the A&P. I saw her from a distance. She'd got real fat. I couldn't dodge 'em all, but I dodged that bullet."

Was that an opening?

"What did you do during the war?"

He put his big hands on the arms of the chair and adjusted his position.

"I was in what's called the signal corps. Carried a radio on my back. Made for pretty good communication in the field most of the time. Things got crazy toward the end. That's when I got wounded."

"You were hurt?"

He rubbed his big hands across his legs. "Just grazed in the thigh. Got infected. Could have been a lot worse. I was lucky. Some of my buddies weren't." He took off his glasses and wiped his eyes. "I don't talk about it."

"I'm sorry. I didn't know."

"You don't wanna."

I did, but I didn't want to probe.

"Are you warm enough? Do you want me to put this throw over your legs?"

"Nah, I'm fine."

The sound of a lawnmower reverberated off the brick walls below.

"Took me a while to get used to regular livin' after I got back," he said. "Your Grandma was a saint. Put up with me when she could've tossed me out on my ear. Later, after I came out of the fog, I guess I just got set in my ways. It creeps up on 'ya, livin' single. Kind'a liked it." He pulled at the lapels on his flannel shirt. "Hard to change as you get older."

"I know what you mean."

With each passing year, the routine I'd fallen into—no, chosen, really—had become increasingly comfortable, seductively familiar. Richard had jolted those patterns. Sometimes it felt refreshing. Still, I had a niggling worry that if I wandered too far beyond my comfort zone I wouldn't be able to breathe.

"But you're young. You've got a lot o' life ahead of ya'." He winked at me. "Nice gal like you, should'a been snatched up years ago."

"You're an old sweetie." Even though I had no desire to be "snatched up" by any man, coming from Uncle Erich, I took it as a compliment.

I walked over to the window. A man in overalls was edging a narrow flower bed that ran the length of the building. He used his foot to push the sharp end of the blade into the soil.

"One of the postcards," I said, "was signed 'your dear sister Anna.' I wondered about that."

"Yep. She was the one your Grandma was closest to. They were only a year apart. After the war, your Grandma sent clothes, food, whatever she could, but there was only so much we could do. Aunt Anna was in the Russian Zone, don' cha know." He ran his hand through his hair—what was left of it.

"We did what we had to do, but that collateral damage you read about in the papers is real people. Aunt Anna had two sons. Both dead," he said. "Just think of it. I had no question about what we were fighting for. Hitler and his cronies were monsters, but I'd been fighting my cousins. Could'a killed one of 'em myself. I worried over that a lot after I got back home."

I was stunned. My impressions of the war were from school history books and Turner Classic movies. In my mind, "the enemy" always had been sinister jackbooted soldiers strutting through defeated Paris, or faceless men bombing our brave boys as they stormed Normandy beaches. It never had occurred to me that some of my relatives might have been German soldiers, drafted with as little say in the matter as my Uncle Erich would have had. I wondered if any of them were still alive, if they had families, if I had relatives in Germany.

"I'd seen so much in the war. Too much. A bar of chocolate could buy you...well, anything. Think of it. A bar of chocolate. Took time to beat back the blue devils after I got home. After I came out of it, I made some decisions. I never was going to get rich. Didn't want to. But I could take care of what I had, share the rest. After all I'd seen, maybe I could restore some balance, if not in the world, at least at home."

There it was, Uncle Erich's philosophy, all wrapped up like a Hershey's Kiss in silver foil.

"Enough of this," he said. "Yesterday is history, and that's where it ought'a stay. I'm fer livin' in the present. That's all we got. Better make the most of it."

I wanted to hear more, but he had clammed up.

I went over and kissed his forehead. "You're a genuine philosopher."

He patted my arm.

"Let me wash up these coffee mugs," I said. I put them in a drain and wiped all the surrounding surfaces. It was approaching 11:30.

"Are you getting hungry? We could head out to lunch. You pick the place."

He scratched his chin. "There's a restaurant not far from Matt's. Used to stop in there for a treat once in a while. They got an 'all you can eat' lunch buffet for 7.99. A real bargain."

"I could take you some place a little fancier, if you like."

"Plain and simple, that fills the bill." He pulled himself out of his recliner and slowly made his way into the bathroom.

"Should we take your walker? I can put it in the trunk of the car."

"Don't want to cause any trouble, but that'd be a help. I'm not too steady on my pins today."

He maneuvered the walker out the door and we slowly made our way to the entrance of the building. Helene and her companion were sitting on the same bench where I'd encountered them the previous day.

"See you've got a new girlfriend, Mr. Petersen," Helene said.

"My niece," he said, standing straighter. We're off to Polaski's for lunch."

Chapter 22

I opened the restaurant door so Uncle Erich could maneuver through with his walker. An aroma of kielbasa and cabbage flavored the air. Tables and chairs were arrayed on either side of a buffet that stretched down the center of the narrow room. An apron-clad cook, who looked like he had indulged in far too much kielbasa, barreled out of the kitchen with a tray of dark rolls that he dumped into a wicker basket.

"We beat the Sunday lunch crowd," Uncle Erich said. "That's good. We have our pick o' seats."

He chose a table mid-way between the entrance and the kitchen.

"This is the best spot. If you get too close to the door, you get a draft every time someone comes through. And if you're too near the kitchen you get a lot o' noise."

I helped him park his walker against the wall and we settled in.

Polaski's was a long way from the Four Seasons. Rain-spattered, dust-covered windows overlooked the parking lot. At least I could keep an eye on my rental car and hope it wouldn't get burgled while we were inside.

I unwrapped a tab containing flatware and paper napkin. A waitress filled our glasses, slopping water over the sides and onto the floor.

"How're ya' doin', Sadie?" Uncle Erich said. "The world treatin' you all right?"

Sadie looked like she'd made a career of waitressing, one that should have been rewarded with retirement twenty years ago. She was bow-legged and stoop shouldered. Her arms were dotted with liver spots. She wore a hair net.

"Better for seeing you in here, Mr. Petersen."

He grinned. "This here's my niece, all the way from Boston."

"My, my. Well I hope you enjoy your stay. We got pierogies today. The cook made 'em last night. Be sure to give 'em a try." She duck-walked back into the kitchen.

"I know what I want, Claire. Would you make up a tray for me?"

And so, per Uncle Erich's instructions, I loaded a plate with a pork cutlet, boiled potatoes, cabbage stew, and "one pierogie, to make Sadie happy." I chose the ones stuffed with mushrooms and added green beans on the side. A far cry from my normal luncheon fare of cottage cheese and fruit, the food was delicious.

Uncle Erich wasn't as talkative as he had been on Saturday. He seemed distracted. I wondered if I had tired him out, or if talk about the war had disquieted him. I filled in conversational gaps with comments about Grandma. I had been thinking about the courage it would take to make such a radical change, to set out for a new land and an unknown future. What inner strength did she draw on? Where did it come from?

Every time new patrons—"the after-church folks" he called them--walked in the door, Uncle Erich's head jerked up. It was as if he were expecting someone who had failed to arrive.

Lunch was finished in twenty minutes. When Sadie returned with the bill--$15.98 plus tax—I grabbed it before Uncle Erich had a chance and hauled out my American Express Platinum card, only to discover that the restaurant was a "cash only" place. I left a five dollar tip under the sugar bowl and retrieved his walker.

We never made it to Matt's ice cream stand. I don't know exactly what happened but one minute I was holding the door so Uncle Erich could maneuver through the tight space with his walker (the Americans with Disabilities Act apparently had not impacted this corner of northern Ohio), and the next minute, he was on the sidewalk. The walker flew forward, its trajectory halted by a parking meter. Sadie saw it and came running. Between the two of us, we managed to get him seated upright. He shook his head as if to clear it of some unseen fog.

I didn't think he'd tripped. I couldn't see any uneven places on the sidewalk, no pesky doormat with an upturned edge.

Sadie and I hovered over him. I wanted to call an ambulance, but he wouldn't hear of it.

"Just let me collect myself," he said. "I'll be all right. Happens sometimes. I trip and end up ass over tea kettle. The old bones get shook up a bit, but nothing's broken."

He seemed coherent. I didn't think he'd hit his head. I couldn't see any noticeable bumps or red spots.

"Didn't mean to scare you," he said.

"Well, you did. Are you sure you're all right?"

"I'm a tough old bird."

"Sometimes it takes a few minutes to discover that you've hurt an elbow or sprained an ankle or something. I know from experience, and I'm a lot younger than you."

"Don't worry about me. But I think I'd better get back home and lie down a while. Let my system get readjusted."

He was adamant. No hospital emergency room. Just home.

Sadie helped me get him into my rental car and put the walker in the trunk. I drove us back to the Lakeside Retirement Community, stealing glances at him along the way. I hovered over him as he gingerly made his way to the elevator and navigated the left turns to the door of his apartment. I accompanied him inside, helped him into bed, and covered him with Grandma's soft throw.

"Now don't you go fussin' over me. I'll be all right. Why don't cha take your car and head over to the lake. It's real pretty this time o' year."

"I'll come back later. I still think we should have gone to the hospital to have you checked out."

"Only thing wrong with me is old age, and that's nothin' they can cure."

He already had closed his eyes when I kissed him on the forehead and tiptoed out of the room.

Chapter 23

I clutched the steering wheel so hard that my knuckles were white. The pierogi was giving me heartburn. I felt guilty leaving Uncle Erich alone. Should I have stayed in his living room and checked on him periodically? What if he had a seizure or something?

When I calmed down, I re-entered the building and went to the front desk. Robert Miller, assistant manager of Lakeside Retirement Community according to his nameplate, was staffing the phones. He had over-combed gray hair, plastered to his pink forehead with gel. I explained who I was, told him that Uncle Erich had fallen (he looked relieved when he learned the fall had occurred off premises), that he had refused to be taken to the hospital, but I was concerned and wondered if someone on the staff could check on him.

When he found out my uncle was in "independent living", he explained that only persons in "assisted living" had access to such services. Furthermore, it was a Sunday afternoon and their regular staff only worked Mondays through Fridays. Besides, Mr. Miller said, they had to respect the privacy and wishes of their residents. If Uncle Erich needed help, he had a pull chain by his bed and a medical alert around his neck. At that point the phone rang and he became otherwise engaged. It was clear I would get no help from Mr. Miller.

The information about the medical alert system gave me some comfort. I dithered in front of the desk, but finally turned around and went back to the car.

My options were limited. Retreating to the motel room in the middle of the afternoon was a non-starter. I didn't feel like driving twenty miles to get a copy of the *New York Times*. I was tempted to call Richard and tell him what had happened, but I didn't want him to think I was growing too dependent, so I decided to take Uncle Erich's suggestion and drive to Lake Erie. Maybe I'd stop at Matt's on the way back and pick up the hot fudge sundae he'd raved about.

The parking lot was filled with cars. I pulled into one of the few remaining spots. Tulips were in full bloom. Gulls swooped overhead, making a racket with their raucous calls. The day was clear, the sky was cloudless, the sun was bright. It was unusually warm for late May. I had on a light sweater, but I took it off and threw it in the back seat.

I was surprised by how attractive the area was. Some Northern Ohio congressman must have done a big favor for a powerful colleague to put that kind of money into what the welcome sign billed as a "recreation area." Mothers and fathers sat on concrete benches and watched their children cavort on the sandy beach. The smell of barbecue was in the air. Families picnicked on tables on a bluff overlooking the beach and lake beyond. A lawn bowling competition, teams with distinctive green and blue shirts, had attracted a scattering of onlookers.

The scene should have been uplifting. Instead, I felt guilty. I should have insisted that Uncle Erich go to the doctor, though I wouldn't have been able to take him. My flight was scheduled for Monday morning, and Monday was a holiday, anyway. Unless we went to the emergency room I'd have to stay until late Tuesday. I imagined the mischief Piper Mangan might get himself—worse yet, "us," as he kept reminding me—into while I was gone. I needed to get back to business, and not just his. Despite the governor's pledge of "no new taxes," the state budget crisis could morph into a search for new tax revenues. Vigilance was required, lest my clients become a convenient target.

I was heading toward the lawn bowling competition when my cell phone rang. It was in my purse—a misnomer for something bigger than a grocery sack. The ID indicated that it was Barbara. "How like her," I thought. She'd known I was going to see my uncle for the first time since adolescence, encouraged me to make the trip. She sensed—perhaps more than I had—how unsettling the visit might be.

"Barbara, how sweet of you to call."

"Oh, Claire!" she sobbed. "Timmy's sick. He's in the hospital. Dana Farber. I'm here now."

"But that's for cancer patients," I blurted out.

"They think he has Hodgkin's lymphoma."

I didn't know exactly what that meant but it sounded ominous. I got back in my car to block the sounds of nearby picnickers.

"You and Caleb were going to take him to Nantucket for the long weekend. What happened?"

"He's been lethargic ever since he came home from school and he's lost a lot of weight. I thought it was because he'd been living off campus." Her words were a kind of high-pitched keen. "You know how boys eat when they're on their own."

I didn't, but I could guess.

"I figured he was exhausted after having studied so hard all semester," she said. "He was supposed to begin work as an intern at a pharma lab in two weeks. He may have been running a low-grade fever for a while, I don't know how long. I finally insisted—just insisted—that we go to the doctor."

Her crying started in earnest once again.

"These damned waiting rooms," she said. "There's no privacy."

"They must have someplace quiet where you can sit down. Why don't you ask at the nurses' station?"

I heard footsteps, voices, beeping machines, a closing door, then quiet.

"The doctor ran some blood tests," she said between hiccups. "When the results came he told us to get to the hospital, said Timmy's white blood count was way too high. They admitted him early yesterday morning."

This was a Barbara I hardly recognized. She was always such a together person—suits immaculately pressed, hair expertly coiffed, never a chipped fingernail. She glided through life as if she were a champion figure skater on a perfectly manicured ice rink. Now she sounded like she'd been butt ended with a hockey stick.

I knew what to say when confronting an obstreperous legislator, but in the face of personal suffering from my dearest friend about a boy who was the closest thing to a nephew that I'd ever get, I was immobilized. Once again, I felt so inadequate. I should be there to support her, even if I didn't know how. I groped for words of assurance but came up empty. I finally said "He's in good hands there. They know what they're doing. I'm sure they'll be able to get this under control." I wasn't, but Barbara didn't need to hear that from me. How could I comfort her when I shared her panic?

I started to cry, too. With my free hand I rummaged around in my purse until I found some tissues.

"You're not alone, are you?" I said. "Where's Caleb?"

"He went to get me a cup of tea from the cafeteria. I don't really want it, but he seemed so helpless. He's no good in situations where he's not in charge."

Mention of Caleb seemed to distract her.

"And where's Timmy?" I said.

"They're running tests to get a clearer picture of what we're dealing with."

"I'm so very, very sorry. I wish I could be there to give you a hug."

"I could use one."

"Timmy must be scared."

More weeping. Did I say the wrong thing?

"I know," I said. "You are, too. But you need to be positive for Timmy's sake."

"I don't know if I can. I feel so alone. And if I come unglued I'm afraid Caleb will fall apart. He doesn't do raw emotion."

"He's a buttoned up kind of guy. That's one of the things you liked about him when you married him."

"It doesn't wear so well over the long haul."

"Look, you can lean on me. I'm in your corner. I'll be your back-up. Be strong for Timmy and you can come as unhinged as you want with me." I hoped I sounded strong—I wanted to, for Barbara's sake. If I'd had any second thoughts about staying to help Uncle Erich, I'd just squelched them, but between Timmy and Uncle Erich, I felt like I'd been thrown into Lake Erie without a life vest.

"When are you coming home?" she said.

"I'm on the first flight out of Cleveland tomorrow morning. I'll call you as soon as I land."

Mangan and my other clients would have to get in line behind Barbara.

"I probably will be at the hospital."

"Well, wherever. I'll find you. In the meantime call me as much as you want. I mean it. Any time, day or night."

"Thank you so much."

"You've been there for me more times than I can count. It's my turn."

"Caleb's back with the tea."

"Give Timmy a hug for me."

And she was gone.

I sat in that stuffy car, too stunned to move. Barbara's whole life revolved around Timmy. She would get into high gear now, micro-managing his care, harassing doctors and nurses, responding to his every need, neglecting Caleb in the process. If she weren't careful, the foundations on which she'd built her life—son first, husband next, the rest a distant third--could come collapsing in on themselves. I'd have to do what I could—talk to her like a stern German Oma if necessary—to prevent that from happening. At least I would try. Thank goodness finances weren't a worry.

I hit the steering wheel so hard it vibrated. Barbara had lived a charmed existence. She'd waltzed through the teen years without a blemish. Sometimes I envied her, but she was my best friend. My only true friend, really. She didn't deserve this. And Timmy? I adored that kid. He was barely into his third decade. He had his whole life in front of him. He had to get well, he just had to.

I felt flush. I turned on the engine and cranked up the air conditioning. All those Sunday afternoon families were frolicking on the grass and there I was, sitting alone in a rental car in Oretown,

Ohio. I needed to get out of there.

On the drive back to Uncle Erich's, I spotted Matt's soft-serve ice cream stand across the road. On impulse, in good Boston-fashion I did a U-turn. I'd misjudged the distance and narrowly missed an oncoming car. The driver, a scruffily bearded male in his mid-twenties, laid on the horn and gave me the finger. When I pulled into Matt's, he drove in right behind me, hemming me in. He got out of his car—a souped-up Chevy with pitted green paint—marched over to mine, fists clenched, a Cleveland Browns football jersey spread tight over his beer gut, and yelled through the closed window. "Whattaya think yer doin', lady? You crazy or somethin'? You could a gotten us both killed!"

I swallowed hard, opened the window part way, and stumbled all over myself with every form of apology I could think of. My motto: when you screw up big time, admit it and hope for the best.

"I'm so very, very sorry," I said. "I'm not from around here. I'm visiting my sick uncle. He likes ice cream. And I just got word that my best friend's son has cancer. When I saw this place, I thought—well, I didn't think. I'm so sorry. I really am." By then my eyes were teary--more from fright than remorse, but if it played on any sense of chivalry in the big oaf, I was going to use it.

"Well, all right," he said as he backed away from my window. "You apologized. But don't pull that kind of stunt again. This is Ohio, you know. We don't do that kind of thing around here."

"I will. I promise."

He stalked back to his car, fists unclenched, burned rubber as he backed out of the parking lot and hurtled down the highway.

My hands were shaking as I walked up to the counter. A man wearing a white paper cap that made him look like a washed ashore sailor slid open a screen.

"You all right, lady? I was just about ready to call the cops."

"I'm OK, thanks. Just a little rattled."

"You must have really wanted some ice cream to pull that trick."

"It was stupid, I know. I'm not from around here. I'm visiting my uncle this weekend. He's sick. He's raved about your hot fudge sundaes and when I saw the stand across the road, I decided to get one."

"You want a cup of water? You look a little green around the gills."

"No, thanks, I'll be all right."

"What'll you have?"

"A hot fudge sundae with all the trimmings."

"Hot fudge, coming up." I put my purse on the shelf in front of the window and searched for my wallet.

"Make that two. I think I'll join him."

Armed with a white paper bag containing two giant hot fudge sundaes, mounds of whipped cream, and maraschino cherries on top, encased in clear plastic covers, I assiduously followed the speed limit for the mile back to Uncle Erich's.

Chapter 24

I had left his apartment door unlocked, and I quietly entered so I wouldn't wake him if he still was asleep.

"Uncle Erich?" I said softly.

"In here. Still in bed." His voice was strong. "Lazy old cuss, don't cha think?"

"How are you feeling?"

He shifted to a sitting position, his back against the headboard. I didn't detect any signs of discomfort.

"Tired but OK," he said. "How long did I sleep?"

"Oh, probably a couple hours. Are you hurting anywhere?"

"No place different than usual."

Was he giving me the full story?

"I brought you a hot fudge sundae from Matt's." I pulled one out of the bag. I wasn't going to tell him about the stunt I had pulled it get it.

"Now that was nice. Real thoughtful-like. I'm not too hungry right now. Could you put it in the freezer?"

"Sure. Actually, I bought a couple, so you can look forward to two treats when you feel like it." I didn't want to eat one if he wasn't having his.

I opened the refrigerator. The freezer contained a couple cans of frozen orange juice, some English muffins, and a partially eaten sandwich in a plastic bag. That was all.

"How about some chicken soup or something?" I said. "I could get it from the kitchen downstairs."

"Don't fuss. I don't much feel like talkin', but come and sit by me for a spell."

He reached out and took my hand. We sat like that, my manicured hand in his calloused one, for ten minutes or more. He seemed content. He dozed off occasionally, but when I gently started to remove my hand he awakened again and tightened his grip.

If Uncle Eric was feeling better, should I get a Sunday evening flight out of Cleveland? I could see Barbara and Timmy at the hospital first thing Monday morning. Then I'd have to re-focus on the office. I'd been neglecting some other clients since I took on Mangan. I needed to redress that situation before any other companies decided they could handle their legislative affairs "in house." But if I walked out on Uncle Erich now, it would compound all those years I had neglected him. I couldn't do that.

"Did you go to the lake? They've done a real nice job sprucin' it up, don't cha think?"

"It's lovely."

I got up from my chair, walked over to the window and talked into the glass. "I got a phone call while I was there. From my best friend. We've known each other since grade school."

"Nice to have a friend like that. Don't have to do so much explainin' to fill in the blanks."

"She has one son, Timmy. He's the sweetest kid. He's got one more year of college, then he wants to go to med school. Calls me Aunt Claire. Next to you, they're the closest thing to family that I've got. He's was admitted to the hospital yesterday. He's only twenty-one and...and now he's got cancer."

"That's real rough. He's just a kid."

"I feel so helpless. Here you are, under the weather, Barbara's in Boston, frantic over Timmy, and I can't do squat to help either one of you."

I was trying, unsuccessfully, to repress tears. I brushed them away and hoped Uncle Erich didn't notice.

"You come here, gal." He patted the mattress and moved over to make room. "I'm gonna talk to you like a Dutch uncle." His compressed lips turned up at the corners. "Guess I can, since that's what I am."

I perched on the side of the bed. He put his arm around me and kissed me on the forehead. His lips felt dry. I leaned into him and put my head on his shoulder.

"Now you listen to me. There ain't nothin' wrong with me but old age. I just get a little wobbly on my pins once in a while."

I pulled away and scanned his face for any sign of strain.

"Are you sure that's all it is? You really scared me."

"My doctor called it a balance issue. Said I should get some physical therapy. They got a place here, down in the basement, with trained people and all."

"Will your insurance cover it? If not, I want to help."

"I'm all right. Doctor said Medicare will take care of it. And I've always been frugal, just like your Grandma. Got a little money set aside. So you can cross me off your worry list."

He hugged me. I hugged back and held on tight.

"Now I'll tell you what I want you to do," he said. "You get on that phone and see if you can fly back to Boston tonight."

"What about you? I hate to leave you like this. Shouldn't we get you checked out in the morning?"

"Tomorrow I'll be right as rain. Don't you worry. We've had a good visit. That'll keep me smiling for a long time."

"Are you sure you'll be all right?"

"The only thing I want you to do before you go is take a picture of the two of us. Can you get my camera out of that drawer?" He pointed to the dresser across from his bed. "Yep, that one. Now come sit here and I'll hold it out so's we can get both of us."

It was a simple little camera with a wrist string. I moved my head next to his, he reached his long arm out and snapped the shutter.

"I'd really like a copy of that," I said. "Will you send one to me?"

"Sure thing. Easy enough to do. They got a place in the shop downstairs where you can drop stuff off, they send it out, and it comes back in a day or two. Now git on that phone and see if you can change your flight."

So that's what I did. The timing would be tight but doable.

"Success?" he said when I came back into the bedroom.

"I can catch a 7:10 flight. With luck I'll make it home by around ten o'clock."

He looked at his watch. "You'd better git a move on. Come here." He reached in the drawer beside his bed. "I have something for you."

He pulled out a small box. Inside, nestled in faded blue satin cloth, was an intricately woven golden chain with a pendant that had a green three leaf clover in the center. I knew real gold when I saw it, and this was genuine.

"It was your Grandma's."

"I never saw her wear it."

"She didn't. It was a gift from Mrs. Fuchs, a neighbor lady. After your grandpa died, Grandma cleaned her house every week and they became friends. It would make your Grandma happy to know you have it." He fumbled with the lid and closed the box.

Yet again, I made liberal use of the tissues in my pocket.

"You'll probably be asleep by the time I get home," I said, "but I'll call you tomorrow morning. If you don't feel better by then, I'm going to insist that you see a doctor on Tuesday. And that's an order!"

"Yes mam! Now come and give yer old uncle a hug and then git on out a here."

He kissed me on the cheek. I had gathered my things and was at the door when I turned around and walked back toward the bedroom. I wanted to kiss him one more time, but his eyes already were closed.

Chapter 25

I called Richard from the airport and told him about my change in plans.

"I'll pick you up."

"You don't need to do that. I'll grab a cab."

"I don't need to, but I want to."

"So much has been going on. I need some time to process it."

"I've missed you. Besides, I want to hear how the rest of your visit with Uncle Erich went."

I didn't feel like talking about it, and I wasn't sure I could sort it out myself. I had retreated into default mode—hunker down, forge ahead, don't look right or left.

"Right now I'm more worried about Timmy than I am about Uncle Erich."

"You help Barbara, I'll support you."

He'd insisted. I gave in. So there he was, waiting as I descended the escalator to the baggage claim. He kissed me, first on the cheek, then on the lips.

"Something wrong?" he said.

"I can't find my Gucci sunglasses." I pulled item after item out of my purse and threw them all on a plastic chair to no avail. "I hope I didn't leave them on the airplane." Why I thought I needed them at night I don't know, but I hated to lose anything.

Richard stood beside me and shifted from one foot to the other. Then he said, "Have you checked your coat pocket?"

Sure enough, that's where they were.

Richard took my rolling suitcase and steered me out of the baggage area, a protective hand on my back. Although the pavement was dry, the air was humid and I thought I heard the distant rumble of thunder.

When we got to the car Richard reached into the back seat and retrieved a small bag, handles tied with blue ribbon. He held the bag and played with the ribbon.

"This needs an explanation," he said. "I picked this stuff up before you told me what's been going on."

He gave me the bag.

I poked around the tissue paper and felt a couple of bottles that exuded a mild fragrance.

"I'm not sure about this," he said, then rushed on with an explanation. "Maybe it wasn't such a bad idea anyway. I'll take you home, and if you want, I'll come in and give you a massage. I thought you needed some TLC."

Under normal circumstances, the gesture would have been thoughtful, even romantic, but the circumstances were not normal. I was exhausted, worried, scared, confused. What I really wanted was solitude.

Drops of rain started to pelt the windshield.

He glanced in my direction. "Like I said, it's up to you."

"I'm in a funny place tonight. So much has happened, and I'm a bit overwhelmed."

"Let's just get you home, OK?"

When he reached in his wallet for a credit card to pay at the parking kiosk, I saw it. Rather, I didn't see it. Laura's picture was gone. He had replaced it with a trimmed-down snapshot of the two of us in birding gear. And off he sped toward the Callahan Tunnel while I tightly grasped the hand support above the passenger door.

It was raining harder. The windshield wipers couldn't keep up with the downpour.

Once we were through the tunnel I called Barbara. I got her voicemail—discordantly cheery under the circumstances—and left a message telling her that I'd come home early so I could see her on Monday, any place, any time.

I updated Richard on the situation with Timmy.

"I can imagine what she's going through. Laura and I spent a lot of time at Dana Farber. Please, God, I never want to deal with that again. In and out of the hospital, hopes up, hope lost, trying to savor the present, afraid of the future. I'll bet I know every elevator in that building."

"I feel so inadequate. I hardly knew what to say when Barbara called."

"You don't have to say anything, just be there."

That may have been sound advice, but I was a fixer. My impulse was to *do* something.

When we arrived at my building, I guided him into the garage, he unloaded the car and we took the elevator up to my condo. Richard headed for the kitchen. I went into the bedroom, threw my jacket on a chair, and kicked off my shoes.

"I didn't know if you'd had any supper," he yelled from the

kitchen. "I picked up some cheese, crackers, and prosciutto to go with the wine, if you want a glass."

I hadn't had anything to eat since Polaski's. I could hear the sounds of dishes and cutlery clanking against my granite counter tops.

I put on a warm fleece and plush sheepskin slippers, then went into the kitchen.

"Did your uncle like the hot fudge sundae?"

"He didn't eat it. I put it in the freezer."

When we settled on the living room couch, I dove into the cheese and crackers. Guilt for abandoning Uncle Erich elbowed out everything except hunger. Between bites, I told him about Uncle Erich's fall. I omitted my encounter with the big bruiser at the ice cream stand. Suddenly I realized that Richard's arm was around my shoulder. I didn't know how long it had been there.

He ruffled the hair on the back of my head. "You've had a rough day. How was he when you left him?"

"All right, I think. I don't know for sure."

"No obvious bruises? No sign of incoherence?"

"Far from it. He was just tired. When I asked if he was hurting anywhere, he said, 'no more than usual.'"

"He has a good sense of humor."

"He was the one who urged me to come home tonight so I could support Barbara and see Timmy. And look at this." I pulled Grandma's golden chain and pendant out of the box and told him the story behind it.

"It's beautiful," he said. "Do you want me to put it on you?"

"Not right now." I placed it back in the box.

"I was so dumb," I said. "I should have reconnected with Uncle Erich years ago, instead of sending him stupid Christmas cards."

"That was then. This is now. You connected this weekend, and you'll keep in touch."

"He could have booted me out the door, said if it had taken that long to visit I might as well have stayed home."

"He doesn't sound like that kind of man."

"People love him. He's a real charmer." I thought of Uncle Erich's easy banter with the waitresses. "He has a gentle, straight-forward gaze that makes you feel like you're the most important person in the world." I had soaked it up like a dry sponge. "He's the real deal," I said. "Not like some of the smarmy politicians at the State House. He lives simply. He's like you that way."

I got up and walked over to the picture window.

"Would you mind if I hop in the shower? It's been a long day and I feel grubby."

"Of course not. And when you finish, if you're in the mood for that massage, the offer still stands." He studied me, looking for a signal.

None was forthcoming. I was not in the mood. Couldn't he see that?

When I came out of the bathroom toweling my hair, swathed in my favorite heavy-weight terrycloth robe and my favorite super soft cotton pajamas, Richard was in my bedroom, seated in a winged back chair in his khaki chinos and polo shirt. He had dimmed the lights. Thick, white candles were on a table near the window, on my nightstand, and on my chest of drawers. Flames reflected off a mirror on the wall behind my dresser. The whole place smelled like apple blossoms in springtime. Under other cir-cumstances I would have been mesmerized. Instead, I felt like I was in a movie theater and had wandered into the wrong show. How could two people be so out of sync? All I wanted to do was crawl into bed in a fetal position.

"Please let me hold you," he said. "Just hold you."

"Oh, all right."

I let him rub my back, massage my shoulders. He nuzzled my neck. I shed tears into my pillow. Eventually my body took over and I succumbed to his practiced touch. Our coupling was different from anything that had preceded it. My mind checked out and I lost myself in the weight of his body pressed against mine. Then he snuggled into me, my back to his front, his right arm over my shoulder, his hand gently caressing my arm, my chest, my breast.

I removed his hand from my breast.

We were quiet for a while. When I talked, it was to the wall. "When you're a kid, what do you know about your parents? You don't see them as persons in their own right. They're your parents, the guardians of your little universe, benign or malevolent, depending on the atmosphere. And if they're not forthcoming, you understand even less."

He stopped caressing. If he'd expected post-coital pillow talk, I had disappointed.

Eventually, he resumed, omitting the breast. "Kids are, by definition, self-absorbed," he said. "It's their right. At least that's what my mom used to say."

"Daddy didn't talk about the past, and I never questioned Mom's version of the Petersen family history. It was more nuanced than I had been led to believe." I adjusted a pillow under my head.

"Uncle Erich and Daddy didn't have easy lives when they were growing up. Their father used to re-sole their shoes with old tire treads. Can you imagine? Then their father died and the family was left to fend for themselves at the height of the Depression. It's a miracle they didn't lose their home."

"How did they manage it?"

"Grandma baked and they sold what she made. She cleaned houses, took in laundry. They ate a lot of soup. No wonder Daddy never liked soup."

"They had a roof over their heads and food on the table. That was more than many could say."

"The family's German heritage raised eyebrows outside their neighborhood. Daddy was targeted at school. Got back at the boys the only way he knew how—not with his fists but with his wit. Took their money gambling. Money meant security."

In that way, I supposed we were similar. And where had that gotten me?

I disengaged from Richard and sat up in bed. He propped his head on his elbow and eyed me.

"Sorry," I said. "My body's here, but my head's still in Oretown."

"I noticed." He leaned against the headboard.

I looked at the clock on my nightstand. It was 12:30.

"Would you mind if we don't spend the night together?"

"I'd hoped we could share breakfast tomorrow morning. It's been days since I've seen you."

Richard was used to thinking of two when I automatically thought as one.

"Sometimes I feel like an afterthought," he said.

"I've had so much coming at me. I need some time alone."

He hopped out of bed, extinguished the candles, and put on his clothes.

"Is this the way it's always going to be?"

"I feel like we're on different planets. You are drawing global consequences from one night, one weekend, one extraordinary weekend, at that."

He was bent over, putting on his shoes, so I couldn't see his face. Then he searched around for his keys. He'd left them on the dresser as if they'd taken up residence.

"Why don't you leave the candles right where they are," I said, "so they're ready for future use."

Had he received the olive branch?

"We'll talk tomorrow?" he said.

"Of course." I crawled out of bed, put on my bathrobe, and belted it tightly around my waist. "I may head over to the hospital in the morning. It depends on what Barbara wants. And I need to get back into the office."

"Tomorrow's a holiday."

"I know."

"Guess a walk in Great Meadows is out."

"I'm sorry." I'd been saying that a lot lately.

I handed him his coat. We hugged. I closed the door before he reached the elevator.

After he was gone, I curled up in a chair by the picture window in the darkened living room and nursed a second glass of wine. Raindrops trailed down the glass. Was Barbara staying overnight at the hospital with Timmy? pacing the halls? camping out on a cot? Had Uncle Erich stayed in bed? skipped his supper? If I had asked for dinner to be brought to him, would they have done it?

An ambulance wove through cars on Storrow Drive, its siren muted by fog rolling off the Charles River Basin.

Chapter 26

When in doubt, work. Just barrel on through. That had been my default position. So on Monday morning after a restless sleep, I was in the office by 8:00. Since it was Memorial Day I had the place to myself.

The thermostat had been programmed for the long weekend and the room was chilly. I turned on the heat.

I called Barbara and left another message. I wanted to be supportive without hovering, though if I didn't hear by lunchtime I would try again. Then I called Uncle Erich. He sounded more like his old self. His voice was strong. He said he'd had a good sleep, and even used his walker to get some breakfast bacon and eggs from the downstairs cafeteria. "Needed the protein," he'd said. I was relieved.

The silence calmed me—at least until I saw the pile of notes from Maura. Piper Mangan had called three times after I'd left on

Friday. Note One: 4:00. Mangan called. Said it's important. Told him you were out of town 'til Tuesday. Tried to pacify him. Note Two: 4:15. Mangan again. Wanted the number where he could reach you. I stonewalled. Didn't want to disturb your Ohio trip. Note Three: 4:45. What is it with this guy? Told him you were on personal business with a sick uncle. (Hope he isn't really.) Mangan said if he didn't hear from you by Tuesday morning at the latest he was going ahead with his plan. He wouldn't give me any more info. Note Four: 5:00. Sorry, Claire. Maybe I was being over-protective. Hope I haven't done anything wrong. But he's a pain in the you-know-where. I'm heading out the door, taking my mother for a drive up to New Hampshire this weekend. I need to get her out of the house. Hope you're having a good visit with your uncle.

I couldn't fathom what was so urgent that Mangan needed to reach me before Memorial Day weekend. Maybe he just liked to jerk me around. I didn't want to encourage such behavior, but if he was hatching some new harebrained scheme I'd better squelch it before it caused more problems. So at 8:30 I called Mangan. After the way he'd harassed Maura on Friday, if I woke him up, so much the better.

"Mr. Mangan, I've been out of town on family business, but I gather you've been eager to reach me, so what's up?"

I could hear bagpipes and raucous male voices in the background.

"Not an ideal time, Claire. Not an ideal time. I'm sponsoring a float in the Apple Grove Memorial Day Parade. Help win over the locals. Very important you know. Win 'em over."

An obscene image of a portly kilt-clad Mangan flitted through my mind. More likely, he'd be in a cream-colored Cadillac with the Mangan logo emblazoned across both side doors.

"Especially in light of what I've heard," he said.

His voice had a sinister tinge. I straightened up in my chair, on high alert.

The state legislature had been in recess since shortly after my visit to Senate Ways and Means. I doubted that anything significant had changed in the interim. If the pace of legislators were any slower, they'd be in reverse.

"What have you heard?"

Politicians were such a gossipy bunch. Who knows what he might have picked up, no matter how far-fetched.

"Can't talk now, but it's important. Call me around noon. Parade's over then, barbecue won't start 'til five."

I didn't like being boxed into Mangan's schedule, but I needed to know what was going on. Mangan was like an unexploded bomb in a hotel lobby.

"I'll see what I can do, Mr. Mangan."

"You do that, Claire. You do that."

I walked to the window overlooking the harbor. It was a clear, sunny late spring day. Sailboats were taking full advantage of the wind. A windjammer in full sail was heading out of the harbor toward the Atlantic. What would it be like to thumb my nose at Mangan, hop on board with only a backpack, hat and sunglasses, and take a cruise to the Bahamas?

I leafed through the pile of mail that Maura had placed on my desk. One envelope stood out, the return address in embossed raised print. The letter, with a dark blue logo on cream stationary, announced that my building had been sold to a real estate investment trust. The space was being turned into condominiums. The letter said it was a golden opportunity for savvy investors. What it said to me was buy up or move out. I was gobsmacked.

My ten-year lease was due for renewal in September. I would have an option to buy—for a whopping $3253 per square foot, not even considering the monthly condominium fee. At 922 square feet, that was three million dollars. I couldn't have afforded it before I'd lost twenty percent of my income to that Texas behemoth. Now it was out of the question. Boston was in the midst of a real estate bubble. The price of commercial real estate had skyrocketed everywhere in the city. I'd have to move. But where?

My neck ached. My back ached. I could feel another headache coming on. I reached in my desk, grabbed two Tylenol, and paced around my office as if that could stimulate fresh approaches to my situation.

The rest of the morning I cast about web sites of commercial real estate agents. I started by investigating other rentals near Rowes Wharf (forget it), roamed through offerings in the Financial District (also pricey, of course), and tried Beacon Street near the State House (fruitless). Some locations near North Station looked promising, but that was the back of the beyond, as far as my clients were concerned.

I glanced at my watch. 12:10. It galled me to be on Mangan's short leash but I couldn't afford to alienate him, especially now.

"Mr. Mangan, is this a more convenient time?" Good thing he couldn't see my curled upper lip as I said it.

"That it is, Claire, that it is. You should'a been here this morning. What a parade we gave 'em."

"So what did you need to discuss with me, Mr. Mangan?"

"Ended up at the cemetery. American flags on all the graves. Makes you real proud of this country. Real proud."

"Maura said you were eager to talk with me." Whatever it was, I would have to drag it out of him.

"Spotted you in Belmont a week or so ago." His voice had an oily tinge. "With that Truitt guy."

I stiffened.

"At first," he said, "I thought, well now, that's real smart. She's checking out the opposition."

"It never hurts." My mouth had gone dry. I reached for a bottle of water and quietly took a sip.

"But then I heard a rumor. Maybe a little something else is going on, if you catch my drift."

I flinched. What should I say now? I couldn't bluff my way out of this one.

"Mr. Mangan, I am very careful to keep my personal and my professional lives separate. Furthermore, my private life is private."

"That's not what I heard." He sniggered. "People around here have long memories."

"I can assure you that whatever my friendship with Mr. Truitt, it in no way is in danger of compromising my professional commitments to you or to any of my other clients. Furthermore, it does give me insight into the challenges we face and how we might overcome them."

"Since the two of you are friends, as you say, maybe you can get your 'friend'" (he dragged the word into two syllables) "to persuade the Tannenbaum daughter to back off, find some other place to put her money. Save a swamp or something. Then we wouldn't need to fart around with Whately and his gang."

"Our agreement isn't all-encompassing. If you need to deal with the Tannenbaum daughter, you should go to a PR firm." Admittedly a reach, my public relations recommendation sailed right by him.

"You hired me to implement a legislative strategy, Mr. Mangan, and that's what I'm doing. I think by the end of July, when next year's state budget is finalized, you'll be satisfied with the results." I wasn't so sure, but I had to find some way to make this work.

He snorted. "We've got two months to go. Two months is a long time. A lot can happen in two months. You know what they say: it ain't over 'til the fat lady sings, and I ain't even heard her hummin' yet."

"You need to trust me on this." I tried to sound confident.

"My sainted mother said that was one of my failings. I wasn't big on trust. I prefer insurance."

I was on high alert.

"You're at the top of my list when legislators start drifting back after this holiday hiatus," I said. "I'll see if we can firm up enough commitments to give you that insurance you say you like."

"By the way," he said, "heard your building's being sold. Price per square foot's going up. Way up."

I tried to keep my voice neutral.

"Where did you hear that?"

"I'm on a couple of boards. When it comes to real estate, I'm a 'go to' guy."

Was he blowing smoke or was he serious? And what if he was?

"Just how 'go to' are you?" Sweat was beading under my armpits.

"Well, that all depends."

"On what?"

"On whether I'm in that circle of friends you've got. See, I can be a real help to those who help me."

What he didn't say, but he didn't have to, was that the reverse also was true.

"I'll be in Boston tomorrow afternoon," he said. "Got some business to attend to. Think you and I need to meet. How about a drink at *When the Gavel Drops*? Say, four o'clock?"

"I'm not a drinking woman, Mr. Mangan, but I'll meet you there if you wish." What next?

"Gotta go now, Claire. The Missus is waving at me. Wants me to take her to lunch. Can't say 'no' to the Missus. You think about this little conversation, OK, Claire? You're a smart woman."

Then he was gone.

I pressed my fists on my eyes. Why, in the name of heaven, had I ever taken on Mangan in the first place? The old skunk had left his scent on everything I held dear, and the residual fumes could threaten it all.

The phone rang. I jumped. Not Mangan again.

It was Barbara.

"Is that you, Claire?"

"Oh, my dear, I haven't thought of anything but you since I got your call."

"Your voice sounds funny."

"Not to worry, just a little headache. But more to the point, how are *you*? And how's Timmy? How's everyone holding up?"

"Caleb fixed us some stiff gin and tonics when we got home last night. They knocked me out until 3:00. After that I couldn't get back to sleep. I spent the rest of the night on the internet searching for cutting edge lymphoma treatments."

That's my girl, I thought. When panicked, go into research mode. She and I were alike that way.

I could hear her weeping quietly.

"So we met with the oncologist this morning. They're still getting test results. If it hasn't spread beyond the lymph nodes, they will attack it with radiation and chemo." The crying became more obvious. "The whole process could take months."

The subtext, what she didn't say, was "if it works." She'd given me the best case. Perhaps that was what the doctors had done. Offer hope. Right now, that's what they needed.

She cleared her throat. "Timmy's eager to get started, but they won't do that until we have a complete picture of the situation."

Once again I felt paralyzed. I didn't know what to say or do. Should I appear at the hospital unannounced? Bring food? Send flowers? Take her out to lunch and let her talk? Stay away until she asked for me?

"Do you want me to come over to the hospital this afternoon?" I said. "I could bring a supply of your favorite espresso cannoli from Mike's Pastry."

I'm not sure why, but that made Barbara laugh.

"I'll take a rain check on the cannoli. You're there. That's what I need right now."

"Wish I could give you a hug."

"You just did. I've got to get back to Timmy."

"Give him a hug for me, too, will you?"

That's how we left it.

Although I'd never liked being on the water, I loved looking at it—the ebb and flow of the tides, wave patterns that shifted with the wind, and beyond the harbor in East Boston, planes taking off from Logan airport. It usually calmed me, but not today.

Richard had warned me about Mangan. I should have listened.

I paced back and forth. The office had been a second home to me for nine and a half years. The location conveyed success, and the appearance of success was almost as important as the reality. The converse also was true. If my clients thought I was losing my edge, that I couldn't deliver, they would bolt without a backward wave.

I decided to go home. I grabbed a cab and, thanks to the light holiday traffic, was there in ten minutes. It was only three o'clock in the afternoon but I put on my favorite pajamas, made a cup of hot chocolate, pulled out paper and pencil, hopped on my bed, and propped plump pillows against my back.

My notes veered from the traditional to the—shall we say—less so: original legislative strategy; ways to speed up the process (sub-heading: legislative or gubernatorial); how to get the Tannen-baum woman to back off; creative tactics (the latter in big bold print). If I chose the last approach, I'd better have a damned good, under the radar way to outflank Mangan, or my other clients would vanish faster than you could say "Piper's Dream."

I had the categories. I was stymied about how to fill them in.

The phone rang. I could see from caller ID that it was Richard. I let it go to voice mail.

Chapter 27

"You're awfully quiet," Maura said when she brought in my mail the next morning.

"I've got a lot on my mind."

"How was the visit with your uncle?"

"Good, I guess. I can't talk about it now. Too much else going on." I waved her away. She'd find out soon enough what was happening, but I needed more time before I could reassure her—hollow comfort if my profit margin took another dive.

"If visiting your uncle puts circles under your eyes like the shiners you've got now, I wouldn't recommend a repeat trip any time soon."

"Just drop it, will you, Maura?"

"OK, OK." She backed out of the office and closed the door.

I felt guilty about pushing her away. I should have asked how her mother liked their drive to New Hampshire. I should have taken her into my confidence. But I couldn't face the prospect of her anxiety on top of my own.

I flitted from one task to another and was completely unproductive.

At four o'clock I opened the heavy wooden door to *When the Gavel Drops*. The bar, across from the State House on Bowdoin Street, was a favorite watering hole for legislators and their staff. The lighting (if you could call it that) was dark. The concept of a smoke-free zone hadn't yet penetrated *The Gavel*. The place smelled of nicotine and beer. It oozed testosterone.

Mangan was seated in a corner booth toward the back. I nodded to acknowledge that I'd seen him. Then I stopped at the occasional table along the way, chatted with a representative here, a staffer there, just to signal to Mangan that I had connections. Two could play this game.

"Claire," Mangan boomed. "What can I get 'cha?"

I didn't want my senses dulled by alcohol, but I figured a light beer wouldn't hurt. He fingered an empty glass. Even in the dim light I could tell that his potato nose was rosy—a bad sign. I wondered how many drinks he had put down before I'd walked in.

Mangan sober was a challenge. Mangan inebriated could be intolerable. If he made a pass at me I'd have to deflect, but he didn't appear to be the type to desist after a diplomatic rebuke.

He waved to the waitress. "How 'bout a beer for the little lady? And I'll take another scotch neat, dirty ice on the side." As the waitress walked toward the bar he yelled, "Make that a double."

I don't like improvising, it's not a strategy, but I hadn't come up with anything better. He fidgeted with a cardboard coaster, flipping it back and forth on the glossy wooden table. Was he nervous about something? He held all the cards, at least I thought he did. I'd need to let him show his hand.

I willed myself to stay calm, appear in control, even if my insides were roiling. I'd let Mangan talk to see what I could get out of him.

Voices ricocheted off the wood paneled walls. Mangan leaned over the table, alcohol radiating off his breath. "I need a favor. A biiig favor." His wiry eyebrows shot up at the word "big."

"I'm listening." I clutched my palms in my lap to keep them from shaking.

"Glad to hear it. But then you can't afford not to, can you?" His face was flaccid but his eyes were hard.

"Then I guess this isn't really a favor, is it?" I said.

The waitress brought our drinks. Mangan dropped one ice cube into the Scotch, stirred it with his finger, studied me as he licked the digit. He took a generous swig.

"I'm getting impatient. It's time to fix that timeline of yours, high time. I always thought it was way too pokey. I like action, fast action. Want to settle this deal and get on with it."

Like a two-year-old child with a short attention span, he wanted what he wanted when he wanted it, and he would bulldoze anything or anyone who got in his way. Richard had warned me. Why couldn't I have seen it?

"You've been around long enough to know that the legislative process is slow even on its best days."

"You didn't like my idea about the golf outing, but this is something you're gonna love, just gonna love, I'm sure of it." His full lips puckered. "How could you not?"

I was sure I wouldn't. "Tell me what you have in mind."

"It's clear that Whately is our problem, don't you agree?"

I nodded.

"He's an obstructionist," Mangan said. "A big obstructionist."

Little droplets of spit sprayed across the table. I wiped my mouth with a napkin and took a sip of beer which, at that point, was a quasi-disinfectant.

"I've decided on a solution, and you're the one to handle it."

He put his hand on my knee. I jerked them together.

"You're the one," he said. "It's why I'm paying you the big bucks."

I hoped no one had noticed. His puffy flesh repulsed me. I picked his hand up and lifted it back onto the tabletop where I could see it. What I really wanted to do was punch him in the nuts, but I kept my composure.

"That is outside our contract, Mr. Mangan. *Way* outside."

"The way you've been messing around with that Truitt fellow, I thought you might like it."

After that remark, I was ready to pour what was left of his Scotch on his crotch, but I was in no position to act on the impulse. "Let's get back to the subject, shall we? As I told you over the phone, my private life *is* private. Just tell me what you have in mind."

"Maybe not as private as you think."

"What do you mean by that?"

"Like I told you, I'm big on insurance," he said, patting his inside vest pocket. "I've got a little policy in here. I can show you if you want." He pulled out a campaign brochure featuring Mr. Public Charities, his wife and two children, and waited for my reaction.

I looked down at the table. I could feel the blood rushing to my face. Even in the dim light he saw it. I had been the victim of a massive deception with that jerk, but the circumstances of the misalliance were irrelevant.

"Look, dearie," Mangan said, "our candidate has been friend-ly to business interests. They're backing him. And many of them happen to be your clients."

My head jerked up.

"That's not a secret," he said, "even if *some* things are—for the time being." He ran his finger around the rim of the glass and sniggered. "You see, his wife thought he was a rover, and I don't mean the canine variety. She hired a private detective to tail him, got some pictures, her own kind of insurance." He waited to let that sink in. "I golf with that detective."

"It's not what you think." I was playing with a weak hand and he knew it.

"What I think doesn't matter, does it? If anything untoward should come out—say, anything about his private life—it'll torpe-do his candidacy. And his supporters, who, let me repeat, happen to be your clients, will lash out at whoever is responsible for taking him down."

"Collateral damage." I slumped in my chair.

"Now you're getting the picture. You're not the only one, but that doesn't matter here, see. His wife's got him back in line, right where she wants him."

When it came to politics, payback was as natural as breathing. Boston was a small town. Grudges were passed along from one generation to the next as if they were the family jewels.

I massaged my forehead. First I had been trapped by economic reversals. Now the door had been slammed shut, I was caged, and Mangan held the key.

I looked around the room. Representatives Cavanaugh and O'Sullivan were laughing at some private joke. Four legislative staffers were sitting on bar stools watching a Red Sox game on an overhead screen. It was an ordinary afternoon when, in a small corner table at the back of the bar, a potential political scandal could be unfolding. Or not, depending on me.

He leaned toward me and lowered his voice. "I want to push Whately out of the box, and here's how you're going to do it."

Despite the beer, my mouth felt dry.

"I'm listening. I'm not agreeing to anything, but I'm listening."

"Whately's wife was institutionalized six months ago. Psychotic break or some such thing. Tragic it was, just tragic." He waited a beat. "But useful."

I must be slipping. I should have known about Whately's domestic difficulties, but I didn't. Was Mangan telling the truth?

"You know how it is with men who lose their women," he said. "They get needy, real needy. They start hitting the bottle and bad things happen, things they maybe wouldn't do if they were sober and satisfied."

I wondered if Mangan was talking from personal experience.

"Has he done something he shouldn't? I haven't heard any rumors."

"Whether he has or he hasn't, we're going to start some. That's where you come in." His eyes washed over my breasts. I felt mauled.

I'd been set up. The first day I met Mangan he said he'd come to me because I was female. Did he have this in his devious mind all along?

"You don't actually have to do anything." He winked at me. The Scotch in his glass was rapidly disappearing. "Unless you want to. I know you have standards, even if they slip once in a while."

I pushed my half-consumed beer across the table.

"Whately's been working late," Mangan said. "I heard about it from one of my golfing buddies who used to play a few rounds with him."

Golf, golf, golf. I wanted to take a club and twist it around his neck with my bare hands.

"He's been staying in the office 'til all hours with one of his aides—a *young* aide."

"That young guy who's a gofer?"

"He wouldn't go in for that stuff. No, he's more traditional. I mean a female aide. Who knows what goes on in there when things quiet down? It's a compromising situation, a very compromising situation." Spittle formed around the corners of his mouth. "I don't think his constituents would like it. If, that is, they knew about it."

"So where do I come into this?" I could see where he was going, but I wanted him to spell out every nasty detail.

"You're gonna make 'em know."

"Just how young is this aide?"

"Old enough to know better, young enough to raise eyebrows, if you know what I mean."

I did know. I remembered with gratitude how protective Big Tom Callahan had been when I started working at his lobbying firm.

"Besides," he said, "he's her boss and he's married, not that you would find that a problem."

Mangan wasn't going to let that go, and he wanted to be sure that I knew it.

"All you have to do," he said, "is ask a few questions, drop a few hints in the right places—say, around the State House News Service. That shouldn't be too hard, should it?"

"What good would that do? Whately wouldn't be the first legislator to misbehave in the office, though I'll admit, standards are higher than they used to be." Even as I posed the question, I knew the answer. Mangan confirmed it.

"See, folks in central Massachusetts are pretty conservative when it comes to the behavior of their elected officials, especially with Whately's poor wife in the loony bin. He already has trouble with the local Chamber of Commerce because of his environmental sympathies, I've seen to that. And who knows where he's getting the money to pay for his extracurricular activities. This would provide a good reason to cut him loose."

"Are you suggesting that he's been dipping into his campaign funds?"

"Can't prove it." He slapped his fist on the table. "If you could, now that would tie things up real nice, wouldn't it?"

"And with Whately out of the way," I said, "you eliminate your chief legislative obstruction."

"It's called innuendo. In-nu-wendo. His campaign contributions will dry up like a stream-bed in an August scorcher. Mrs. Tannenbaum's daughter—a bit of a prude, if I do say so myself—she'll run away from him faster than a gecko on a hot rock."

"How can you be so sure?"

"I've talked to the mayor of Worcester. He thinks more senior housing for Worcester is a real winner. We both went to Holy Cross, graduated in the same class. Those old school ties are tighter than a wide receiver's grip on a football barreling toward the end zone."

"Of course." I should have known.

"He agrees with me that we should name Third Street after Mrs. Tannenbaum's mother, put a nice memorial on a playground at a nearby park—if, that is, she eases off the conservation land cause and doesn't give 'em any more money. Maybe forgets to send a check she'd promised. The Environmental League of Central Mass. can take what she's already given 'em and rescue long-eared bats or something. They'll look like heroes."

"I see where you're going."

"And when we get this little package all wrapped up I just might be able to help you with your situation." If he'd had a handlebar mustache, he would have played with it.

I marveled at his inventiveness. On its face what he was asking seemed relatively tame, so why was that beer backing up on me? It wasn't real hardball. I didn't like it, but I only would be disclosing behavior that was inappropriate anyway. I'd have to think about the right approach. Maybe I could do it without leaving any fingerprints. Then the dirt would be on the inside, a tainted soul. Was I tough enough to live with that?

"If you don't want to contribute, that's your choice," Mangan said.

As if I had a choice. Everything I'd worked for was on the line.

It was time to get Mangan on the record. "And just what would you be prepared to do to 'help me with my situation'?"

He put his forefinger to his lips and smiled.

"First things first. Right now your focus should be on Apple Grove. I want those farmers to think I'm their savior (not to take the Lord's name in vain, mind you). A year from now I'd like to see 'em retired and happy in Florida." He poked my arm with his fist. "Hardworking farmers like that deserve a rest. And I'll be well on my way to getting that land re-purposed for the good of the fifty-five and over population in Worcester County."

"You know, I'm straightforward, above board. When you first walked into my office, you said that was one of the things you liked about me." I scanned neighboring tables. With overhead televisions tuned into sports channels, multiple conversations, circulating waitresses and clinking glasses, no one could hear. "All right, Mr. Mangan, we'll do it your way."

"Good girl. That's what I'd hoped you'd say."

"And I'll hold you to your side of the bargain as well."

"I want that land," he said.

But it was no longer just about the land. We'd tumbled into a power game where Mangan's ego was at stake. And his ego was bigger than all the barns in Apple Grove.

I was so anxious to leave that I bumped into a table and jostled the drinks of the couple sitting there. They looked miffed. I hastily apologized, pulled a twenty out of my purse, threw it at them and kept on walking.

Chapter 28

I should have sensed something was wrong when Richard called. We hadn't talked for four days. He had on his professional voice.

"What's your schedule like today?" he said.

"What do you have in mind?"

"You know how we have this rule about not mixing business with pleasure? Well, this is business. Can we meet at Sal's?"

"What's up? Want to give me a clue so I can put my best game face on?"

"I heard a rumor about you and Mangan. I expect it's not true. I hope it's not, but I don't like to let these things fester, especially between us. Best to get it cleaned up."

Fester. A strong word. My heart was pounding as if I'd run a marathon.

Per Mangan's demand, I had sowed some seeds of mischief about Whately—enough, I hoped, to cover my rear and expose

Whately's without blowback that landed on me. I felt whipsawed.

"Whatever you've heard, Richard, it's not as bad as it looks."

"You mean there's something to it?"

"That's not what I meant." But what did I mean?

"Give me a break. I'm not some hack State House reporter. You sound like you're trying to spin a story."

"Come on, you can trust me. You know me."

"Do I?"

His question burnt through the telephone.

"This conversation is taking a decidedly sour turn," I said. So was my stomach. I'd need to get some antacid medication fast.

I looked at my calendar.

"I can be at Sal's in half an hour. Will that work for you? I'm going to the hospital at four o'clock." I wanted to get my relationship with Richard back on track, if it had, indeed, veered into a cul-de-sac. We had been on different wavelengths when we were last together. Still, there was something true about us that I didn't want to lose.

"I'll meet you at two."

No flexibility there. "Right. Richard, whatever it is…" I was talking into the air. He'd hung up.

Maura walked into my office. "What was that all about? You look like you've been hit in the face with a dead cat."

"I don't know, but I have an uneasy feeling. Can you cancel my meetings for the rest of the afternoon? I have to see Richard and then I'm going over to the hospital to see Barbara and Timmy."

"Right. Will do." Maura straightened the papers at the edge of my desk. "Just keep your priorities straight. Richard is the best thing that's happened to you in years. Even if Mangan has bulked up our bottom line, it's not worth it."

I waved her off. She had no idea.

I was heading out the door when Maura ran after me. "Don't you want your briefcase?"

"Oh, yah. Thanks."

I saw Richard through the window of the diner before I walked in. He was in the same booth he'd occupied when we first met, hunched over a cup of coffee, hands together under his chin in a tight fist, wavy hair all a-tumble. Oh that curly hair!

I had been so anxious that I hadn't even thought to get coffee. "Hey, you," I said, kissing his forehead before I sat down. He drew back. That gesture was like a slap in the face. No "Hi, I've missed you." Nothing like that.

"You look like a kid whose favorite baseball glove got left out in the rain," I said. "What's up?"

He launched straight into it. "I bumped into a stringer for the Worcester *Telegram and Gazette* in the State House cafeteria yesterday afternoon. He said there was a nasty rumor about Representative Whately and he was looking for confirmation from a second source. He asked me if I'd heard anything. I hadn't. He only gave me sketchy details, but what I heard could be damning if it were true."

Richard studied my face for any sign of confirmation.

I moistened my lips. "And how does this relate to me?"

"Come on, be straight with me. This has Mangan's fingerprints all over it. He's your client. If Mangan is involved I'm guessing you are too. And if you aren't, you should drop him in a very public way. Otherwise you're as complicit as if you *had* done something. I don't know why you took him on in the first place but it's high time you extricate yourself."

"I don't know what to say."

So far, I'd only planted a discrete question or two—"say, I heard a rumor, there might not be anything to it, but if there is, Rep. Whately has some explaining to do." That was an understatement. Whately would be burnt toast. But I hadn't *confirmed* anything, just raised questions. I thought I was being clever. Give Mangan enough of what he wanted without implicating myself or risking what was left of my reputation. I should have known Richard would see through the subterfuge.

"Can you categorically deny you've had a hand in this?" He waited, hands clasped around his mug.

"Let me get some coffee. I didn't sleep very well last night and I need a jolt of caffeine." The break also might give me time to prepare a plausible defense.

As usual, I put too much cream in the mug and the contents slopped over the rim when I sat back down. I took my time wiping up the spill with multiple napkins.

"I'm not saying I've done anything wrong, but what if it is true?" I said. "Shouldn't Whately be held accountable?"

Argument weak, shout here.

Richard stared at me. "I don't care whether Whately's behaved inappropriately. What I do care about is how the rumor started."

"You don't care?"

"You know what I mean. Right now what I want to know is whether the woman I loved…"

Did he say "love" or "loved"?

"has behaved in a way that I can't respect."

He hadn't mentioned that word before. I hadn't either, yet was that what had been unfolding, walk by walk, bird by bird?

"So it is true," he said. "You've admitted as much by your silence."

"I haven't admitted anything."

What would Richard do if I explained? Could I tell him about the bind Mangan had put me in? Could I trust him that much?

No, it only would make things worse. I hadn't told him about Mr. Public Charities. With an election to the office of attorney general at stake now, and his even loftier ambitions beyond that, Whately's situation would look like a minor sub-plot in an afternoon soap opera.

"We need to take a break," he said.

The coffee I'd just swallowed started to make a trip back into my throat. "'A break?' What do you mean, 'a break'?"

"Where is our relationship going? I mean, really going? What kind of woman are you, anyway? I thought I knew, but now I'm not so sure."

I wasn't either.

For an instant, his eyes reddened. He looked away. When he turned back, whatever had been there was gone.

"You'll do what you have to do," he said. "And I'll keep plugging away in the coalition. But I can't make love at night to a woman I don't trust during the day."

That was a gut punch.

He shook his head. "The funny thing is, I thought you might be winning in any case. With state tax revenues coming in below estimates, the governor probably can't find money for conservation land anyway. Too many competing claims are chasing too little money."

He had just confirmed what I'd told Mangan, but the jerk couldn't wait. Mangan had to do things his way and upend my life in the process.

"I was worried from the start that our professional interests might clash with the personal," I said. "And now they have."

"That's not the point. The point is, there are rules, ethical boundaries, about how to fight fair. This crosses the line."

"A line? What line? Don't tell me you're a purist. You can't be and work in the system." I knew, as I said it, that Richard was as clean as the environmental causes he espoused.

"I can't help thinking there's something else going on here," he said. "I just can't figure out what it is."

I wanted to tell him. Oh, I wanted to tell him, but I didn't dare.

Richard fingered his coffee mug. "You have high security needs," he said. "I know that. Your survival instincts are finely honed. They may have served you well in the past, but they've got downsides. This one's a stunner."

I stiffened. "If I want a psychiatrist, I'll go out and get one. I don't need you to do the deed pro bono."

"Look at me. I'm your friend."

"I thought we'd moved beyond friendship."

"You know what I mean."

"OK, you said it. Whether he intended to or not, Daddy taught me that it's always good to be prepared for the unexpected. I wasn't sufficiently prepared. I'm paying the price now."

"I don't know what you mean."

"I've said as much as I can."

"You're as bad as a dry drunk, except you're not addicted to booze or drugs. With you, enough is never enough."

I'd let down my guard with him, and that's how he treated me? That was his parting shot? Bull's-eye, right through the heart.

I didn't want him to see how much he'd hurt me. If I didn't get out of that diner fast, I'd start to cry.

"We've already said too much," I said. "You've said too much. I don't think we can accomplish anything further here, and I've got to get to the hospital to visit Barbara and Timmy. I'll see you around."

    I jumped up and barreled through the door.

Chapter 29

I grabbed the first cab I could find and slunk into a corner. What I wanted to do was sob, but I didn't want to arrive at the hospital with eyes that looked like over-ripe cherries. Barbara didn't need that. I shut my eyes, squeezed my fists together so tightly they hurt, and took some deep breaths.

A woman at the Dana Farber information desk gave me directions to Timmy's room on the seventh floor. When I exited the elevator, I was hit with a parallel universe of beeping machines, antiseptic smells, soft-soled shoes, and nurses in blue scrubs. It all boiled down to life and death, and I was somewhere down there, thrashing around in the scum. I ran into a bathroom and splashed cold water on my face. The least I could do to salvage an iota of self-respect was put a lid on my troubles so I could be a good auntie to Timmy and the friend Barbara needed.

The patients' rooms were arranged at right angles in a confus-

ing maze. Just as I walked up to the nurses' station to ask directions
to Timmy's room, Barbara came down the hallway.

"Claire!" she said. She threw her arms around me in a tight
hug. "It's so good to see you! Timmy's resting now and I'm going
to the cafeteria for a cup of tea. Come on along. You have time,
don't you?"

"As much as you need."

I had expected her to look tired and drawn. Although her eye
make-up was more abbreviated than usual and her nails were un-
polished, she appeared unexpectedly composed. Were both of us
wearing masks?

We got our tea and found a corner table facing an inner courtyard.

"How are you?" I asked. "Really? And how's Timmy?"

"I'm so much better than the last time we talked."

"I didn't know if it was real or if that was your 'game face.'"

"The doctors are very encouraging, thank God!" She acknowledged one of the nurses who walked by our table. "Timmy is
healthy, well, except for this. The cancer hasn't spread beyond the
lymph nodes. They think we can beat this."

I covered her hand in mine. "That is such good news!"

She went on to describe, in numbing detail, all the tests, pro-
cedures, and logistics. I suspected she hadn't had anyone else with
whom she could unspool the narrative. Although my mind was
back in Sal's Diner, I tried to be attentive. "What kind of woman
are you, really?" Richard had asked. I didn't know any more.

My tea had grown lukewarm. When Barbara finally wound
down I asked how everyone was coping.

"We have our good times and our bad. Caleb has his work. It
distracts him." She pushed a stray wisp of hair off her face. "You
know how he is."

When I was a teenager, Barbara's home felt like a sanctuary. She had taken that template and replicated it with Caleb. Even in the hard times they had an easy familiarity. How did they do that? How would it feel to be so intimate with another human being that you could both be disappointed and forgiving at the same time?

"When he's at the office, he can wall this off." She waved a hand at all the hospital staff in scrubs around the cafeteria.

"And you?" I said.

She finished her tea. I waited.

"I guess you're catching me on a good day," she said. "Timmy sleeps a lot. His immune system will be compromised from all the chemo and radiation, so he can't be in groups. That means no school for now, and of course, no summer job."

A sparrow fluttered around a nest in a tree outside the window, feeding her fledglings. Squawking sounds penetrated the glass.

She leaned against the back of the chair. "So he misses a year or more. I keep telling him it's a small price to pay for your life. Everything else can be managed. If we can get through this, nothing else matters. And we will get through this."

There was something sacred about that fierce kind of love.

"It does tend to shift one's perspective."

"We've already talked with the academic dean. He's been very understanding, told us not to worry. Yale will be waiting for him when he's ready to come back for his senior year."

Barbara's father, grandfather, and who knows how many other members of the family had been alumni, so I wasn't surprised. I was relieved. I really loved that kid, and I didn't want his career derailed any more than Barbara did.

"Want more tea?" she asked.

"No thanks. I'm drowning in caffeine."

"Do you mind if I get another cup?"

"Of course not."

A long line had formed at the cashier's table. Barbara chatted with a woman ahead of her. I checked my cell phone to see if Richard had called. The screen was blank. Damn him. He was abandoning me in the middle of one of those ponds he took me to. "A delicate freshwater ecosystem," he'd called it, "threatened by all the pesticides Mangan and his ilk use to keep their precious golf courses manicured."

What about *me*? I was stuck in the middle of the pond, feet balanced on a slippery rock, not sure if the next one would hold, peering at a steep embankment on the other side. I couldn't turn around and go back. It was too late. But how could I go forward?

Just then Barbara re-appeared with a mug of tea in one hand and a bag of cashews in the other. "It's so good to see you," she said. "Hey, I've been rattling on for forty-five minutes and I haven't even asked you about the visit with your uncle. How did it go?"

I needed to call and see if he'd recovered from that tumble in front of Polaski's.

"It was…interesting."

"'Interesting' is an interesting word." She poured some nuts on a napkin and pushed it in the middle of the table.

"I don't want to bother you with my troubles," I said. "You've got enough of your own."

"Look at it this way. You'll do me a favor by distracting me. So how was your visit?"

I picked a few cashews off the napkin and ate them one by one.

"Oh, it was fine. Right now my mind is on work. And on Richard."

"Richard? He's the best thing that's happened to you since— since I don't know when."

"I know."

"You don't sound convinced. What's going on? You haven't pushed him away, have you?"

I dove into my purse, allegedly to find a breath mint, but really so she couldn't see my eyes. I was sure they were reddening again.

"We had a fight, a big one, over one of my clients who's in direct conflict with an organization in his coalition."

"Surely you can agree to disagree. You've always been able to maneuver through political minefields. You're not perfect. Richard's not perfect. The imperfections are part of what you grow to love in each other. What's so different now?"

I choked on a cashew, which led to a coughing spell. Heads at nearby tables turned.

"I've done something I probably shouldn't have," I said. "Richard called me on it. Said we needed to take a break, that I'd crossed some invisible line—'an ethical boundary,' he said. Sometimes I think he missed his calling. He should have been a rabbi, not a lobbyist. He's so damned Pharisaic."

"This doesn't sound like you. Is something else going on?"

I looked at my hands. They were vibrating. I'd had too much caffeine.

"I'm in a bit of a bind--nothing I want to trouble you with. You have your own problems, and they're far more consequential."

"I still can listen to my best friend."

"I really can't talk about it now."

"Can't, or won't?"

"I need more time to sort it all out."

It often took me a while to figure out how I felt about something, especially when the feelings were complex. These were like a Rubik's Cube.

"From everything I've heard, Richard is one of the good guys. He certainly has been good for you."

"Not now."

"Don't be so sure. You don't think you have the right to depend on anybody. Maybe if you trusted him he could help you."

Just then my cell phone rang. The call was an Ohio area code.

"Richard?" she asked.

"No, I think it's from Uncle Erich. I'd promised to call him after I got back, and I haven't connected yet." More guilt. I was drowning in it.

Barbara looked at her watch. "I should be getting back to Timmy anyway." She tucked the rest of the cashews in her purse, we zigzagged between tables and into the hospital corridor.

"Thanks for coming," she said. "It means a lot."

"I'm glad the news is encouraging. But I meant what I said. If I can help, just ask. You know you can call me anytime, day or night. And let me know when Timmy's up for a visit from his Aunt Claire."

No air-kiss this time. We hugged tightly. She turned toward a bank of elevators and I headed out the door to a secluded bench in a courtyard by the hospital where I could return the call from Uncle Erich.

Chapter 30

I expected to hear Uncle Erich's voice, but a woman at the Lakeside Retirement Community switchboard answered instead. When I asked to be connected to Mr. Petersen she said "Oh, my dear, just a minute. Let me put you through to Chaplain Wolf."

"The chaplain?"

She hesitated. "We've got some sad news. Let me transfer you to the chaplain. She'll talk with you." She put me on hold before I had a chance to ask for more information. I sat on the bench, chewed a hangnail, and waited.

I never should have left Uncle Erich on Sunday. I should have insisted that he go to the hospital. He probably was there now. Maybe he'd fallen again. Broken a hip. Or worse yet, had a heart attack.

I bit off the hangnail. My finger bled. I licked off the blood. Then my finger started to ache.

"Is this Claire Petersen?"

"Yes, just tell me what's happened to my uncle. Where is he?"

"Are you somewhere quiet where we can talk?" The chaplain's voice was modulated, steady.

"Just tell me what's going on."

"I'm so sorry. Your Uncle was found dead in his apartment earlier this afternoon."

"Dead? Are you sure?" I felt stupid even as I said it. Of course she was sure. You don't make a mistake about something like that.

"He was supposed to have lunch with one of his neighbors. When he didn't show up, she notified us. We found him lying on the living room floor where he'd fallen. He must have had a stroke."

My brain froze.

"I know this is sudden," she said. "It's a lot to absorb."

"I was just there."

"I know. Mr. Petersen saw me in the hallway on Tuesday. We stopped for a chat."

How much had he told her?

"He said you'd been to see him, how much it meant to him."

"Me too." I suppressed a sob. "We'd been out of touch."

That was an understatement. Now I'd lost the chance to make it up to him.

"I'd been busy with work," I said. "Then he sent me this box of things from my grandmother."

Just when I saw an opening to reclaim what was left of family, the door had shut. Doors were slamming in my face in all directions.

"Your visit gave him so much pleasure. I could see it in his face when he talked about you. He was beaming. That's something you can hold onto forever. He was very proud of you."

He wouldn't be now. Not if he knew the mess I'd gotten myself into.

I held the phone in one hand and clutched my waist with the other. That was all I could hold onto, and it was nothing.

"I've lived in Oretown all my life," she said. "I knew Mr. Petersen before he joined us here. I used to see him in the produce section of the old A&P. He always had a kind word and a friendly smile."

"Can you give me a minute? I need to get a tissue."

"Of course."

I put the phone down and rummaged around in my purse.

"I'm back now."

"Let me give you my cell phone number," the chaplain said. "When you've had a chance to absorb this, please call me. Your uncle listed you as next of kin. We should talk about how you want to handle the arrangements."

"Arrangements?"

"Whenever anyone becomes a resident here, they fill out detailed forms about how they want matters handled after they die. Your uncle was very explicit about some things, less so about others. He'd already purchased a cemetery plot. We can hold a service in our chapel if you'd like. He hadn't lived here very long, but he'd made a lot of friends in that short time. Or you can talk with the minister at St. John's where he was a long-standing member. Those are things we should work out when you've had a little more time."

In some ways, Chaplain Wolf knew more about my uncle than I did.

"Where is he now?"

"Now?"

"Yes. Now. Where is he?"

"The funeral home has taken his body, per his instructions. And we've notified his lawyer."

"His lawyer?"

"Your uncle apparently had a good mind for details. He'd arranged with a lawyer in town to be the executor of his estate. I don't know anything about the particulars, but Ohio law usually requires that assets over a certain amount go through probate."

I felt lightheaded. "I'm sorry. This is too much for me to take in right now. Can I get back to you?"

"Of course. You can reach me any time until ten o'clock tonight and all day tomorrow. Am I correct in assuming that you'll want to come to Ohio for the funeral? We can schedule it at your convenience. And after you've spoken with his lawyer, his personal effects will need to be cleaned out of his apartment."

"What? I'm sorry, what did you say?"

"The retirement community gives a week's grace period in situations like this. We're used to handling these things, and a social worker on staff can advise you about where donations can be made—furniture, clothing, that sort of thing."

I was getting dizzy. "I have to go now. I'll call you back as soon as I can."

"I understand. You've had a great shock. You have my number?" She repeated it slowly.

"Yes. Thank you. I'll call you as soon as I'm able to sort out the logistics at this end."

"Take good care of yourself. I'll be here to help in any way I can. God bless."

After we disconnected, I vomited. Little bits of cashews dotted putrid pink fluids on the green grass. Fortunately, no one was around to witness it. I wiped my mouth, made a hasty retreat from the evidence, and hailed a cab.

"Lady, aren't you going to tell me where you want to go?" the cabbie asked after he'd navigated his way out of the hospital curbside. He adjusted the air freshener hanging from his visor.

"Oh, yes. Sorry." I gave him the address.

His round black face studied me in the rearview mirror. "That's all right, miss," he said in a lilting accent rooted somewhere in sub-Saharan Africa. "Don't you worry. Abraham gonna get you there lickety-split."

Chapter 31

I fell into bed with all my clothes on and pulled a comforter up to
my chin. I kept thinking about Uncle Erich lying on a cold slab in
a funeral home somewhere in Oretown, and I couldn't get warm.
"Home." Why did they call a place like that home?

When I was seven I found a dead black crow in my backyard,
lying on its side, stiff, eyes open, yellow legs pointing out. I was
afraid to touch it, but Barbara and I got a shovel from my garage,
carried it to the back of the yard, and solemnly buried it under a
bed of leaves. That was my only brush with death before my father
died. Whereas the crow was an object of fascination, the sight of
my father's dead body horrified me.

It was the family custom to have an open casket. When we
arrived at the funeral home, my mother held my hand and walked
us up to a shiny mahogany box with brass handles. (She didn't yet
understand that every penny spent on the funeral was one less we

would have to live on.) There he was, a waxen figure with frozen lips and cold, cold hands, lying on puffy white satin. Mother kissed his forehead. I screamed and ran out of the room. I couldn't touch that lifeless body. It wasn't my Daddy anymore.

Mother and I, she in a chic black suit, me in a black dress with ruffled white trim on the sleeves and around the neck, stood next to each other in the funeral home parlor. The ruffles scratched my neck.

A line snaked around the room and out the door for what were called "visiting hours," as if ladies were coming for tea. My back kept bumping into huge floral arrangements. Their fragrance made my nose itch. I didn't know what to say to people, and the middle school friends who had come—maybe out of curiosity as much as anything—didn't know what to say to me, either. I wanted to run into the bathroom and hide.

Barbara was the only one who had understood. When she arrived with her parents, she hugged me, then pressed a silver bracelet into my hand. It had a charm that said "friends forever." I still had it.

This time I would be standing alone.

Oh, Uncle Erich! Why didn't you let me take you to the emergency room after you'd fallen? Why did I convince myself that it was all right to leave you? Were you just putting on a good front? I never should have done that.

All those years I missed. I could have visited. I was just too damned focused on work, and what did I have to show for it? A bankrupt life.

I'd always thought yours was pathetic—a single old man who lived with his mother in the house where he'd grown up. You could have been like the father I'd lost, maybe like one I'd never had— loving, loyal, honest, principled—a man I could trust. Now look who's pathetic!

I wanted to call Richard and tell him what had happened, but I was afraid. Would he see it as another tactical maneuver from an underhanded lobbyist? I didn't think so, but I couldn't be sure. "With you enough never is enough," he'd said. His words seared my heart.

My hands and feet were freezing. My muscles ached. My mouth was dry. I went into the bathroom, rummaged around the medicine cabinet, and struggled to open a bottle of aspirin with one of those child-proof plastic caps. I dropped the bottle and pills scattered all over the tiled floor. "To hell with it," I muttered, kicking the pills out of the way as I stomped out of the room.

My work ethic may have ruined my personal life, but it was the ability to focus, to blot out all distractions, that got me through the next twenty-four hours--that and caffeine I consumed as if it were an IV drip straight into my veins.

I made lists of everything I needed to do before I left for Ohio. Then I called Maura at home. The way she talked about "that kind old gentleman," you'd think she had known Uncle Erich. When she offered to make my flight arrangements, I let her. We agreed that I should go to Oretown the next morning, but not too early, and return on the following Tuesday--three and a half days, including the weekend. That, I hoped, would give me enough time to deal with Uncle Erich's things. With Mangan's threats hovering, I didn't dare stay longer.

Maura promised to deflect any business calls before then. A death in the family was a legitimate excuse. Piper Mangan wasn't mentioned but she knew who needed managing. What she didn't know was why.

I took Chaplain Wolf at her word and called her back. After explaining my abhorrence of an open casket, she recommended that we have a private burial followed by a memorial service at a separate time. If I wished, she said, I could use the dual-purpose hall at the retirement facility. They were used to handling such things. She suggested that I speak with the manager of the cafeteria to arrange for simple refreshments following the service. The residents would expect it, and it would give people a chance to express their condolences.

I left all the arrangements for the memorial service in the chaplain's hands. She asked if I knew Uncle Erich's favorite hymns or verses from Scripture. I had no idea. She said she would consult with his pastor, and we made plans to meet after I flew to Ohio. We decided to hold the memorial service early Monday afternoon. The schedule would be tight, but I hoped that would give me time to handle the rest of the logistics. Besides, if I was busy I would have less time to think.

When I called the funeral home I discovered that Uncle Erich had pre-paid for everything. He'd even purchased a cemetery plot next to my grandparents. A headstone already was there with his name and year of his birth. They only needed to add the date of death. All I had to do was tell them the plans for a service and pick up the death certificates. I had no idea why I would need them, but the funeral director, who spoke in a modulated baritone, assured me that some would be required.

Then I called Barbara. When she didn't answer, I left a message, told her about Uncle Erich, said I'd be preoccupied for the next few days, but she knew how to reach me. I left phone messages for the lawyer and social worker, whose contact information Chaplain Wolf had supplied, telling them I would be arriving in

Oretown early Friday afternoon and hoped it would be convenient for me to meet with them before the weekend.

By the time I'd accomplished all that it was eleven o'clock. I was hungry. The only edible thing in my refrigerator was ice cream. I sat in the dark living room with my feet curled up, stared out the window at car lights as vehicles whizzed along Storrow Drive, and dug out a spoonful at a time.

Uncle Erich loved ice cream. A "simple pleasure," he'd called it. The rich texture didn't sit well on my empty stomach, so I put the container back in the freezer. Uncle Erich wouldn't be eating any more ice cream. I couldn't, either.

Chapter 32

The social worker at the retirement home was a portly woman with tightly permed gray hair and bifocals on a chain around her neck. After expressing her condolences and offering me tea or coffee (I declined. Counting the Grande I'd purchased from an airport Starbucks before boarding the plane and the two cups of coffee I'd had in flight, my teeth were afloat.), she produced a prepared folder with different colored pieces of paper containing "all the information I would need to make an inherently difficult time a little less stressful." She put on her glasses and handed me papers in dizzying succession. She was a model of efficiency, while my mind flitted like the nervous chickadees Richard and I had watched on our last nature walk.

She had lists of organizations that accepted used clothing, used furniture, used books, used kitchen utensils; shops which traded gold and silver for cash; names of antique dealers from a nearby flea market; and a local church with volunteers ready to pick up anything that either could be recycled or used in their next rummage sale. I wasn't in Back Bay Boston anymore. "Use it up, wear it out, make it do or do without" was the modus operandi here. Uncle Erich would have approved.

My stomach started doing another fandango. How was I going to get everything done in the next three days?

"Are you sure I can't get you anything? Some water or something? You look a little pale."

"No thanks." I clutched my purse as if it were a security blanket. "It's just that I've never had to do anything like this before."

When my mom and I had to move to Nonantum, she handled the packing while I was in school. All I remembered were boxes everywhere and her mandate that I sacrifice some of my bulky sweaters and my collection of stuffed animals, since there wouldn't be space in my new pea-sized bedroom. "You're almost fourteen," she said. "Stuffed animals are for children. You're not a child anymore."

I was so angry at her, at my father, at the situation. I slammed the door, ran out of the house and across the street to Barbara's. She tried her best to comfort me, but at thirteen, her capacity to offer genuine solace was limited. Eventually her father intervened and escorted me back to my mother.

"I know," the social worker said, taking off her glasses and wiping them on the edge of her jacket. "It seems daunting at first, and it isn't easy to go through a loved one's personal effects when they've passed on."

Personal effects. Passed on. She had a whole vocabulary to sanitize Uncle Erich's death, yet it couldn't be glossed over. The uncle whom I'd lost, no, I had to be honest, the uncle whom I'd neglected for so many years, who had welcomed me with warmth and hugs and love only a few days ago, was dead.

"My advice to you is, start with The Salvation Army and Goodwill," she said. "They'll take almost everything. You can use the Lutheran Church as your back up. If you call them this afternoon, they may even be willing to help you on Saturday. Most of the church folks are volunteers."

"Saturday?" I stuffed the papers into my purse. "I'll be lucky to get it all sorted out by Monday."

"They do a lot of their work on the weekends, but some of the men are retired and they're more flexible. Just stock up on garbage bags and wade in. That's the only way to do it." She waved her hand in a northerly direction. "There's a CVS two blocks from here."

Garbage bags? Was that the culmination of a life? If someone were to go through my worldly goods, what would they say about me? Who would do it? Who would care?

She offered to go up to Uncle Erich's apartment with me, but I declined. I didn't want her to see me when I walked through the door.

I postponed the inevitable as long as I could. I phoned the chaplain and told her I had arrived. We agreed to meet on Saturday morning to discuss arrangements for what she called "the committal" (translation, put Uncle Erich in the ground) and the memorial service. I contacted the lawyer, a Mr. Schneider, whom Uncle Erich had designated as executor of his estate. There probably would not be much to do, nevertheless, Mr. Schneider seemed eager to meet me. We scheduled that for Saturday morning, as well. Then I lined up The Salvation Army and the church folks. Both assured me that they could come on Monday afternoon. We planned their arrival for 3:30. I hoped that would give me enough time to handle Uncle Erich's "personal effects." Then I picked up a supply of thirteen-gallon extra strength garbage bags (the black color seemed fitting for the occasion), begged a few empty boxes from a nearby liquor store, and headed to his apartment.

I stood outside the door, key in my hand, and resisted the weird impulse to knock as if he were still inside. Which, I realized after I walked in, in a way, he was. A copy of Thursday's *Oretown Sentinal* was on a TV tray next to his recliner, opened to a half-completed crossword puzzle. Breakfast dishes were in the drain next to the kitchen sink. He had washed them right after he'd eaten. He was meticulous that way.

I sat in the recliner, threadbare where Uncle Erich's elbows would have rested, and fingered the stubby pencil he'd used to fill in the blanks of the puzzle. Had he been working on it right before the stroke? How much pain had he been in? For how long? How awful to have been alone, no one around to comfort him as he died.

It was so quiet. The only sound I heard was a ticking clock somewhere in his bedroom. His slippers were under the end table next to his recliner. The worn inner fleece conformed to the shape of his big feet. The insides still smelled of liniment. It seemed sacrilegious to throw them in the trash, but who would want them?

I took off my sweater and put my purse in an out of-the way corner. What I could do was get to work. I had always found salvation in work. But where to begin?

I walked through his apartment and made a list of furniture that The Salvation Army could pick up. It was such a modest list: sofa, coffee table, recliner, end table, bookcase, little television, TV stand, twin bed, nightstand, dresser, chest of drawers, chair. That was all. Much of it looked like it might be returning to The Salvation Army for a second visit--so different from my condo with its oriental rugs, drapes in matching hues, upholstered chairs and silk throw pillows selected in consultation with my decorator on a whirlwind tour of the Boston Design Center.

I started in the kitchen. He'd kept three of everything—plates, cups, glasses--just three. I supposed he figured if one broke, he'd have two left. The accumulation didn't even fill one box. The refrigerator had a few plastic containers of half-eaten cakes and cookies, probably brought back from the community dining room. When I opened the freezer, for whatever reason, the dear man never had eaten the sundaes I'd brought from Matt's. They looked so forlorn, the whipped cream shrunken from prolonged exposure to the cold. I pulled the plastic lid off one, pressed my finger in the hard chocolate sauce, licked it. The chocolate still had a sharp, tangy flavor. Then I tossed them in a garbage bag.

A beige two-drawer filing cabinet was sandwiched in a corner of his bedroom with a key in the lock. He apparently hadn't thought anyone would be interested in stealing its contents. I opened the drawers, bulging front to back with neatly labeled filing folders. How would I ever get through all that paper? I closed the drawers with such force that the key fell out of the lock. I had to get down on my hands and knees to find it.

I thought turning my attention to clothing would be easier, but I was wrong. It felt weirdly intimate, pulling a pile of neatly stacked briefs and slightly yellowed undershirts out of his dresser. I had a new understanding of how Richard must have felt when his wife died. He had told me her clothes stayed in their drawers for months afterwards. He couldn't bear to get rid of them.

Buried beneath some handkerchiefs in the back of the bottom drawer was a little leather-bound commonplace book. It appeared to be a collection of quotations co-mingled with personal notes. I tucked it in my pocket so I wouldn't lose it.

Hanging in the closet were five ties, one suit (his "church suit"?), three pairs of pants, and six shirts--two white dress and four flannel. I buried my face in the soft flannel, remembering his bony ribcage the first time I hugged him.

Richard wore flannel shirts like that. It was his standard dress whenever we went hiking. I was tempted to take them home (could I give them to him as a peace offering?), but after a moment's hesitation, I stuffed them in a garbage bag along with the other clothes—all but one. That I would keep and use in the winter as a nightshirt—not my standard Chambray cotton, but who would see it, anyway?

A little pile of memorabilia was accumulating on the living room coffee table: the flannel shirt, Uncle Erich's Bible, the retirement plaque he'd been so proud of, his small music collection, Grandma's crocheted throw, her old photo album. Now I never would get the chance to ask him about more of the pictures. Or the postcards Richard had translated.

In the bathroom a bottle of Old Spice was on the counter. I inhaled the scent, plunked down on the toilet seat and sobbed like a lost child.

"Oh, Uncle Erich, I'm so sorry. You were my only family. Why didn't I take more time to be with you? God knows I've had plenty of free weekends with nothing to do, no place to go. And now you're gone. I miss you so much!"

Eventually I washed my face and dried it with a towel that hung neatly on a nearby rack—a towel Uncle Erich would have used just a day ago. My blotchy cheeks and red eyes were a sorry sight in the medicine cabinet mirror.

Gradually the garbage bags got filled with books, linens, stuff from his medicine chest. I still had more to do but I began to see my way clear. This, in large measure, because of the modest way Uncle Erich had lived. It didn't take much to make him happy.

I had done all I could for the day. I was finished. The rest would have to wait.

It had been less than a week since I'd been in the motel. The gum-chewing teenage receptionist remembered me. Maybe she thought she was doing me a favor by giving me the same room.

When I flopped on the bed, my eyes fixed on the generic landscape which looked like it had been plucked from a cereal box. I remembered lying on the same bed, looking at the same picture in its black plastic frame, talking with Richard.

What was it he'd said? "Don't try to stuff all your feelings. Just let them be for a while."

My feelings were like mice that had chewed their way out of a cardboard box and darted about, leaving mess in every corner of the room. Even if I'd wanted to, there was no containing them.

Chapter 33

At nine o'clock on Saturday morning I dropped Uncle Erich's one good suit, white shirt, tie, and underwear (it would seem strange for him to be buried without his undies) off at the funeral home. Everything was in earth tones ranging from loam brown leather chairs to beige drapes and cream-colored walls, all designed, I surmised, to foster calm in grieving families.

We were sitting in the funeral director's office.

"I seem to remember that your uncle wore glasses," he said.

I must have looked startled—how would he know? He added, "It wasn't too long ago that Mr. Petersen came in to make arrangements. You don't need to worry. Everything's pre-paid."

Had Uncle Erich had a premonition that death was near? This further evidence of his thoughtfulness only added to my feelings of guilt and loss.

"Would you like us to put them on him? The glasses, I mean.

We can give them back to you before we close the casket."

"Oh, leave them on, whatever, he might need them." I didn't know what I was saying. I just wanted to get out of there as fast as possible.

The visit with the chaplain didn't go much better. A box of tissue rested prominently on a corner of her desk. I supposed that it got frequent use.

"Would you like to say something about your uncle during the service?" she asked.

The prospect terrified me. When I didn't answer she ploughed ahead. "If that is too daunting, you could read one of the Scripture lessons, or a poem he especially liked. Perhaps you could share a story or two. It doesn't have to be long. As a matter of fact, it shouldn't be."

I was embarrassed. How could I tell her my adult interactions with my uncle had lasted less than two days.

"I don't know if I can handle it," I said.

"I understand. It's a perfectly normal reaction." A large silver cross on a chain she wore around her neck bumped against the metal desk when she leaned forward. "Think about it."

Then I remembered his commonplace book. "He kept a little journal. I haven't had time to look at it yet. I thought I'd do that tonight. Maybe I can find something there. Could I get back to you?"

"Of course. And if you find some Scripture you want me to use, you can put it in my in-house mail cubby. It's in the lobby near the reception desk."

After clarifying logistics for the committal and the memorial service, I drove to the lawyer's office.

Frederick Schneider, Esq. was located on the second floor of a non-descript yellow brick bank building on Main Street, sandwiched between a "New to You" clothing store and "Ye Olde Sub

Shoppe." The place was respectable, not flashy—nothing like the plush offices of big corporate law firms in Boston. I assumed that if Uncle Erich had entrusted his affairs to this man, he had his reasons.

No receptionist was in view, probably because it was a Saturday. The door to the inner office was open. As I walked in, Mr. Schneider, a short, slender man with close-cropped salt and pepper hair (more salt than pepper) with a receding hairline, got up from his desk and shook my hand.

"Mr. Petersen was a prince of a man," he said. "Until recently, my wife and I saw him in church almost every Sunday. When he wasn't there, we noticed. He loved to sing. He sat in the same pew, left side, right in the middle. We'll miss him."

He motioned for me to sit down and pulled a chair so he and I were on the same side of the desk.

"He was my Sunday School teacher for several years. He put up with us unruly boys all the way through junior high school. He even managed to teach us a few things. I still can recite parts of The Heidelberg Catechism. He drilled it into us."

I didn't know what the Heidelberg Catechism was, but I was about to find out. He straightened his shoulders and flattened both feet on the floor as if he were back in Sunday school, looked up at the ceiling and said "'Why is prayer necessary for Christians? Because it is the chief part of the gratitude which God requires of us.' It goes on from there. I can't remember the rest, but that stuck with me."

I was coming up empty in the gratitude department. I had lost the two men who, recently and all too briefly, had pried opened a life previously dominated by the only thing I knew how to do well, work. And now I had messed that up, as well.

"So that's how you know—knew—each other," I said.

"Oretown is knit together by neighborhoods, churches, organizations like the VFW and the Polish Club. By the way, they've got a terrific fish fry on Saturdays, if you're looking for a good place to eat tonight. Your uncle wasn't a joiner. He kept to himself. I'm sure you know that. But if he could help somebody he was right there, every time. When my wife and I adopted our baby, his was the first card of congratulations we received. You must be missing him terribly."

"More than you know." More than I could have envisioned.

"He had a soft spot in his heart for you."

I swallowed hard.

"You're a beneficiary in his will," he said. "That's why I was eager to meet you."

What could that mean? I'd just been through all his earthly possessions. The most valuable thing he owned he already had given me—my grandmother's gold necklace.

Mr. Schneider went over to a locked cabinet, rifled through some files, pulled out a manila folder, and returned to his chair. "Your uncle left quite a large estate," he said. "Not enough to go through probate according to Ohio law, but still, substantial." He put on his reading glasses. "He has stipulated three gifts of $25,000 each to the charities that meant the most to him—his church, a scholarship fund at Oretown High, and the local chapter of the VFW."

"$25,000? I thought my uncle was—well—poor."

"Poor, my dear, he was not. He just believed in living simply. There's a difference. What he didn't need, he salted away, invested wisely over the years, and once in a while (I know, because he consulted me) he anonymously made a monetary gift to someone in difficulty."

"I didn't know." So much I didn't know.

"It's always satisfying at a time like this," he said, "to see how love gets shared. Mr. Petersen was a quiet man, some might say he was shy, but not much escaped him. He cared about people. You could see it in his face. Folks responded to that."

I told him about the way he'd spoken with the girl who'd waited on us in the dining room at the retirement community. Zofia? Was that her name? And how he'd joked with the women sitting on the veranda as we made our way to Polaski's for lunch.

He leafed through some papers in the folder. "I can't be precise, but after expenses, I estimate that your bequest will come to about $750,000."

"Could you repeat that?"

"About three quarters of a million dollars. Impressive for a grocery clerk, isn't it?"

I was dumbfounded. I didn't know what to say.

"Actually, Mr. Petersen called me last Monday. I guess you'd been to visit him. It didn't change his plans in any way, but he talked about how proud of you he was."

I looked down at my feet. A big scuff mark was in the black leather of my left shoe.

"He talked about you. He said things had been hard for you when you were a kid, and he regretted he couldn't help then, but he hoped whatever he had left after he died—he didn't know it would be so soon after our conversation—would help you."

The rest of my time in that office was a blur. I may have signed some papers. I think we exchanged contact information. When I stood on Main Street in blinding sunlight after I left Schneider's law office, I didn't remember whether I'd walked down a flight of stairs or taken an elevator, the color of my rental car or where I'd parked it.

Chapter 34

$750,000! Uncle Erich could have traveled the world, moved into a bigger apartment, or bought some new clothes, but none of that was important to him. It couldn't compare with Barbara's bequest, but it wasn't chump change, either.

The car was hot. I powered down the windows, turned up the air conditioning, and started driving. Where do you go on a Saturday afternoon in Oretown, Ohio when your options are a non-descript motel room, your dead uncle's apartment, or a strip mall with empty storefronts? I ended up at the lake.

The park was bustling with activity. An aroma of hamburgers and hot dogs wafted through the air. People were lined up in front of a food truck. I hadn't eaten anything for breakfast and I was ravenous, so I joined the queue. When my turn came, I ordered a chili dog with all the trimmings, French fries, and a diet cola. On impulse I added a peanut butter cookie the size of a dinner plate. I

carried the bag to a picnic table with an unobstructed view of Lake
Erie. Uncle Erich would have liked sitting there watching children
chase the incoming waves. Had he and my father done that when
they were children? The chili dog and half the cookie disappeared
and I had no recollection of having eaten them. Even with a bunch
of napkins, my palms felt greasy.

Birds flitted around the picnic table, searching for crumbs.
Richard would have been able to identify them in an instant.

I picked at the French fries. They'd been too hot to handle
when I got them. Now they were cold and limp. I tossed a few to
the birds, who swooped in, seized them, and flew off to nearby
bushes.

Uncle Erich and my father had experienced deprivation as
children. To compensate for his embarrassed circumstances, Daddy lived larger than life, and we saw where that ended up. My uncle
lived modestly—below his means, on less than what others considered necessary—yet he seemed content, secure, fulfilled, and
he had accumulated $825,000 by the end of his life. Something
gnawed at my insides, and it wasn't the effects of the chili dog.

When I reached into the pocket of my slacks for a roll of breath
mints, I discovered Uncle Erich's commonplace book. His hands
were so big. Why had he chosen such a small book? I stroked the
soft brown leather cover, worn from years of use.

The pages contained a hodgepodge of phrases, sentences,
paragraphs, apparently from whatever he was reading at the time.
Dates skipped months, sometimes years. He had gone to school in
an era when penmanship was a normal part of the school curric-
ulum, and most of the writing was clear and elegant. That made
one jagged entry, pressed into the paper, all the more remarkable.

"Veteran's Day 1951." That would have been five or six years
after he came home from the war. "Tear into smallest pieces any

itinerary for the journey which your imagination may have drawn up. Nothing will fall out as you expect."

A gust of wind scattered my napkins and luncheon detritus all over the ground. I didn't want the book to go flying and was afraid to leave my purse untended, but I didn't want to litter the park, either. I put my purse on top of the book and dashed around to pick up the trash. The thin napkins were like white paper airplanes, traveling farther from the picnic table with each new burst of wind.

Two children came running to help. They made a game of it, giggling as they scurried around and captured yet another airplane on the fly. After the last of the napkins were deposited in a nearby receptacle, I retrieved my purse.

"These," I said, choosing lofty words as I placed fifty cents in each of their grimy hands, "are tokens of appreciation for your invaluable assistance."

They received the silver coins with sober expressions. Then they grinned and ran off to show their mother their newfound wealth.

I swung my legs back under the picnic table and leafed through a few more pages of the commonplace book. In 1962 Uncle Erich had written "Many refuse to be still with themselves because they dislike what they are. So what? Don't we all?" He'd underlined "Don't we all?"

I was only four years old in 1962. Barbara and I were playing on the elaborate jungle gym my mother had paid workers to assemble in our backyard.

What demons had dear old Uncle Erich been wrestling with that made him dislike what he was? And what, or who, had helped him achieve the peace that grounded him in later years? I wanted what he had, though it was clear that his contentment had not come easily or without cost.

Then, "June 20, 1987, The Day Mother Died," in heavy black ink. "I now think that to be united with Christ is to be making progress in seeing life as it is, not as the child within you wishes it to be, and receiving grace to love its real presence."

I picked at a splinter in the gray weathered wood of the picnic table. Eventually it pulled away from the plank. Ants had made a home under there. Now they ran around in confusion. I brushed them off.

Wave action on the lake had intensified, with whitecaps skittering over the surface of the gray-green water. Gulls were screeching and flapping their wings, eager to swoop down and consume leftover scraps of food before any other creatures had a chance. I hurried to my car, lest I get bombarded in the melee.

I started to head back to my motel, but then I wondered. Could I find the house where Uncle Erich and my father had grown up? It would be my last chance to see the old place. After the funeral I had no intention of returning to Oretown.

I turned around and headed south on Main. After crawling down Fourth Street, eliciting more than a few stares, I found it and parked across the street.

Where did we stay when we came to visit? It couldn't have been there. The house was even smaller than I had remembered, with one window on either side of the front door.

As a child, I was oblivious to these matters. What I did remember was Grandma sitting on the thread-bare living room rug, flowered print house dress pulled up to her knees, nylons sagging around her thin ankles, bunions pushing out the sides of her worn black leather shoes, playing tiddlywinks with me as long as I wanted. What stamina! When Timmy was a kid, after two rounds of Chutes and Ladders I was finished, no matter how much he begged for another game. Did Grandma get bored? Did sitting on the hard floor pain her back?

She kept strawberry flavored kool-aid in a noisy old refrigerator that hummed and burped. She never put enough sugar in the mix, so the bright red juice had a slightly sour taste. Still, the color was enticing, and I drank it, imagining that it was a secret potion to make me invincible.

Uncle Erich kept his collection of tools and a pile of old newspapers on a workbench in the basement. Once when I crept down the wooden stairs to get a jar of Grandma's home-made dill pickles, a mouse scurried across the floor in front of my bare-toed sandals. After that, I never ventured into the basement again.

That was forty years ago. I was nine years old.

I must have gazed at the house for five minutes when a young black woman came out the front door, a baby on her hip. She put the baby in a bouncer on the porch and called to someone inside. The next thing I knew, a tall man—he must have been six-four and looked like a linebacker—walked down the stairs and across the street to my car.

"Can I help you?" he said, his voice an authoritative bass. He bent over to look at me through the open window.

"I'm sorry. I hope I wasn't bothering you and your family. It's just that my grandma and my uncle used to live in your house. I haven't been here for years and I wanted to see it, that's all. Sorry if I troubled you."

By the time I'd finished my hurried explanation, he stood up, smiled, and motioned to his wife. She picked up the baby and walked over to the car. I released my grip on the steering wheel.

"Honey," he said, touching her shoulder, "this lady is Mr. Petersen's niece."

Then he turned back to me. "We heard about his passing."

"You knew my uncle?"

"Sure did. He was so nice to us when we bought the house. I've got to work on Monday," he said, "but Delia plans to go to the memorial service."

"How kind. That's so thoughtful." How many people would be coming? Would I know any of them? I still had a lot of work to do to prepare, and I had no idea what to expect.

He stepped back while I got out of the car. "I'm Earl Rodman. This is my wife Delia, and our baby girl, Coretta." His voice softened as he spoke their names. The baby had bright eyes, dimples, and a mop of curly black hair.

"She's so cute," I said. "How old is she?"

"Ten months." Delia shifted the baby from one hip to the other.

"I'm Claire Petersen." I offered my hand. "From Boston."

"Would you like to come in? See the place?" Delia said.

"I don't want to bother you."

"We really don't mind," Earl said, "if you take us as we are. I've still got a lot of projects I want to do. It's hard to find the time between work and the baby."

"Earl's really handy," Delia said.

"He sounds like someone else I know. If a toilet's running, he knows just what to do to fix it."

"That's my Earl."

That could have been my Richard.

We walked across the street and up four wooden front porch steps, freshly painted white with dark green trim, not a mark on them.

"Come on in," she said as her husband opened the front door, practically filling the frame. "I've got some lemonade in the fridge. I'll show you around, then we can sit outside."

"I don't want to inconvenience you."

"It's no trouble at all," she said.

The skeleton of the house hadn't changed but the heating system had. The old distinctive smell which had perfumed everything—clothes, furniture, curtains, the dollars Uncle Erich sent me—that was gone.

The living room furnishings were utilitarian contemporary. A long sofa, probably chosen to accommodate her tall husband, filled one whole wall. A good-sized television was directly across from it. A few toys were scattered around a playpen nearby. But Grandma's old upright piano still was there, the round swivel stool tucked under the keyboard.

"Look familiar?" Earl said.

I brushed the ivory keys.

"Mr. Petersen said we could have it, so it's right where he left it," Delia said. "I don't get a chance to play much, but sometimes Earl sits down and bangs out a tune."

Delia flashed him a smile in an unspoken language that was all their own. A foreign tongue. Was it hard to learn?

Delia led us from the living room through the dining room, which had just enough space for a round table, three chairs and a highchair for the baby, and to its right, into the kitchen. The backdoor was open. Grandma's rose bushes still leaned against a back fence.

"My Grandma used to throw breadcrumbs into the backyard," I said. "She would make a kind of swishing sound to let the birds know food was available."

"That's why it feels like we have a bird sanctuary back there," Earl said. "They have expectations. I guess we'd better carry on the tradition, honey."

He took the baby and cradled her gently against his big chest. She snuggled into him. Delia poured lemonade into glasses, put them on a tray, and got some cookies out of a tin. When I looked again, the baby's eyes were closed.

"Nap time," Earl said. "I'll take her upstairs and meet you two out on the porch."

In another sign of domesticity, they had managed to squeeze two rocking chairs into the small space. The floorboards creaked when we sat down.

"I taught kindergarten until Coretta was born," Delia said. "We'd been saving for a house ever since we got married. Earl's a member of the Oretown Police Department. This section's part of his beat. One afternoon your uncle was sweeping some leaves off the porch and Earl saw the new For Sale sign, so he stopped and asked about it. I'm not sure the realtor would have approved, but Mr. Petersen told him a little about the place and invited him in."

By then Earl had come outside.

"Am I sitting in your chair?" I started to get up.

"Please," he said. "you're our guest." He folded himself onto the steps and leaned back against the railing.

"I called Delia and told her I thought I'd found our dream house. She came with me the next day, looked it over, gave the nod, we made a bid, and as quick as that, we had our home."

Even with its two floors and basement, the square footage was probably smaller than my condo, yet they had called it their "dream house." And I could see by the gentle way they looked at each other that it was. They made it so.

The cold lemonade was a perfect balance of tart and sweet.

"My uncle would be so pleased that it's working out for you," I said. I was, too. I liked thinking of the house warmed by family love.

It was nice to be in a rocking chair. There was something soothing about the motion, back and forth, back and forth.

"Before Mr. Petersen moved he made a list of things, asked if we could use any of 'em," Delia said. "We had our own furniture from the apartment we'd been renting."

She was being polite. Based on what I'd seen at the retirement home, Uncle Erich's stuff was worn, dated, and certainly not her style. Their furnishings had simple, modern lines. Somehow, in that eighty or ninety year old house, she'd made it work.

"But Earl wanted that piano." Delia winked at him.

"Coretta loves it when I play," he said. "We put her in a little bouncy chair and she practically jumps out of the thing. We have a high ol' time." He laughed. It started somewhere deep in his belly but by the time it came out of his mouth it was more like a raspy whistle.

The three of us laughed together. It felt good.

A woman in jeans and a t-shirt with large sunglasses and flowing dark hair came out the door across the street and waved as she got into her car.

"That's Mrs. Martinez," Earl said. "I think your uncle gave her some of his furniture."

"She called him when I was here last weekend," I gulped some lemonade, "before he died. They had planned to visit."

"I lost my mama a year ago," Earl said. "She'd been sick with diabetes for a long time, so it wasn't a surprise, but that didn't make it any easier. Still doesn't."

"So we understand," Delia said.

We rocked in silence. I'd never met these people, yet their companionship was surprisingly comforting.

I finished my lemonade and stood up. "This has been such a welcome respite, but I should get going. I've still got a lot to do before the service."

When I reached for Delia's hand, she pulled me toward her and hugged me. She must have been twenty years younger than I, but with that hug, the roles felt reversed, she the mother, I the child. The strength of that hug carried me through the rest of the day.

"See you Monday," she said.

"Thank you. Thank you so much."

Earl walked me to my car. "You take care, ya hear?"

It was close to six o'clock by the time I left the Rodman's. After the overdose of picnic junk food, I decided to pick up a salad from a nearby grocery store, go back to my motel room, and see if I could cobble together some ideas to give to Chaplain Wolf for the memorial service.

I sat cross-legged on the bed, picked at my salad with a plastic fork, and leafed through Uncle Erich's commonplace book. A few weeks after Grandma died, he had made another entry.

"One learns a great deal about people by discerning what they deem important enough to fight over." And "Trust that when you are the most vulnerable and the most broken, there you will find the presence and love of God."

He had been older than my forty-nine years when he had written those words.

Uncle Erich spoke about God like some people talk about close friends. It was that intimate. Did he intend for his journal to be found and read? Or would he have destroyed it if he had known about his imminent death?

Spirituality wasn't part of my vocabulary. I didn't even fit into the sociologists' "spiritual but not religious" cohort. Yet now, when I was unmoored, rootless, alone, and yes, I had to admit, ashamed, Uncle Erich had stretched his long arms toward me through those pages. I longed for what had grounded him in some apparently very dark days. His faith, years in the making, was like a strong root round hard rocks.

I slapped my fist on the mattress. What did I want? What did I really want? And how far was I willing to go to get it?

Chapter 35

Bright light streamed through the motel room drapes and woke me up. Limp lettuce sat in a plastic container on the nightstand. I'd slept until 9:30.

I had just come out of the shower when the phone rang. It was Barbara.

"How are you holding up?" she said.

I sank down on the bed. "I should be asking you that question. How's Timmy?" I dried my legs on the edge of my bathrobe.

"The doctors think we can beat this. They're discharging him tomorrow. From here on most of his care can be managed on an out-patient basis."

"Tomorrow?" Was she being overly optimistic? "That's such good news."

"We've agreed on a treatment plan. They'll use a combination of therapies. It will involve regular trips back to Dana Farber, periodic PET scans."

She was talking so fast that her words were tripping over each other. I could sense the relief. The sound was uplifting.

"He's lost weight, so I'm stocking up on all his favorite foods."

"That sub-zero refrigerator of yours will be overflowing. By the way, I've ordered some books for him. Nothing too heavy, just fun stuff. I know he likes science fiction." I didn't tell her, but I also had ordered bottles of lotion and perfume in her favorite scent.

"That's so sweet."

"It's the least I can do. I've felt so helpless."

"Can you wait a sec?" she said. I heard voices, then a door closing. "Caleb's going over to the hospital, I'll go this afternoon, so I've got some time. How are you? I was so sorry to hear about your uncle."

"Shouldn't you take a bubble bath or something? You don't want to listen to me."

"I'm sitting at the kitchen table with an espresso and a nice, big croissant Caleb brought from that French bakery in West Newton. I'm fine, so I'll ask again: how are you?"

"I don't know how to answer that."

I crawled under the covers.

"I wish someone could bring me hot coffee and a bagel--a fat sesame seed bagel slathered with cream cheese," I said. I shifted pillows behind my back.

"I remember when my Mom died. There were so many details. It was overwhelming."

Given the size of her mother's estate, it probably took a team of lawyers months to sort out all the trust funds.

I told her about the social worker, the chaplain, the lawyer. "People have been very helpful."

"Just listen to yourself. You've been there only two days and you've got everything organized. I'm not surprised, but I can tell that you're stressed. I can hear it in your voice."

"You don't know the half of it." I took a drink of water from a glass beside the bed. "It's not the logistics I'm worried about."

"What's the other half?"

I chewed the inside of my cheek.

"Are you there?" she asked.

"Do you know what my uncle did? Left me some money. It may not seem like a lot to you, but his lawyer tells me it will be about $750,000."

"Let's not get into comparisons."

"Sorry. It isn't even about the money. Well, it is and it isn't. He was just the produce manager in a grocery store, for heaven's sake. He only had one suit, and he'll be buried it."

"So how did he get it?"

"Not through gambling. According to the lawyer, he lived simply, invested wisely, squirreled away what he didn't need, and still managed to give to charity. It's astonishing."

"Sounds like he was in the wrong field. He should have been an investment advisor at Caleb's firm."

I giggled at the thought of Uncle Erich among all those Boston Brahmins.

"Look," she said, "if he hadn't wanted you to have it, he wouldn't have left it to you, so what's your problem?"

I got up and started to pace around the room. The cheap carpeting felt rough under my bare feet.

"I found this little journal he started after the war. It's a window into his soul. It's poked a hole through mine." Or maybe it was trying to fill an empty space.

"Whoa! That must be some diary."

I told her about visiting the Rodman's, about how Uncle Erich had left an imprint on his neighborhood.

"If I died tomorrow, what difference would it make?"

"Come on. Maura's devoted to you. You have a successful career. Your clients respect you."

Not for much longer, if I didn't finesse the hand I'd been dealt. More to the point, how much respect did I have for the causes I championed on their behalf? What did I care if their corporate taxes got raised four percent? Maybe it would provide more social services to foster kids. God knew they needed it.

"That's a pretty thin list," I said.

"You're my best friend. I depend on you."

"You have Caleb." I wasn't sure how well their marriage had been working recently, but I wasn't going to open that up. Not now. Maybe Timmy's situation had brought them closer again. The fear of loss could do that to you. Or the opposite.

"I say things to you I never could tell him," she said.

"I feel like my whole life is upended." I grabbed a tissue, blew my nose, and slumped into a chair. "I want to run away from everything and everybody. I know, I know, the only way out of this is through it, but right now I'm stuck in a tunnel without a flashlight."

"Have you tried to patch things up with Richard?"

"I don't know if he'd take my call. I don't know what I'd say if he did."

"You told me the fight was about one of your clients. Surely you can work your way through that."

"It's complicated. I took on this developer a few months ago. He builds golf courses. If you want to know the truth, he's a bit of a seedy character."

"You've been on edge lately. I thought it was because of Richard."

A spider inched its way across the ceiling.

"I don't know why I did it. Well, yes I do. In January I got word that one of my clients was taken over by an out-of-state firm, and twenty percent of my revenue walked out the door. My operating costs have been skyrocketing. So the prospect of new money was enticing."

"You didn't say anything."

"What could you have done about it? I regretted it soon after I did it, even more after Richard, but I thought I could handle it. Now I'm in over my head--way over."

"Why would Richard dump you? That doesn't sound like him. I hardly know him, but when the four of us had dinner together, he seemed like a down to earth guy. Surely he knew about the businesses you represent before he asked you out."

I walked over to the window and peered through the curtains to the parking lot beneath. It was close to eleven. A man was stashing luggage in the back of a van while his wife corralled their two young children and buckled them in the back seat.

"Remember Mr. Public Charities?"

"How could I forget?"

I played with the curtain pull cord. "You may have noticed that he's running for attorney general."

"Yah, we got some campaign literature in the mail. I saw the picture of the wife and kids. I told Caleb to keep his distance."

I closed the curtains.

"The developer found out."

"He what?"

"He knows."

"You were the wronged woman in that sorry episode, so how can he use that against you?"

"Politics, pure politics."

"Not so pure."

A knock on the adjoining room was followed by a loud female voice saying "housekeeping."

"I let him talk me into doing something that was, shall we say, questionable. This married legislator whom we need to neutralize has been fooling around with one of his young aides, and I...well, I happened to run into one of the reporters at the State House News Service, and I...well, I..."

"You didn't."

"Richard found out."

"That's not who you are."

"It's who I've become." The air had grown chilly. I wrapped the bathrobe more tightly around my chest.

"I don't believe that."

"Look, I gambled and I lost. The developer has me over a barrel."

"Fix it. It's not too late. If you don't, you won't be able to live with yourself. It's a little like cleaning out a closet. It's hard, dirty work, but you'll feel better afterwards."

"You should see my closets."

"You've worked hard and played by the rules. Don't let this bastard mess you up."

"I don't know how."

"You'll figure it out. It might be painful, but you've got to do it. If I can help in any way, ask. And talk with Richard."

I put a "do not disturb" sign on the handle outside my motel room door. I had left open the question of whether I would speak at the memorial service. I wanted to make this parting gift to Uncle Erich, but could I manage to speak without indecorous weeping?

I sat in my bathrobe at the faux-wood desk, pencil in hand, and stared at a blank sheet of paper. It looked so empty. How do you capture a life in seven paragraphs?

I turned on the desk lamp and adjusted the shade so light showed less directly on the paper. I picked at a hangnail until it bled, made several false starts, scrunched up the papers and tossed them in the trash.

By the time I finished my head ached and my fingers were sore from having clutched the pencil so hard. I swallowed two aspirin, got dressed, and drove over to the retirement community to finish packing before the Monday afternoon pick-up. Around four o'clock I took a break. Boxes ringed around me, I sat cross legged on the floor and leafed through Grandma's photo album, brushing my fingers over the stiff paper. In one picture, my father and Uncle Erich stood side by side. Uncle Erich's arm was draped protectively around my father's shoulder.

I loved how my father dried my tears when I fell and scraped my knee on an uneven patch of sidewalk. I loved his silly rhyming songs. I loved the way he tousled my hair. Tender, oh so tender. Was it possible to hold together two seemingly opposite emotions? I had nursed the anger, with good reason, but had blocked out the love. I didn't want to live that way anymore. Uncle Erich had managed to embrace life as it was, in all its ambiguity. That was what I wanted to do. I slammed the album shut. My father did love me, and I loved him. It was time to forgive him.

I hadn't eaten since breakfast, and I was hungry. I decided to pick up an ice cream sundae from Matt's. I would need all the nourishment I could get for what lay ahead, and I wasn't thinking only about the funeral.

Chapter 36

A black limousine arrived in front of my motel on Monday morning. Both the funeral director and Chaplain Wolf got out of the car to greet me. They were dressed in black. I wore a navy-blue pants suit. At least it was dark navy. I had packed so distractedly that I'd given little thought to funereal clothing.

The one item I did remember to bring was the gold pendant Uncle Erich had given me. I'd kissed it before I put the chain over my head.

We followed the hearse to the cemetery in somber procession. It was on the outskirts of Oretown. Chaplain Wolf had on a clerical collar surrounding her thick neck. I wondered if it pinched. She occasionally patted my arm, but she didn't try to engage in conversation. I appreciated that.

I never had visited my grandparents' graves. Come to think of it, I hadn't been back to my parents' graves, either. Although I wasn't sure my mother would have wanted it, my parents were side by side in a cemetery in Newton. Reeling from Mother's sudden death, I was on autopilot when decisions had to be made. Barbara had said it was a sensible approach, so that's what I did. The burial was handled with decorum. The casket was above ground, surrounded by green astro turf and floral arrangements. The minister spoke. Barbara held my hand. We left. Then someone took care of the rest. That's all I remembered.

The grounds at the Newton Cemetery were extensive, beautiful, well-manicured, reportedly a haven for birds in spring migration. Did Richard know that? What would I do if I went back? Bring flowers? They would wilt. Should I tell Daddy about Uncle Erich? Do people talk to the dead? What if someone saw me? Would they think I was crazy?

When the limousine arrived at the Oretown cemetery gate, I was surprised by how inviting the setting was. My grandparents' graves were located near a pine tree which must have been over forty feet tall. It sighed in the wind, the pine fragrance heightened by exposure to the morning sun. The surrounding earth was covered in brown pine needles. Someone—Uncle Erich? had given careful thought to the location. If your body had to lie in the cold, hard ground, it was a better place than many.

The casket was removed from the hearse, wheeled over a gaping hole in the ground, Chaplain Wolf read some Scripture ("Jesus said: So you have sorrow now, but I will see you again and your hearts will rejoice, and no one will take your joy from you."), I placed a bouquet of dark crimson roses on the coffin, and it was over. No joy in sight.

Chaplain Wolf started to return to the limousine.

"No, wait," I said. "Can I stay a while? Do you mind? I don't know why. I need to see them put him in the ground. It doesn't make any sense, I know. Am I violating some custom? I just need to see it."

She assured me that it was all right. The funeral director already had opened the door of the limo, but after a quiet word from the chaplain, he closed it, leaned against the hood and lit a cigarette. I was annoyed by the cigarette. It seemed disrespectful.

Chaplain Wolf stood at a discrete distance. A big dump truck, filled with dirt, pulled up to the site, and three burly workers in faded overalls hopped out with shovels. Chaplain Wolf hurried up to them and assured them they hadn't made a mistake with their timing.

I watched, transfixed, while they used a system of pulleys to lower the casket into the ground. The pulleys creaked with each turn of the winch. The workers maneuvered the truck into position so the load of dirt could be dumped into the hole. And then, for some reason, I asked it if I could touch the dirt. The lead man nodded. He motioned for the workers to stand back. They moved away, but not too far. I suppose they wanted to be prepared should I get unsteady and topple into the grave.

I took a fistful of dirt and threw it onto the casket. I needed to absorb a reality I wanted to deny, to feel it on my skin. Good practice. Once I'd thrown that dirt, I brushed my hands, turned around and headed back to the limo. The soil made a thumping sound as it was dumped into the hole. And that was the end of Uncle Erich.

We'd scheduled the memorial service for 1:00 so I could return to the apartment in time to receive workers from The Salvation Army and the Lutheran Church. The service was held in the retirement facility's all-purpose auditorium. It doubled as worship space and recreation center. When folks weren't belting out hymns, they were shouting "Bingo!"

I was surprised by how many people showed up. There must have been seventy-five in the auditorium. The ushers needed to set up more folding chairs.

I sat by myself in the front row. Never have I felt so alone. No relatives. No friends. Just me.

Chaplain Wolf read Uncle Erich's favorite Scripture. "He has told you, O man, what is good; and what does the Lord require of you but to do justice, and to love kindness, and to walk humbly with your God?" (Micah 6:8) I had spent twenty minutes searching for that verse in the Bible the Gideons left in the drawer of the nightstand.

I had been clutching the service bulletin so tightly that it felt damp from my sweaty palms. I was next on the program. I climbed the carpeted steps to the stage, stood behind the podium, adjusted the microphone, fiddled with my text. My hands trembled as I shifted from one piece of paper to the next. Normally strong and confident when I spoke before a legislative committee hearing, I didn't recognize my soft, halting voice. I couldn't look at all the people in their folding chairs. My eyes focused on what I had written.

"Erich Petersen lived by his faith," I read. "He taught Sunday School at St. John's Evangelical and Reformed Church for many years. He was devoted to his church, his family, his neighborhood, his work at the A&P.

"He was a faithful companion to his mother until she died." I paused and looked at Chaplain Wolf. She gave me an encouraging nod. I pushed on.

"Between their father's early death and the Depression, Erich and his brother had a hard childhood." I clung to the sides of the podium.

"He served honorably in the Army during World War II. If those experiences scarred him in some ways, they strengthened him in others. They taught him to make do, use it up, wear it out. He had budgeting skills that would impress the most scrupulous auditor." I heard a few chuckles in the congregation. I lost my place and had to scan four paragraphs before I found it.

"He was generous with his modest income. He believed in tithing—10% to worthy causes, his church chief among them. He got far more joy from giving than receiving." This made me smile involuntarily.

"He was gracious. He rarely, if ever, uttered a harsh word. He was thankful for even the smallest kindness that came his way." I had kept my composure, but with those words, I wasn't able to hold it anymore. "Our time together was all too brief, and I shall miss him very, very much."

When I returned to my folding-chair I used all the tissues left in my purse.

The next thing I knew the congregation was singing the closing hymn. "Lead, kindly light, amid the encircling gloom, lead thou me on; The night is dark, and I am far from home; Lead thou me on!" I felt so far from home, and not just because I was in Oretown. "Keep thou my feet; I do not ask to see the distant scene; one step enough for me." I didn't even know how to take a first step. I was lost. Completely lost.

After the chaplain pronounced a benediction, I hardly had time to blow my nose before I was surrounded by people. Delia was the first one to appear. Coretta was sleeping in a baby carrier, her little head with the tight black curls tilted against Delia's shoulder. She put a bag of cookies in my hand. "Peanut butter," she said, "with a chocolate drop in the middle."

"My Grandma used to make those. They were my favorites."

"I baked them this morning, so they're nice and fresh. Comfort food is important in times like these." She smiled and moved out of the way as other people pressed in.

Mrs. Martinez, the neighbor who had called when I was visiting Uncle Erich, pressed a rosary into my hands and, in heavily accented English, reminisced about how Uncle Erich had saved his coffee grounds so she could spread them on the soil under her roses. A man who introduced himself as a representative from the United Food and Commercial Workers said Uncle Erich had been his mentor when he started out in the produce section of the old A&P, and "taught him everything he needed to know about how to keep vegetables fresh and display them to their full advantage." Two women from St. John's Evangelical and Reformed Church said for ten years Uncle Erich was the only baritone in the church choir. "He didn't say much, but he sure could sing!" Zofia, the young waitress who had remembered Uncle Erich's love of chocolate cream pie, had on her uniform. She said she'd been given time off from her dining room duties to attend the service. "I might not have applied to nursing school without his encouragement. He told me I could do anything I set my mind to, and you know what?" she asked. "Last Thursday I heard I've been accepted." She started to cry. "I wanted to tell him, but I didn't get the chance."

In story after story, I heard about how Uncle Erich had touched people's lives. I was enveloped by hugs. I knew none of these people, yet I felt comforted. There was power in those circles of communion, a different kind of power from my quid pro quo world. At the same time, their stories about my uncle—his modesty, his compassion, his generosity—magnified both my sense of loss and my own inadequacies. His purpose in life had been to help others. What was mine?

Several bouquets of flowers were arranged on the podium. After people drifted away I read notes attached to the bouquets. One was from the produce section of the grocery store where Uncle Erich had worked. It had been around fifteen years since he'd retired, yet they still remembered him. Another was from "St. John's Church Women." Maura had sent one "in loving memory of your dear uncle." A lavish spray of white lilies had come from Barbara, Caleb, and Timmy. Their perfume filled the air. A simple vase of yellow roses sat on the altar between candlesticks and a huge Bible. Richard knew I liked yellow roses, and I had a faint, foolish hope that he had sent them. It turned out they had been left from the previous Sunday's service.

It occurred to me that the bouquets might brighten up some of the common spaces around the building. Uncle Erich would have liked that.

By 4:30 all the boxes and bags had been removed from Uncle Erich's apartment. I gave twenty dollars to of each of The Salvation Army workers. The men looked like they could use it. The astonishment on their faces (I guess they were more accustomed to fivers, if that) made me glad I had stocked up on loose bills. The church volunteers said they didn't accept tips, but they would be happy to give the money to folks who served meals to the homeless.

So that was that. I walked through the empty rooms one final time. Not even a whiff of Uncle Erich's after shave was left in the bathroom. The sliding doors to his bedroom closet were open and there, crumpled up in a dark corner, was a polyester black tie with a picture of a hot fudge sundae in a glass cup with whipped cream and a bright red cherry on top. I couldn't picture Uncle Erich wearing it. Who had given it to him? I couldn't imagine anyone wearing it. I sat down on the floor, buried my face in it, and wept, snot comingling with the ripples of chocolate.

Ten minutes later I tucked the tie in my purse, locked the door, turned in the key to a secretary in administration, stopped by Chaplain Wolf's office to thank her (she wasn't in; I'd write a note), and walked out of the building. Helene and her companion, the "professional greeters" as they'd called themselves, were not at their customary stations outside the door. They had attended the memorial service. It must have worn them out.

I barely had enough strength to hold the steering wheel. My rental car intuited its way back to the motel room. Not even taking off my suit jacket, I threw myself on the bed and replayed images from the reception after the memorial service until I fell asleep.

I dreamt I was back in my dorm room at U Mass. I kept reaching for something to lean on—a table, the back of a chair—but I was surrounded by boxes and anchored to the spot. My dad appeared and said he was there to help. I said that wasn't possible because he was dead. He didn't answer. Empty garment bags were hanging in a closet. I thought, why had I needed all this stuff?

I awakened two and a half hours later, bathed in sweat. Grandmother's pendant was plastered against my neck. My navy suit was an accordion of wrinkles.

I shed the suit, took a shower, and put on my old gray fleece pants and jacket. They made me look like a boxer ready for a workout, which, in a way, I was.

Chapter 37

For the mid-morning flight back to Boston, I'd booked a seat in business class with the expectation that I would be left alone as occupants nursed their Bloody Marys, read *The Wall Street Journal*, or stared out the window.

I stared out the window. The clouds were just as ill-defined as my thoughts. What I wanted to do was shred my contract with Piper Mangan and throw it in his face. Regardless of the fallout, with every passing mile that became clearer. The rest was murky. Was that all I wanted? If I ever was going to reorder my life, the time was now, but how would the revised version look? Who would it help? Who would it harm? Even if I could figure that out, how would I do it?

I turned off the air vent and asked a stewardess to fetch my coat. After I spread it across my body I still was shivering. My seatmate inched away from me as if I had the plague. I assured him that I wasn't sick and made up a story about living in Costa Rica and not being used to the northern climate.

When the plane landed I went directly to the office.

"I didn't expect to see you until tomorrow," Maura said.

She came around her desk and enveloped me in a hug. Then she looked at my suitcase.

"You didn't even stop at home."

"I've got too much to do."

She trailed me into my office. "You shouldn't work on an empty stomach. Have you had lunch? Let me get you something from the Greek Deli. A cup of lemon egg drop soup? Tuna salad with pickles?"

She knew my favorites. I opted for the soup, pulled a twenty out of my purse and handed it to her.

"Back in a jiffy," she said.

Maura had left a stack of mail in one corner of my desk and a pile of phone messages under Grandma's paperweight. Piper Mangan had called four times. Damn him, he wouldn't let up.

He would have to wait.

Somewhere outside, a jackhammer was tearing up pavement. The sound made the windows vibrate. I was paying big money for this?

I poured myself a cup of coffee, retrieved a yellow legal notepad from the supply cabinet, and shoved a new pencil in the electric sharpener. Armed with fresh supplies, I sketched out the issues I would need to address.

My attempt to sully Representative Whately distressed me more than anything else in the whole sorry episode. I needed to fix that and fast. I'd always fought hard for my clients, but never before had I fought dirty. It wasn't who I had been. It certainly wasn't who I wanted to become.

I chewed the pencil. I kept reaching for some vulnerability in Mangan I could exploit without sliding into the same morass from which I was trying to escape. His threats were not empty. He had made it quite clear that he could cause mayhem, innocent people would get hurt along with the guilty, my reputation would be damaged, my business ruined.

Uncle Erich's favorite Bible verse--"do justice, love kindness, walk humbly"—crowded out most of the possibilities I considered. The prospect of the chaos ahead made my jaw freeze.

I had forgotten to close the door. When Maura walked in with the soup I hastily covered my notes.

"They had some baklava right out of the oven, so I got a piece." She put a brown paper bag on my desk. "Are you sure you're all right? Maybe you should take the week off. I can hold people at bay a few more days." She meant Mangan.

"Who's the boss here?" I tried for a smile.

"Look, I know you've been under a lot of pressure. I'm just trying to ease the load."

Maura was used to mothering her mother. Now she'd adopted me as well.

"I appreciate the offer, but I need to settle a few things."

She wasn't accustomed to my being so guarded. I lifted the white cup out of the bag and took a spoonful of soup.

"Delicious. Thanks so much."

Maura stood next to my desk and waited.

"And now, the sooner I get to work, the faster I can get out of here."

She didn't need to know the rest. Not yet. Especially since I hadn't figured it out, myself.

Next morning I put on a conservative beige suit and soft knit cream blouse, my power outfit, along with Grandma's pendant. I went directly to the State House. It was too early for legislators to have arrived. My low heels resonated on the marble floors and reverberated off the walls as I walked along the fourth floor to where the news service was located. Keyboards were clicking. A few reporters had started early. I sat down on the ledge overlooking the three floors below.

A delivery girl passed me carrying a small spring arrangement of tulips and miniature daffodils. It must have been somebody's birthday.

Seeing them brought back a memory that still made me blush with shame. Pretty yellow daffodils and multi-colored tulips were in full bloom near our house. I picked some and brought them to my mother. Instead of being pleased, she was angry. I was four years old, and I didn't understand. Hadn't I done something nice? "Those are our neighbor's," she said. "They don't belong to us." She took me by the hand, marched me down the sidewalk, and lifted a big brass doorknocker with a lion face. I stood in front of the door, my knees shaking. I would have bolted if Mother hadn't had such a firm grip on my hand. "Now you're going to apologize to the lady," my mother whispered through clenched teeth. The neighbor, a grandmotherly type, listened to my mumbled confession and assured me that no harm was done. She introduced me to a big bushy gray cat circling around her legs and invited me to visit her any time. The rest of the exchange was a blur, but I never forgot the terror I felt before that door opened. The scene was like a bad movie stuck in my brain and replayed in a continuous loop.

I straightened my shoulders and walked into the newsroom. The reporter from the Worcester *Telegram and Gazette*, a paunchy guy in his mid-thirties with a receding forehead, was focused on his computer screen. He didn't look up until I was standing in front of his desk.

"Can we take a walk?" I said.

He looked at me, looked at his watch. "Yah, sure. Just let me save this."

He followed me down the hallway to an alcove. I looked around to be sure nobody was within earshot.

"You remember what I told you about Representative Whately? Forget it. There's nothing to it. I was wrong. I'm sorry to have sent you on a wild goose chase."

"I know."

"You do?"

"I couldn't run the story without a second source. Couldn't find one. Then Richard Truitt comes to see me. Tells me some shenanigans are going on over some farmers' land in Apple Grove. Puts me off Whately, tells me to go digging."

"Richard Truitt?"

"You know the guy?"

I wondered if he knew just how well I knew the guy.

"Yah. Director of the Environmental League of Massachusetts," I said.

"Any idea about what's going on in Apple Grove?"

He didn't get out pen and paper, but he might as well have. I could almost hear his brain clicking in a direct link to his computer.

"You should know—you probably already do," I said, "that Piper Mangan has been, is, my client, though for how much longer I'm not sure."

There. I'd said it, and not just to myself.

He raised his bushy eyebrows.

"So I can't comment," I said. "But I'll be interested in what you dig up."

He tilted his head with an unspoken question.

"In a day or two," I said, "it's possible you may receive some additional information."

"With or without attribution?"

"That remains to be seen."

He stared at me, his eyes magnified through his rimless lenses.

"Aw, come on," he said. "Tell me more."

"I can't. Yet."

He looked at his watch. "You've got my number."

"Thanks. I owe you."

"And I've got yours," he said as he headed down the hall with a backhanded wave.

What was Richard up to? Was he trying to save my skin even after he'd told me off? Was he acting out of principle to protect a legislator with a chronically sick wife? Did he know something about Mangan that I didn't?

I stepped off the curb at the corner of Beacon and Tremont Streets and almost was run into by a bicycle courier who whipped around the corner. A businessman a few feet behind me, who had just exited the corner bank, yelled at the cyclist, but he was in the next block before the words were out of his mouth.

"That was close," he said. "Are you all right?"

"I think so."

"Too bad a cop wasn't around. That bastard could have killed you."

"Guess my luck hasn't run out...yet."

"Take care," he said as he headed toward One Beacon.

When I got back to Rowes Wharf my adrenalin still was pumping. I ducked into the hallway bathroom, went into a stall, and did something new. I prayed.

I didn't know if Uncle Erich believed in saints, but whether he did or not, he was the closest I'd ever come to encountering one.

"Uncle Erich, if you're up there, out there, wherever, I really need your help."

I took a few deep breaths, then walked into the office.

"Are you OK?" Maura said. "Your face is flushed."

"I had a near collision with a bicycle demon."

"Want me to get you a bottle of water?

"I'll be fine." I toyed with some pencils in a jar on her desk.

"Would you come into my office?" I said. "I need to talk with you."

"Sure," she said. Did she mutter "finally" under her breath?

"Have a seat," I said.

She moved the chair to an angle next to my desk so she faced me directly.

"What's up?" she said.

"What isn't?"

Maura's fate was tied to mine. She knew it, and I knew it. We were a team. Still, it wasn't a union of equals. I pulled at a loose thread on the sleeve of my blouse.

"As you're well aware, our lease comes up for renewal in September. A few days ago I received word that the owners of this building are selling it to a real estate investment trust and our space is being converted into condominiums."

Maura knew what came in, what went out, how much we had in reserve. She sat very still.

"None of our options look good," I said, "and all of them are expensive, even more since we lost that big account. They're offering an option to buy—so generous of them—for $3250 per square foot."

She did a quick calculation in her head. She was good at that. "That's almost three million dollars! And that doesn't factor in the monthly condo fees."

"I know. It's one of the reasons I've been so stressed. But it's not the only one. Taking on Mangan was a big mistake. Because of him, I've gotten myself tangled up in something that I now have to untangle."

"He's a real piece of work."

"You've had more than your share of encounters with him while I was in Ohio. I'm sorry about that."

She didn't deserve to suffer for my mistakes.

She jiggled her foot in a nervous rhythm. "What does that mean for us?"

I suspected that her personal expenses were escalating, and if her mother had dementia, the situation only could get worse.

I brushed my hands on my thighs.

"Bottom line?" I said. "We can't afford this place anymore. For the rest, I'm working on it. Believe me, I'm working on it."

She looked out the window. "I know how much you like being near the harbor, though I've never once seen you so much as use the water shuttle to Logan Airport."

"Point taken." She knew me so well. "I've been thinking through the options. Maybe it's time to downsize. Go lean. Reduce our overhead."

She picked a paper clip off my desk and twisted it. "Just how do you plan to do that?"

"However this unfolds, I won't abandon you, I promise. We're a team. I couldn't have functioned without you all these years. I depend on your good judgment."

She sat up straighter in her chair.

"If that's true, why didn't you tell me earlier? Maybe together we could have worked on some solutions."

I felt like I'd been slapped, and I deserved it.

"I'm sorry. I'm so used to not being able to lean into anybody. I thought I could handle this myself. I was wrong."

I rubbed my thumb on the smooth glass of Grandma's paperweight. "I'm thinking out loud here" I said. "If, for example, we could find a location that reduced our costs by, say, a third or more, maybe I wouldn't need such a large book of clients to make the whole thing work."

"You place great stock in appearances, but most of our clients never come here anyway. They probably wouldn't care if we moved to East Boston."

"They might care more than you assume, but I've been thinking. Maybe we could take on a different kind of client. If we did that, who knows? We could follow the legislative pattern—take Fridays off, do a half day on Mondays. Get a life."

Even if, with Richard out of the picture, I had no idea how I would use the time.

She threw the paperclip in the waste basket. "What happened to you in Ohio?"

"You know how a person fills a space so full, they're still there when they're not? That's Uncle Erich. The way I've been living isn't working anymore, if it ever did. I don't fill enough space to occupy a broom closet, and I want to change that. I'm sick of this damned place. The only good thing about it is seeing you when I walk in the door in the morning."

"Are you serious? Don't say it if you don't mean it."

"Yes, I think I am."

"Three day weekends would give me more flexibility with my mother," she said. "I like the sound of that."

"I hope it might give you more time for *yourself*."

"Look who's talking."

"Can you do some sleuthing and see what office properties

might be available? Check the price per square foot for something in one of the older buildings. Don't go to East Boston, for heaven's sake, but how about something not too far from Post Office Square?"

"Just how old? I once got stuck in an elevator between floors in one of those places. The super had to lower a ladder from the ceiling to get me out."

With Maura's generous hips, that must have been quite a production.

"Not *that* old. Run the numbers. Maybe we could make more efficient use of space, hire a decorator so the insides don't look like we shopped at K-Mart for our furnishings."

She uncrossed her legs and leaned forward. "A lot of what we have here is transferable. That, for example." She pointed at my coffee table—a symbol of the elegance to which I had aspired.

"Most of it doesn't seem so important anymore," I said, "but I still like that table."

"I'll get right on it."

"Do it quietly," I said. "Some other pieces of this puzzle haven't fallen into place yet, so I'm not ready to let the word get out."

"I'll be careful."

"And Maura? Thank you. It could be a wild ride for a while, but I'll make sure you're OK."

Chapter 38

Two hours later I was sitting in the reception area of McLennan, Myers, and Fish, LLP, wondering whether there was any available space in their building. It was just the sort of place that might be feasible—not too far from The State House, on an obscure side street near the financial district, decent first floor entry way but nothing too fancy, security at the front desk. I hadn't been there more than two minutes before Dave Fish came striding down the hall.

We'd known each other almost thirty years. He'd been in the research office of Speaker Dunleavy when I'd interned there. I'd gone the lobbying route, he'd stayed with the Speaker, married Representative Lombardi's secretary, had a kid, and gotten a law degree by taking night classes at Suffolk University. He'd joined McLennan and Myers about the time I formed Petersen and Associates. I trusted him. He was street smart and he didn't have an ounce of bullshit in him.

He ushered me into his office. The view outside his window was of a neighboring brick building. A black fire escape snaked its way down the side. A foot-high stack of papers occupied one corner of his desk. The opposing wall was lined with legal tomes, any one of which could serve as a doorstop. Propped against the books were pictures of his wife and son at varying stages—stroller, soccer field, high school graduation.

I studied the photos. "Your son looks like you did when we were young and green."

"I hope he manages to keep his hair."

Dave's close cropped gray was thin at the crown.

"He's at Boston College now. Doing great."

"You made it work."

"We're still digging our way out of debt but he's a terrific kid. Hasn't caused us a lick of trouble. And how about you?"

"Not much has changed in the personal department."

A secretary walked by his glass fronted office, arms laden with papers up to her chin.

After a few more pleasantries, I explained that I needed good, solid legal advice about how to extricate myself from Piper Mangan. It took an hour and a half to lay out the whole situation.

Dave listened attentively, took notes occasionally, asked questions periodically. At one point he said, "Whatever made you take him on in the first place? He has quite a reputation around town. He's a sleaze bag."

"A friend tried to warn me." Richard had done everything but paste a skull and crossbones on my briefcase. "I didn't listen."

"He cuts corners by whatever means are available. He wouldn't know a scruple if he tripped over it."

"I know that now. I thought I could maneuver around him.

Boy, was I wrong."

I studied the rug on the floor. It was an imitation oriental, the patterns too exact to have been hand-woven, but it looked fine. Why did I pay ten thousand dollars for one instead of a machine made?

"I needed the money," I said. "I'd just lost my biggest client. Once I get this Mangan situation resolved I still have to find a new place for the office. I've got to move out of Rowes Wharf. It's expensive and they're converting it into condos."

"You're not the first one of my clients to face a reversal of fortune. Your ego may be bruised, but you've built a solid reputation over the years. As long as you continue to deliver for your other clients, you'll survive."

I felt like I'd been in a confessional, except I wasn't seeking absolution—at least not from him.

"Would you like a bottle of water? A cup of coffee? You look like you could use a breather."

Rather than ask a secretary, he went out himself. He was gone a full five minutes, while I stewed in a brew of humiliation, shame, and remorse. He returned with water and a few butter cookies on a plastic plate.

He leaned over his desk. "Are you all right?"

"Revisit this in a year and I'll let you know."

"Let's start with the straightforward stuff," he said. "Then we'll talk about how to clean up the dirt."

Dave had prepared the contract Mangan signed. It was a standard agreement I gave to all my clients. He pulled one out of his file and scanned it.

"I remember when I drafted this," he said.

He ran his finger down the back page to a spot near the bottom. "It says, 'This agreement may be severed by either party without prejudice for any reason.' From a legal standpoint, all that's required is to tell him he's no longer a client of Petersen and Associates. If he were anybody else, you could hand him a check for the retainer he paid you and that would be that. In Mangan's case, as a sweetener, I suggest you tack on the interest."

"If only it were that simple."

It was like handing a sling to a patient with a severed limb. Dave had answered the legal question but not the political one. That was where Mangan had placed the land mines.

"Do you want me to be there when you hand him the check?"

"Let me think about it."

I hadn't yet told him about the compromising photographs of me with Mr. Public Charities. When I did he jolted upright.

"That's attempted blackmail. Have you seen them?"

"Come to think of it, I haven't. He patted his coat pocket and brought out the family photo being used in the campaign. I just assumed..."

"Never assume," Dave said. "He knows something, that's clear. Whether he can prove it or use it are separate questions."

I choked on a cookie, took a gulp of water, spilled some on my skirt. Dave started to come around his desk but I waved him away.

"Just give me a minute," I said. "I'll be OK."

He made notes on a legal pad. Outside his window two sparrows were making a racket. Their wings flapped spasmodically as they battled it out.

"I'm at a loss for how to handle this," I said.

"If you don't put a stop to it now, you'll be forever beholden to him. Besides, that's not who you are."

"Someone else said that to me recently."

"Whatever you do next with Mangan, don't do it alone. You'll need a reliable witness, and I don't mean your secretary."

"You're right. Otherwise Mangan will run over me like one of those John Deere tractors he plans to use on all the trees in Apple Grove."

"When you decide to set up a meeting, let me know and I'll be there to back you up. If you want to test out some tactics, give me a call. In the meantime, I'll make some inquiries to see if he's got any vulnerabilities that will force him to back off."

By the time I left his office every muscle in my body felt like it had been pummeled with a wooden mallet. I called Maura and suggested that she chat up the security staff in Dave's building to see if they knew about any future vacancies. They often knew these things before the real estate agents.

She said Piper Mangan had phoned twice. I told her to put on the answering machine and take the rest of the afternoon off.

I headed home. I needed to regroup before the next round. Not only that, I decided I should call Richard, and that was a conversation I didn't want to have in the office.

Chapter 39

Compared with Uncle Erich's apartment, my condo had no personality. All it said was that I'd hired an expensive decorator.

Richard was everywhere. In the bathroom where, of all improbable places, we'd first kissed. In the kitchen, leaning against the countertop while I poured coffee into a French press. In the living room, where *The Audubon Society Field Guide to North American Birds* sat on the coffee table. In the bedroom. The candles, with only a faint scent of apple blossoms, were where he had left them, on the table, the nightstand, the chest of drawers.

I lit a candle, sat in the winged back chair, and flipped through the pages of the bird book. A folded paper fell out. It was the Audubon Society checklist of Massachusetts birds. I counted sixty-six entries on five separate outings, many repeats. Written in Richard's distinctive block print were the dates and locations of the birds we had seen. Together, we—no, he—had identified a Rufous-sided Towhee, an immature Black-crowned Night Heron, and a male wood duck. I'd complained about the bugs swirling around my head ("Birds have to eat," he'd said) and spider webs hitting my face (he called the spiders "frog food"). Despite my protestations, I savored those outings with Richard. It was as if, before then, I had been watching movies in black and white, and afterwards, the screen had exploded into Technicolor.

By the time I pulled my cell phone out of my pocket, puddles of wax had accumulated in the center of the candle.

As soon as I punched in the numbers I was tempted to disconnect. With caller ID he could see who was on the line. Maybe he wouldn't answer. I could leave a message. And what? Beg for forgiveness?

Richard picked up on the second ring.

"Claire. Are you still in Ohio?" His voice sounded business-like. My throat constricted.

"No, I came back on Tuesday."

"I was sorry to hear about your uncle."

"How did you know?"

"Barbara called me."

My friend may have been a full-blooded member of the DAR but she was acting like a Yente.

I got up from my chair, circled the bedroom and rattled on.

"It was a nice service. A lot of people were there. I didn't know my uncle had so many friends."

"I know how important friends are, especially at a time like that."

"Of course."

Missed the mark again. Now what?

"I went to see that reporter today. I said I was wrong about Representative Whately. He said you'd already told him."

"That's right."

"Why did you do it? Trying to clean up the mess I made?"

I could hear a door bang shut. Bird calls were in the background. He must have moved to the upstairs back porch.

"If it helps you, I'm glad, but that wasn't my main goal."

That squashed any hope I'd had of Richard, my rescuer.

"What was your 'main goal'?"

"Whately's a decent guy going through a bad patch. I didn't want to see him trashed, that's all. Look, I can't tell you more. Just watch yourself. This could get messy."

Little did he know just how messy it could get.

"I learned a lot in Ohio. I'm going to make some big changes."

"I hope you do."

He sounded so detached.

"Well, thanks again for talking with that reporter. For…for everything."

"Yah, well like I said, watch yourself."

Then he hung up, and I wailed. I'd lost him, lost him for good.

It wasn't long before I heard a loud, persistent knock on my door. I ran into the bathroom, toweled my face, then headed into the living room and looked through the keyhole. My elderly neighbor was fidgeting in the hallway. I opened the door partway.

"Are you all right, Miss Petersen? I heard some—well, I don't know what to call it—sounded like screaming. Most of the time it's so quiet we don't even know you're there. I just wanted to be sure everything's OK."

"I had some bad news, Mr. Marshall, but I'm fine. It was sweet of you to check on me."

"We neighbors have to look out for each other. Just wanted to be sure," he said as he backed away and turned toward his unit.

"Fix it," Barbara had said. "If you don't, you won't be able to live with yourself."

I zombie-walked into the bathroom, opened the medicine cabinet, took out a bottle of sleeping pills, dumped the contents into the palm of my hand, sat on the toilet and stared at the little round tablets.

When I glanced at the bathroom door, there was Uncle Erich's tie, the one with the picture of a hot fudge sundae with the bright red cherry, hanging from the knob.

"You take those pills and dump 'em in the toilet right now, my gal," Uncle Erich said, as if he'd seized my brain. "You've messed up. I know what that feels like. But you can find your way out, just like I did."

Chapter 40

A heavy blanket of fog had enveloped the city overnight, but as I walked down Beacon Street, somewhere between the Frog Pond and the Saint-Gaudens Civil War monument, the fog began to lift.

"You look like you're ready to run the Boston Marathon," Maura said I when barreled into the office. She was pouring water into the coffee maker.

"Let's hope I get to the finish line without collapsing." I already had encountered my own Heartbreak Hill.

She spilled some water on the floor. I grabbed a fist full of paper towels to help clean up the mess. We were on our hands and knees, and I noticed lines on her forehead that I hadn't seen before.

I leaned back against a nearby cabinet. "I know how much is riding on the outcome of all this. It would be easy to say 'Don't worry,' but I promise you, I'll do everything I can to make sure that you come out all right."

I pulled her up and threw the wet towels into a waste basket.

"I'm so sorry," I said. "I really am determined to fix things."

"I know," she said, without conviction.

She returned to the coffee. I waited until she had finished.

"One thing you can do to help," I said, "is pull together some figures for me: the retainer Mangan paid us, plus five and a half percent interest. And tell me what we have in reserves after we cut him a check."

She raised an eyebrow. "You're sure about this?"

"It's the one thing I am sure of. When you have a boil on your butt you have to lance it. It might be sore as hell at first, but that's the only way it can heal."

That was the first hint of a smile I'd seen on Maura's face for a while.

I would follow the advice of my lawyer. That was straightforward. For the rest, I wanted to stuff Piper Mangan's jowly face with rotten fruit from Apple Grove until his insides exploded.

Then an alien thought slapped me sideways. "What would Daddy do?" It was as if that wily S.O.B. were sitting on my shoulder, whispering in my ear to fight Mangan with weapons he would understand. And I had a crazy idea of how to do it. I didn't know if it would work, but at that point, what more did I have to lose?

Judging from a photograph in the campaign brochure, it appeared that Mr. Public Charities and his wife still lived in the same five bedroom Colonial in Weston they'd had when he and I began our relationship. If the unlisted phone number hadn't changed, I still had it. I didn't think. I picked up the phone and called.

"Mrs. O'Rourke?"

"Yes."

"This is Claire Petersen. You don't know me—well," I hesitated, "perhaps you know of me through your husband. I wonder if you would be willing to talk with me about something."

Silence. A vacuum cleaner hummed in the background. Of course she had household help.

"How did you get this number? It's unlisted."

"Your husband gave it to me when we were—when we were friends. I want to talk with you about something that happened a few years ago when you were with your sick mother in Nebraska."

That got her attention.

"What do you want from me?" she hissed into the receiver.

"It's complicated. I owe you an apology and an explanation."

If I could shield her from the consequences of my stupidity, I wanted to try.

"I wouldn't be disturbing you," I said, "if it weren't for some extraneous circumstances that have arisen. Could we talk? I can explain if we meet."

"Does my husband know?"

"No, and I have no intention of involving him unless you want to."

"I need to think about this."

"I understand." I gulped in air.

"Where can I reach you?" she said.

I gave her both my office and cell phone numbers.

"Let me get back to you." She hung up.

I buried my head on my desk. I had just made a very risky bet. I had decided, in the Gamblers Anonymous vernacular, to make amends, and it started with Susan O'Rourke. Where it would end was anybody's guess.

She had chosen a sandwich shop on Route 20 in Sudbury for our meeting, an easy drive for her, the hinterlands for me. I had miscalculated the amount of time it would take to get there. If I was late she might bolt. I'd dashed through a traffic light shading from orange to red and got stopped by a vigilant Newton cop whose motorcycle was tucked behind some bushes. He gave me a speeding ticket and a stern warning. By the time I arrived I desperately needed to pee, but I was afraid to take the time.

She sat in a corner booth, her back to the wall. It was ten o'clock on Friday morning, too late for the breakfast crowd, too early for lunch. The place smelled of burnt toast and fried bacon.

"Mrs. O'Rourke, I'm Claire Petersen." I reached out my hand. She ignored it. Hers were clasped around a mug of tea.

I slid into the booth across from her. With jet black hair that framed her face, flawless skin, and violet eyes, she was even more beautiful in person than the campaign photograph had suggested. The yellow diamond on her finger was the size of a chick-pea.

"Thank you for this," I said. "My call was very unorthodox." I stuffed a scarf in my purse and shoved it in the corner of the booth. "You just as easily could have hung up on me."

"You didn't give me much choice, did you?" Her voice was taut as a viola string. She tapped her long, manicured forefinger on the Formica countertop.

I rubbed my forehead. "I don't quite know where to begin."

"You can hardly expect me to help."

A waitress came. I ordered coffee with lots of cream. Mrs. O'Rourke studied me as if to say, "Whatever did he see in you?"

I pushed my hair back off my forehead.

"Seven years ago," I said, "I had a relationship with your husband. It only lasted five months." Why did I say "only"?

Her face was impassive, whereas my cheeks felt hot and my

scalp was sweaty.

"But then, you already knew that, otherwise you wouldn't be here."

Her finger kept tapping. The sound grew louder with each sentence.

"It happened when you were in Nebraska," I said. "He told me you were separated, getting divorced. I believed him."

The tapping stopped.

"When I discovered the truth I broke it off. I'm so sorry."

She scanned the tables to double check that no one was within earshot. "Why are you telling me this?" Her voice was low, her words clipped. "To make yourself feel better?"

Should I have refused Mangan, let him do his worst, and watched the fallout wherever it spread? If I had miscalculated, it was too late to regroup.

The waitress appeared with my coffee. I added two packets of sugar and topped it off with as much cream as the mug could hold. When I took my first sip some slopped over the edge. I grabbed a bunch of napkins and wiped up the mess.

"I think you know there's more to the story," I said.

"Go on."

Car doors slammed outside the window and an elderly couple emerged. She held his arm, he used a cane, and they inched their way toward the entrance. The man was tall and thin with ears that stuck out like Uncle Erich's.

"I'm a lobbyist. I deal in tax policy. Most of my corporate clients are in the utilities industries in Massachusetts. Many of them, I believe, are supporting your husband in his bid to be elected attorney general. But for reasons that are irrelevant to this conversation, last January I was hired by a developer named Piper Mangan. That was a grave mistake. It's because of Mangan that we're sitting here today."

I looked for some sign of name recognition. There was none, so I asked, "Have you ever heard of him?"

She shook her head.

"Well he's heard of you. And your husband. He's got several golf courses around the state. He apparently played with someone you do know—a private investigator you hired. He isn't as discreet as you may have thought."

She leaned across the table. "What do you know?" she whispered.

I wanted to slide under the seat and disappear.

"I'm not here to cause you more pain, I can assure you. And regardless of his duplicity, I have no intention of hurting your husband if I can avoid it." Banished to the woods of Northern Maine as dog catcher, maybe.

I forged ahead. "Mangan says he has compromising pictures of me with your husband. He's threatened to spread them around if I don't do what he wants."

Her left eye began to twitch.

"And what he wants," I said, "is to prevent some farms in Apple Grove from becoming conservation land. Mangan intends to scoop them up at rock bottom prices and turn them into another golf course." I dabbed at a film of sweat on my upper lip. "In exchange for his discretion, I'm supposed to spread lies about a legislator who could thwart his plans."

She twisted her wedding ring.

My hands were tightly clasped in what, in another setting, may have appeared to be an attitude of prayer.

"I almost agreed to do it," I said, "but once you cave to a blackmailer he owns you forever."

"I thought it might be something like this," she said. "I didn't know my husband lied to you. It probably wasn't the first time, and it definitely wasn't the last."

I wanted to ask her why she didn't leave the jerk, but I had succumbed to his charm readily enough.

"I've lost whatever self-respect I had because of Mangan," I said. "I won't give him what he wants, regardless of the consequences. But because of my stupidity, naivete, whatever, with your husband, you could be collateral damage. That's why I wanted to forewarn you. If there were any way I could undo this, believe me, I would. I'm so very, very sorry."

She shook her head. "I told my husband I would stay with him during the campaign. What happens when it's over, I'm still sorting out. This is a complication I didn't need."

She slapped the table. "Damn it! I'm going to have it out with that S.O.B."

I thought she meant her husband. But then I realized she was talking about the private investigator.

"A private investigator is supposed to be just that—private," she said. "He had no business giving pictures to that Mangan guy."

"If, in fact, he did," I said. "He may just have shown them to him. Or, knowing Mangan's penchant for exaggeration, said something casually that Mangan embroidered. I never saw the pictures."

The restaurant was beginning to fill up with the lunch crowd. Two uniformed crossing guards sat down in the booth directly behind ours.

"Let's get out of here," she said. She spotted our waitress and made a motion to signal that we were ready for the check. "The Assabet Wildlife Refuge is not too far away. Have you ever been there?"

"I don't think so."

Richard always drove when we went birding. I was more interested in Richard than in the places he took me. Maybe I would recognize it, maybe not.

"You can walk for two miles and not see a soul," she said. "We can finish our conversation there."

I went to the counter and paid the bill, made a quick bathroom stop, and we walked to our cars.

"Follow me," she said. "I know a short cut."

She slid behind the wheel of her Mercedes. I hopped into my Volvo. She backed out of her parking space with such intensity that she almost clipped a car coming in the opposite direction. He laid on the horn.

I felt like I was in a road race to keep up with her. At times I wondered if she was trying to lose me, but at two different stoplights she put on her blinker well in advance so I could see where she was going.

Only two other cars were in the sanctuary parking lot.

"Good," she said. She closed the car door with a heavy thump and clicked on the alarm. "Almost nobody's here. There's a spot a few yards in where we can sit."

I followed her along a dirt path. Neither of us was dressed for outdoor activity. My shoes were covered in dust when we got to a wooden bench. She pulled some campaign literature out of her purse and spread it on the seat so our clothes wouldn't get stained by bird poop.

I had been too busy trying not to lose her to think clearly about what I should say next. That, apparently, had not been her problem.

She sat down, leaned forward, elbows on her knees, hands clasped, face forward.

"Here's what I think," she said. "I'm going to talk with the private investigator. I want to know exactly what he said or did or showed to this developer of yours. That's crucial information and he'd better give it to me."

"Believe me, Mrs. O'Rourke, I want to disassociate myself from Piper Mangan as quickly and cleanly as I can." I batted away a buzzing fly.

"Not that we're destined to become friends or anything, but I think it's time you called me Susan."

"All right. Susan."

"After that, I'm going to tell my husband."

I felt like I was getting a hot flash. My cheeks were warm.

"He may know how to stop this Mangan guy. Whether he does or not, here's what I'm thinking."

Then she spun out a strategy I never could have foreseen.

Chapter 41

Monday morning was unseasonably chilly and damp. Boats anchored in Boston Harbor threatened to come unmoored in the fierce wind. I leaned forward, walked fast, and arrived at the office out of breath.

"You're here early," Maura said.

I wiped my eyes with a tissue. "Piper Mangan is coming at 9:00."

"Should I put rat poison in his coffee?"

"You've been reading too many mysteries. But you'll need to make extra this morning. There will be four of us."

She raised an inquiring eyebrow.

"Dave Fish. A woman will be accompanying him."

I didn't want to tell her about the risk I'd taken with Susan O'Rouke. That would heighten her anxiety even more which, in turn, would send me into orbit.

"They should be here in about half an hour," I said.

"O-kayeee."

"I'll explain afterwards. In the meantime, you can help by continuing to research alternative office locations—the cheaper the better."

"You're serious?"

"Damned right. We could go for a whole new look—funky retro."

It was the wrong thing to say.

Maura twisted a paper clip back and forth until it broke.

"A few more pieces need to fall into place, but you've got to trust me on this. We're going to be all right."

"If you say so."

She didn't look convinced, which wasn't surprising, since I needed to convince myself.

"And if you're so inclined, get out that rosary you keep with your pencils and say a prayer for us."

"It's that bad, huh?"

"Please."

While rushing to take off my raincoat, I dropped my purse. Wallet, glasses, pens, cosmetics scattered all over the floor. "I'll get it," I said, waving her away. "You fix the coffee."

I was wearing Grandma's pendant. It bumped on the carpet, so I tucked it underneath my blouse while I scooped up the contents and restored them to my purse. Then I scurried into my office and closed the door before Maura could ask any more questions.

It took three configurations before I was satisfied with the seating arrangement. I decided to position Susan O'Rourke's wing-backed chair close to mine, directly across from my office door. I would place Dave Fish next to Mangan, but at an angle. Mangan would be in a wooden straight-backed chair. I wanted him as uncomfortable as possible. If Mangan tried to look directly at Dave he would have to turn sideways, whereas I could detect any subtle signals that Dave sent my way.

When that was done, I paced around my desk, flipping Grandma's paperweight from one hand to the other. Maura knocked, opened my door, and announced Dave Fish and a guest. I dropped the paperweight. It rolled across the floor, landing at Dave's feet. He picked it up, gave it back to me, and said "How're you doing?"

"As well as can be expected under the circumstances."

Maura reappeared with a tray of cups and a pitcher of coffee.

"Would you like me to serve?" she asked.

I could tell from her puzzled squint that she hadn't figured out who Susan was.

"Thanks, Maura, I'll do it. Mr. Mangan should be arriving any minute now."

Susan O'Rourke had on a navy St. John suit with gold buttons and red piping which reminded me of Marine dress blues. Her long, polished nails matched the red trim. The tips of the toes on her pumps were so pointed that they could have been registered as lethal weapons.

I didn't really know Susan. Could I trust her? Would she back me up? The cup jiggled in the saucer as I handed it to her. I loaded mine with two heaping teaspoons of sugar.

Dave rehearsed the strategy he'd recommended. He spoke in a slow, measured cadence. "Remember," he said. "keep it short and simple. In a situation like this, less is best. Claire, you take the lead. He's your client."

"Right." I chewed my lip.

"Rule number two: avoid unnecessarily inflammatory language."

"You mean I can't call him a son of a bitch?" Susan said.

Nervous laughter ensued.

"I wouldn't recommend it." Dave adjusted his glasses and looked at me. "You're in charge, but if you're in doubt, give me a signal and I'll intervene. All right?"

I nodded. Susan's lips were pursed in a tight smile.

"Let's all take a deep breath," Dave said.

Just then Maura knocked, opened the door, and Piper Mangan swaggered in.

When he saw Susan O'Rourke he almost tripped over his pigeon toes. I looked down and realized I hadn't changed out of my New Balance sneakers.

Susan's legs were crossed. She jiggled one pointed toe toward Piper Mangan's empty chair.

"Have a seat, Mr. Mangan," I said.

My heart was pulsating in my ears. Voices sounded like they were in an echo chamber. I swallowed several times before sounds returned to normal.

Mangan squeezed his big butt between the arms of the wooden chair.

"This is unusual, Miss Petersen, highly unusual," he growled. "I thought we had agreed that our business—*all* our business—was private. *Very* private."

He leaned forward in his chair, elbows out, beefy hands on his thighs.

Calm down, I said to myself. Breathe. Don't talk too much.

"Mr. Fish is my attorney. I asked him to be present because he was responsible for drawing up our contract, the one you signed."

Mangan eyed Fish as if he were a noxious creature crapping on one of his greens.

"I don't believe you've met Mrs. O'Rourke," I said, "but based on our previous conversation, you know of her."

Susan straightened her frame, red talons out, ready to strike.

His eyes darted around the room before they settled on me. "What business do you have..." he sputtered.

"You *made* it my business, Mr. Mangan." I clutched the pendant underneath my blouse. "And based on our contract, as of today, I am severing our relationship. I've prepared a check to refund the retainer you paid us. I'm not charging you for the billable hours I've accrued."

There it was, the first step. There was no going back.

Mangan's bulbous nose and jowly cheeks morphed from pink to red to purple.

With a slight tilt of his head, Dave offered me encouragement.

"And," I said, "we have cut a separate check for the interest. At today's rates, Mr. Fish advises me that it should be five and a half percent."

I tried to hand the checks to Mangan. He swatted them away. I laid them on the coffee table.

"This. failure. to. deliver," Mangan punched out each word, spit landing on the glass, "is gonna cost you plenty more than a coupla checks. You don't know how many people I know. Bob Matthews? Dutch Wolf? Pete Farkas?"

These men were my clients.

"Golfing buddies," he said. "Didn't know that, did you, missy?" He waved his arm and snapped his fingers.

"You wouldn't be threatening my client in any way, now, would you Mr. Mangan?" Dave said.

Mangan pulled at the knot on his tie. "All I'm sayin', all I'm sayin' is, actions have consequences. Con-see-quences. Some things are out'a my control, you know? So if Miss Petersen's reputation flushes down the ter-let," he shrugged his shoulders, "I can't help that, now can I?"

"My reputation…" I started to say. Dave moved his head slightly, which said "Don't go there."

My self-respect had taken the biggest hit in the whole debacle. He knew it. I knew it. I was the only one who could repair that damage, but more immediate matters needed to be settled.

"Here's how you *can* help." Susan's voice was controlled, clipped. Her hands clasped the sides of the chair, knuckles white against the blood red upholstery. "You can banish all thoughts about embarrassing *my* family, do you hear me? I've spoken with a mutual acquaintance who, I gather, has decided to take up archery instead of golf."

Mangan jumped.

"He now assures me," she said, "that he misspoke on that golf course. And if you want to do any more business that in any way requires the cooperation of public officials—permits, variances, contracts, you name it—you'll bury this unfortunate episode so deep that not even a bulldozer could unearth it."

This was new information, and she was driving it home with force. I was in awe.

"Are you threatening me?" Mangan said.

Susan's lips creased in a thin smile. She opened her hands, palms up, shrugged her shoulders. "This is merely a suggestion, Mr. Mangan. I'm only speculating, but you've been around long enough to know how things work in this state. And I assume you have no immediate plans to move to Kansas."

Mangan pushed his way out of his chair and hovered over the coffee table.

"You haven't heard the last of this," he growled.

He swiped up the checks, stormed out, and slammed the door.

My hands were shaking.

"He's a real piece of work," Dave said.

Susan sank back in her chair. When she spoke, I had to lean forward to hear her.

"He never did see any pictures. The private investigator also has a reputation and client base he's eager to protect. He has assured me that I will get the prints *and* the negatives."

"Thank you," I said.

"Oh, I didn't do this for you. I did it for me and the kids. Whatever happens after the election, it's going to be on my terms, not some sleazebag's. And now," she said as she picked her purse off the floor, "I am going home."

When I started toward the door she said "I can see my way out. I don't think you and I will have occasion to meet again. Good luck."

"That was interesting," Dave said. He put some papers into his briefcase.

"Claire! Are you OK? You look like you're going to pass out!"

He leapt out of his seat and guided me into a chair.

"Maura," he yelled, "can you bring us some water?"

She took one look, ran out and returned with a bottle of Poland Spring and a paper bag.

"Breathe into this," she said. "You're hyperventilating." She had one hand on the bag, the other on my back. "Take nice, deep breaths."

I leaned into her, sucked in air from the bag, and the room stopped spinning.

"It smells like orange peels," I said.

"An old lunch." She rubbed my back. "Feeling better?"

"Much better now that Piper Mangan is banished."

"For good?" she said.

"At least I hope he is." I looked at Dave.

"You and Susan are a formidable team," he said.

"She wouldn't describe it that way, but I guess it worked."

"Wow! Free at last!" Maura said, and punched her fist in the air.

"Thanks. You're an angel." I drank more water. "I'm all right now. Dave and I still have a bit of unfinished business, then you and I will talk."

"You're sure?"

"I'm sure."

After Maura exited, Dave said "Mrs. O'Rouke is a real ball buster. Thanks to her, I'd be surprised if Mangan tried anything."

"We'll see. I've done what I can. Now I'd like your help in a different direction."

Dave sat back down and pulled a yellow legal note pad out of his briefcase.

"Mangan is circling that farmland like a hawk ready to pounce on a mouse," I said.

"He looks more like a turkey to me."

That made me smile. I hadn't done that for a while. "All right," I said. "Poor joke." I sipped some water. "I need to know just what a reasonable asking price for that land might be. If the figures aren't too stratospheric, I might leverage a donation to top them off."

"Careful," he said. "You don't want to open yourself to a lawsuit from Mangan based on insider information."

"If the donation, which I assume would be tax deductible, is voluntary, and if it goes to the environmental group for land conservation but with no particular location designated, could I pull it off unscathed?"

"Let's take this one step at a time. My firm can make some

discreet inquiries, then I'll get back to you. We also need to find out exactly how much money those Worcester environmentalists have amassed for this project."

"An inquiry from an unknown attorney might be suspect. I have—had," I swallowed more water, "a friend who might know. He may not be willing to talk with me but I have to try."

"You work your end, I'll work mine."

He made a few more notes on his legal pad and stuffed it in his briefcase. "You're sure you want to do this?"

"As sure as possible when you've decided to make a mid-life U-turn. Whiplash is one of the risks."

He left and I rearranged the furniture. Then I invited Maura into my office. The conversation I needed to have with her was, in some ways, harder than the one I'd just finished. When I told her what was happening, she asked a lot of questions. I didn't hold anything back. We'd been a team for fifteen years, and she was entitled to know the truth.

She said she wasn't surprised. She said I hadn't been the same since Mangan first walked in the office. She shed a few tears, blew her nose, then described, in cringe-making detail, how obnoxious he had been on the phone.

I was ashamed at the degree to which I had failed to protect her. I apologized, both for what I had done and for how it had impacted her. I laid out my hopes for the future and said that, if she still was willing to stick by me, both our lives would be better. She could have abandoned me right then, but thank goodness, she said she was all in.

On impulse, I presented her with Grandma's paperweight. I said it was a token of my commitment to making a fresh start and doing it together. Consultation would be my new guiding principle. I trusted her instincts.

Chapter 42

I felt like I'd been in a triathlon. I closed the office for the rest of the day. At my suggestion, Maura, who ordinarily was prepared to soldier on regardless of circumstance, recorded an "out of the office" message on our voice mail and we walked out the door arm in arm.

I had just got home when the phone rang. Barbara was calling to thank me for the gifts I'd sent—Chanel for her, books for Timmy.

"I'm sorry," I said. "I should have called *you*. I've been too preoccupied with work. How's Timmy?"

"So so. He wanted fried onion rings last night. That was a good sign. Caleb came home with three family size portions. We'll be eating onion rings for a week."

"It's good to hear you laugh again."

"How about you? Have you talked with Richard?"

I loosened the ties on my sneakers, slipped them off, and threw myself on the couch.

"I'm trying to repair the damage. I've made some progress, but not with him. He's so angry. He says he can't trust me. As if he's never put a foot wrong."

"That's the problem with these do-gooders. They're so self-righteous."

I put one pillow behind my head, the other under my knees. "I really did screw up."

"I suspect he likes things neat and tidy. So do you. Life's not like that."

"I really messed up this time."

"What are you doing this evening?"

"Licking my wounds. It's been a trying day."

"Why don't you come over and help us eat some onion rings? They go great with beer and Caleb's stocked up on a new German export."

"That's so sweet, but I'm exhausted."

My back ached and my arms and legs felt like lead weights. After all I'd been through, I couldn't picture the four of us gabbing idly around her big kitchen table.

"Listen to me. You take a shower, throw on some sweats and come over. If you're too tired to go home, you can stay in our guest-room. I'll send a cab to pick you up if you don't want to drive."

When Barbara was determined there was no stopping her. Now that Timmy's situation had stabilized, she'd turned her focus on me.

I protested. She was insistent. Then she said "I'm worried about you. I don't think you should be alone. So get your ass on over here, all right?"

Sometimes she knew me better than I knew myself.

Barbara and Caleb's front porch, bigger than my whole living room, looked out on a quiet, well-groomed, tree-lined street, much like the one where we had lived before Daddy died. Casually arranged white wicker furniture with cheerful print cushions, magazines strewn around, suggested frequent use. I hadn't even rung the bell when Barbara opened the door and enveloped me in a motherly hug.

"I'm so glad you're here," she said. "Come in and say 'hi' to Timmy and Caleb."

Timmy was sprawled on a couch in their family room, watching a movie. His face was pallid and he looked even thinner than I had remembered. My hand flew over my mouth with the shock. Thank goodness he didn't see it.

"Hey, kid," I said, kissing him on the forehead.

He pressed pause on the remote. "Hi, Aunt Claire."

I loved it when he called me that.

"Thanks for the books," he said.

"I'm glad you like them. More are on the way." I looked at the screen. "Is that an old Star Trek movie?"

"'The Wrath of Khan.' Dad got me the whole series. I'm starting from the beginning."

"Well don't let me interrupt the flow."

Barbara and I moved into the hallway. Just then Caleb appeared from his study, a bunch of papers in his arms.

"I hear you've been making special restaurant runs," I said.

"Whatever it takes. Hell, I'd order an eight pound lobster if he'd eat it."

"Now that's a good idea," Barbara said, nudging his arm. "Even if he doesn't, I will."

"Would you two mind if I'm anti-social this evening?" Caleb

said. "I've got some reading to catch up on. I haven't been paying as much attention as I should in the past month, and in my business, that's not good."

"I won't tell," I said.

He headed up the stairway.

"He'll probably fall asleep," Barbara whispered. "He crashes at nine and doesn't wake up until six. It's the stress. If he remembers to set an alarm, I turn it off before I go to bed. He needs the rest."

"How about you?"

She shrugged her shoulders. "I'm made of sturdier stuff."

That's it. Tough it out until the crisis passes. Barbara was in mama bear mode.

"So, it looks like we're on our own," she said.

I suspected she had planned it like that all along. I followed her into the kitchen.

"What can I get you?"

She pulled out a tray and started arranging an assortment of cheeses, crackers, a big bowl of grapes, a huge plate of onion rings, and two bottles of Beck's.

"There are only two of us, you know," I said.

"Just think of it as an impromptu supper. I'll bet you haven't eaten, anyway."

She was right.

We went into the library. The floor was covered in an oriental rug with only a square foot of bare hardwood visible around the edges. She put the tray on an ottoman and we curled up on either end of a long brown leather sofa. Barbara poured a glass of beer for each of us.

"So how are you, really?" I asked.

"I had a massage two days ago," she said. She rolled her shoulders. "My back muscles were so tight I could feel them pop when the masseuse kneaded them."

Then she recounted Timmy's appointments schedule, doctors and other health professionals on whom they had come to depend, her anxieties about his future.

She wiped a touch of foam off her lips.

"Timmy's moody, Caleb's exhausted, and I'm trying to put one foot in front of the other without stumbling. But I'm coping. That's what mothers do, isn't it?"

That's what my mother did, too. I'd been so mad at her when I was a teenager, never given her the credit she deserved for pulling us out of financial quicksand. I wish I could have apologized, made it up to her in some way. It was too late now.

"When you get through the worst of this and Timmy's back to some semblance of normal, I'd like to take you to a spa for a couple of days."

If I couldn't do something for my own mother, at least I could do something for this one, although I would have to monitor my impulses lest they get ahead of my reduced circumstances.

I picked up a pillow, put it behind my tired back, and tried to get comfortable. The grandfather clock chimed softly. It was only 7:30. I thought it was much later.

"You've finished your beer," Barbara said.

"What?"

"You downed that beer like a pro," she said. "Let me get you another." She was out of the room before I could protest. When she came back, she said "Enough about me. It's your turn."

"Turns? We're taking turns now?"

"If you talk about you it takes me out of myself. You're actually helping me, see?"

She put a throw over her bare feet and settled in. "So what's happening?"

"Do you want excerpts, a short story, or the novel?"

"Whatever works. If I get confused, I'll interrupt."

When I got to the part about Susan O'Rourke she said, "You didn't!"

"I knew it was a big risk, but I decided to take the chance. She's a smart cookie. If Mangan followed through on his threats, she could get swept up in the mess, too. What I couldn't have anticipated was her determination to confront him directly."

"Wish I could have seen it."

"By the time she was done, Mangan's face was purple. I thought he'd have a stroke."

"Sounds like you've fixed the old goat. Now what?"

"I've been thinking a lot about what matters most in life. Some of my relationships, if they even deserve the word—the dry cleaner I see twice a month, the clerk at the pizza parlor who works the late shift and takes my orders—they give me a sense of place, but that's all. If I disappeared tomorrow, they might miss my business, but they wouldn't miss me. The thick relationships, the kind Uncle Erich had, what you and Caleb have with Timmy and your family—those are missing."

Barbara gave me a "what about us" look.

"Of *course* I have you. I don't know what I'd do without you. And Maura's been a brick, but that's at the office. There's nobody else. After I visited Uncle Erich it began to sink in. I have a hole in my heart, and I've been trying to fill it with the wrong things, the wrong people. The wrong men. I don't want to live like that anymore."

"You were on the right track with Richard. I'd like to box his ears for being so self-righteous."

"He's far from perfect but look who's talking."

Barbara put on her authoritative, "pay attention, child" voice.

"As my mother used to say, 'Never let the perfect be the enemy of the good.'"

"Richard doesn't like ambiguity. He wants things to get resolved, and quickly."

"Actually, the two of you are alike in that respect."

"Point taken."

I studied the pattern in the oriental rug. With a dark red field, it was covered in olive leaves, red and blue blossoms, and a mass of cream vines with ragged edges outlined in blue thread. Somehow, the mismatched parts converged into a coherent whole.

"You're defending him now?"

"As you well know, Caleb and I have had our ups and downs. Timmy's illness has brought us right again, thank God. Take it from me, real love ebbs and flows. That's why commitment is necessary."

"Even if I were willing, Richard has closed that door."

"He's hurt, and all you see is the anger. Give him some time. At the very least, you know what a good man looks like. That's a step in the right direction."

I started to pace the room. "I've made some decisions. I'm going to wrap up commitments to my current clients, close the office, sell my condo, and take a sabbatical." Testing, testing.

"This sounds like black and white thinking. Couldn't you try to live in the gray for a while?"

"I need to get away from everything, get some perspective."

"Everything, or everybody?"

I went over to a shelf filled with books and played with dust on the woodwork.

"I miss him. Oh, I do miss him. And if he wanted to start over, I'd become a card-carrying member of the Mass. Audubon Society, the Appalachian Mountain Club, the Nature Conservancy---you name it. But this is much bigger than Richard. Maybe he was trying to show me something about life by introducing me to all those birds. With him or without him, I'm going to change."

"The Appalachian Mountain Club?" she said. "Somehow I can't see you hiking the Moat Mountain Trail."

Barbara topped off the beer in her glass and sipped it slowly. "You know how they say you shouldn't make any major decisions for a year after a significant life event? When it comes to stress, on a scale of one to ten, you're at eleven. You lost one big client, banished another, your uncle died, and Richard's exited the stage."

"Don't forget about Timmy."

"I know. So how about, instead of trying to figure out the whole thing, you take this one step at a time? Don't make any drastic moves until you recover."

"You know me, I don't do anything by half measures. I want a life, even if Richard isn't in it." That came out louder than I had intended. "He was right about some things. I'm good at what I do, but I don't want to do it anymore, at least not the way I have been. If I scale my expenses way down, I could reach out to some non-profits, see if they'd like my help, lobby for causes that will make a difference where it matters—the poor, the elderly, the forgotten." Remembering Uncle Erich's passion, I added "local veterans' groups."

"A real Emma Lazarus."

"If I could pull it off, I'd be a Lazarus, all right, but of the Biblical kind—dead and brought to life again."

Then I told her I had decided to give most of Uncle Erich's inheritance to the environmental folks to help them buy the land in Apple Grove.

She slapped a pillow. "You're out of your mind. You said you took on Mangan because you'd lost one of your biggest clients.

When this windfall lands in your lap you're going to give it away? You're the one who told me to hang on to my aunt's bequest."

"Uncle Erich said 'You learn a lot about people by seeing what they're willing to fight over.'"

"I suspect Uncle Erich wanted to make life easier for you. He must have known how hard you'd had it after your dad died."

I threw myself back on the sofa. "My uncle lived simply, and he was happy. He was always thinking about somebody else. He made it seem so attractive. Maybe it's time I try that, too."

"You're serious about this."

"You should have seen the people who showed up at his memorial service. When I die, you could fit the mourners into a closet and still have room for the coats."

She reached over and slapped my arm. "Listen to me. From what you've told me, your uncle also saved. *Saved*, Claire. Not spent."

What would Uncle Erich say if he were sitting in that library? Would he understand?

"Do you know how much money it would take to buy that conservation land?" she said.

"Richard probably could get me the information, if he's willing." I chewed a piece of skin on my thumb. "I'm guessing about two million. Why Mangan couldn't come up with the cash himself I'll never understand. I guess he refused to plunk down his own money when he could leverage it from other sources."

"It's a funny old world, isn't it?"

Barbara retreated to her corner of the sofa. The clock ticked.

"Let's say it's two million," she said. "If the folks in central Mass. have, say, three quarters of a million, and you put up another half million (not that I'm saying this is a wise idea), you'd still need to come up with seven hundred and fifty thousand before Mangan finds the means to get that land."

Barbara's brain had turned into an abacus.

"I know." It sounded impossible. "And I don't know how much time we have before Mangan finds an alternative."

"I still wish you'd pace yourself. However, if you're determined, I'd like to help. What if I could find some of that money?"

Barbara threw out the idea with casual ease.

I started pacing again. "What do you mean?"

"Don't hold me to it," she said. Then she proceeded to tick off ideas, starting with her index finger. "My parents have a charitable gift fund administered through Caleb's firm." Middle finger. "Mother sits on the board of a foundation that includes, as part of its mission, care for the whole inhabited earth." She smiled. "That covers a lot of territory." Ring finger. "And if neither of those work out (though Mother does listen to me), I've got that bequest coming from my aunt."

"I can't take your money."

"Technically, it isn't my money, it would come from a foundation. Or if necessary, my aunt's bequest. How is that different from what you, against my advice, want to do with your uncle's money?"

"A foundation grant would be one thing, but you shouldn't use any of your inheritance. Especially now, with all Timmy's medical expenses looming in the months ahead."

"Caleb has us insured to a hilt. Trust me, we're fine. So we'd better get moving if we're going to give it to—what's its name?"

"Environmentalists of Central Massachusetts."

Her offer knocked me flat. Barbara had stood by me through thick and thin. The bond between us had never wavered, but now we had moved to a whole new plain. I felt a reverence for our friendship beyond words.

She twirled a lock of her hair. "What would you do on that sabbatical of yours?"

So she didn't think I was out of my mind, after all.

"I don't know. Volunteer in a soup kitchen, read to kids in an afterschool program."

"What alien has snatched this body?"

"All right, I'd probably go crazy with boredom, but if I don't give myself time, I'll never know."

A giant globe rested on a pedestal in the corner of the library. I spun it around, stopped it on Western Europe.

"Maybe go to Germany where my Grandma grew up, where Uncle Erich was during the war."

It was the first time I'd been excited about anything since Richard.

Chapter 43

It was Tuesday morning. By the time I arrived at the office, I'd already had enough coffee to propel a squad of soldiers through a forced march. I hoped the caffeine would focus my mind as I figured out what to say to Richard. All it did was give me an overactive bladder. I barely made it to the hallway bathroom.

Once there, I turned the commode into a seat of contemplation. I studied the pattern of alternating black and white hexagonal tiles on the floor. The grout had turned brown from dirt in the crevices. The white had aged to gray.

Our first kiss had been in a bathroom. Richard might have drawn a parable from the setting, but I couldn't see it. I tried out several opening lines.

Surprised to hear from me?

This is strictly business.

A lot's happened since we last talked.

I need to see you.

I experimented with tone of voice, emphasis on key words. Everything sounded lame. What I really wanted to say was "I'm changing. That should count for something." But that was too risky. It sounded like begging, and I still had some self-respect.

"Now," I said to Maura as I came back into the office, "I need to call Richard."

"Another step in the right direction."

"You think?" Her opinion mattered to me, more than I'd realized. "God knows I'm trying."

I kissed Grandma's pendant for good luck, then phoned Richard's office and identified myself. I still had no idea how to begin. The woman who answered said, "May I tell him what this is about?"

"He'll know me."

She put me on hold. Woody Guthrie's "This Land is Your Land" played three times on a continuous loop.

The "roaming and rambling" made me think of Broadmoor, an Audubon sanctuary where Richard had shown me my first towhee. He had shushed me in mid-sentence and pointed to something scratching around in the underbrush. Richard was so close that I could feel him breathing on my neck. What I would have given to go back to that place again, bugs and all.

Woody sang. I doodled birds on a notepad. They looked more like freshly hatched tadpoles with lumpy bodies and long tales, vulnerable to all sorts of predators.

"Claire," he said, his voice clipped. Not even "How are you?" I heard him drumming his fingernails on his desk, something he did when he was nervous.

Sweat formed on my upper lip. I brushed it off. "This is about work, otherwise I wouldn't have called there." Why did I say "there"?

"If this is about Whately…"

"It's not about the State House, at least not directly."

"I've got a board meeting in a half hour, so I can't talk long."

"Look, would you meet me at Sal's later today? I have an idea that I'd like to run by you about how to help the Environmental League get that farmland."

"Are you serious? This isn't some new ploy, is it?"

That was a gut punch. "No, I mean it."

"Wouldn't that contradict the wishes of your client?"

I chewed my lip, drew blood, blotted it with a tissue. "He isn't my client anymore."

"He's not?"

"I sent him packing yesterday."

"You've been busy."

"You don't know the half of it." I took a deep breath. "I know I disappointed you. I've disappointed myself. But I'm determined to make things right—at least as right as I can."

The finger drumming picked up a notch.

"I could do 4:45 if you think this can't wait."

"That works for me."

"I'm doing this for my members, you understand."

Not even a little for me? For us?

"Thanks, Richard. You won't regret this." But he'd already hung up.

When I walked into Sal's Diner at 4:30, the place was hopping.

"Two, please," I said to a teenager who was monitoring the tables. A streak of purple dye ran down the front of her jet black hair.

"Are both of you here? I'm not supposed to seat people until all members of the party are present."

I looked out the window. "I'm expecting him any time. Look, this is a very important meeting and we really need somewhere quiet. Can you help me out?"

I would beg if I had to. I was getting good at it.

She rolled her eyes. "Like I said, I'm not supposed to."

I spotted a workman on a ladder, replacing a light fixture in a dark corner. "Could you put me there?"

"I guess so."

"That would be perfect."

It was, as long as Richard didn't think I was trying to arrange a tryst. I started for the booth before she had a chance to change her mind. I made sure to walk around the ladder.

She trailed me and threw two plastic covered menus on the table. A wall blackboard announced early bird specials: a burger with guacamole; a chicken, avocado, and mango salad; and an avocado energy booster. There must have been a glut of avocadoes south of the border.

The place was noisy. Generic music—a base beat with violins—drowned out nearby conversations. White garbed cooks banged pots in an open kitchen. Rattling dishes and sizzling burgers added to the cacophony.

I kept glancing out the window to see if I could spot Richard. A waitress appeared and asked if I was ready to order. I looked at my watch. It was 4:45. I assured her my friend should be arriving any minute. At least I hoped so. In the meantime, I asked for water.

"Bottled or tap?"

I preferred bottled but Richard said paying for what nature gave us for free was a waste of money, so I requested tap. As an afterthought, I asked if they still had any cinnamon scones. When she gave me a "will that be all?" look, I assured her I'd be placing a full order after my companion arrived.

I jumped as the sound of crashing metal pans exploded from the kitchen, followed by a string of vigorous Spanish that I didn't understand but could imagine.

A line of people had formed, waiting to be seated. What if Richard took one look, thought I wasn't there, turned around and left? What if he decided not to come? I went back to the hostess.

"The name of the man I'm expecting is Richard. He's kind of tall with wavy hair."

"Hope he's worth the wait," she said. "OK. If Richard comes in, I'll send him in your direction."

The workman folded up his ladder and exited. Harsh light now flooded the area around my table. I looked at my watch again. Richard was never late. He said he would come, and I had trusted him in the past. Was that a mistake? Yet another error of judgment? I had no fallback position.

At five o'clock I was about ready to leave a huge tip and give up my seat when he dashed in.

"Sorry," he said. "One of my board members wanted to talk after our meeting, one thing led to another, and…well, you know how it goes."

"You're here. I was afraid I'd have to bribe the waitress to keep the seat. I've never seen it like this."

"Sal's was featured on Channel Five a few weeks back. 'Local deli hits all the right spots.' After that business really picked up."

He took off his backpack, threw it in the corner, and slid into the booth across from me. He had on a blue button down with rolled up sleeves, a casual look that always turned me on. Wisps of hair touched the back of his shirt collar. He needed a cut again.

The waitress appeared with the scones.

"I ordered cinnamon scones," I said. "I know you like them."

"We had a working lunch so I'm kinda full."

"Well, you can take them home, have 'em for breakfast, whatever."

The waitress glared at me. "Do you want anything else?"

"I'll try that energy booster. Do you want one, Richard? It's made with avocado."

"I'm fine but go ahead and order. You probably haven't eaten since breakfast."

"Why don't you bring us some chips and guacamole," I said. "And one of those chicken salads." I had to run up enough of a tab to justify holding the seat.

"What's this all about?" he said. No preliminaries, just that.

"I've severed my relationship with Mangan. Broke the contract. Gave him back his fee with interest. It's over. I'm out of it."

Richard drummed his fingernails on the table.

"This could have serious consequences if word gets around. Don't get me wrong. I'm glad you did it. You're taking a big risk, though. The only rules he follows are his own. What makes you think he'll walk away without a fight? He probably plays golf with some of your clients."

"He does, and he emphasized that point." A vision of Mangan's spittle on my glass coffee table flashed through my mind. "I can't be sure, but I had some outside help that could make a difference."

I had never told him about Mr. Public Charities. I'd been too embarrassed. I wished I'd come clean about that, too. Maybe another time. Not now.

He flipped a cardboard coaster back and forth.

"What's this got to do with us?"

I'd hoped Richard might receive the news like an olive branch.

"He'll be even madder if I'm able to pull off what I want to do to—well, to make amends."

"You don't owe me anything."

"You're wrong, but this isn't about us. It's about that land." It *was* about us, but it went far deeper than that.

He leaned forward, elbows on the table, chin on his clasped hands. "What do you have in mind, and where does the Environmental Coalition come into it?"

The waitress appeared with our food. The scones looked out of place next to the avocado dishes.

"I'd like to see if I can put together enough money to help the folks in central Massachusetts buy that property outright before Mangan can get his hands on it."

There, I'd said it. I studied his face for some reaction. He would have been a good poker player. I couldn't read a thing.

He surveyed the room, then leaned across the table. "What's going on with you? Mrs. Tannenbaum's daughter has tried every angle she could think of to buy that farmland. She hasn't succeeded. Why do you think you can do any better?"

"I don't know for sure, but I want to try."

"What? A little birding has turned you into an environmentalist?"

I could feel my cheeks warm. "That was a cheap shot."

Barbara was correct. He was self-righteous. Couldn't he show even a little compassion?

"Whether or not that was your intention," I said, "maybe it has, just a little."

I snapped a chip in half and studied the uneven ridges. "Looking back on it," I said, "things have been stirring inside me for some time--Timmy's illness, losing Uncle Erich, and you may not want to hear this, but you've made a difference, too."

"Not enough of a difference to keep you from trying to derail the career of a decent legislator who's having a tough time. I warned you about Mangan in the first place. He's a snake."

"I was a responsible lobbyist before this happened and I could be again if I want to. Are you so bloody perfect? Haven't you ever made any mistakes?"

He looked away and brushed his hand over his face.

Barbara said he was hurt. Was she right?

"Look, are you going to help, or not?"

"That all depends."

"On what?"

"On whether it's on the up and up."

"Am I always going to have that scarlet letter tattooed on my ass?"

"Sorry. That's not what I meant. Tell me more."

"It wouldn't be illegal if that's what you were thinking. I'm consulting my lawyer to make sure. And doing an end run around Mangan wouldn't be immoral, either. Listen, I'm not looking for insider information. I only want to know how much money the Environmental League thinks they need to buy that farmland. Do they have a relationship with the apple growers? Do the farmers care whether their land goes for conservation or a golf course? That sort of stuff." Then I landed the big one. "If I could amass the cash they need, could they pull off the deal?"

"Where could you get that kind of money?"

"It depends on how much we're talking about. Uncle Erich left me over a half million dollars."

"A half million? I thought he was a grocery store clerk."

"He managed the produce department. Actually, I'm inheriting about $750,000." It still was hard to believe. "He was frugal, and he was smart. Material things didn't mean much to him. He was like you that way."

Richard had been studying his knuckles. Now he looked straight at me with those dark brown eyes.

"I wish I could have met him."

"He would have liked you. A lot. The last thing he did was help me in ways that go far beyond money." I could feel tears forming. "You know, it's not such a bad way to live. Some things are more important than...well, than material things. Uncle Erich might be pleased to know that my inheritance had been used for such a worthy purpose."

Richard reached in his pocket and held out a handkerchief.

"It's clean," he said. "I put a fresh one in my pocket this morning."

"Thanks, but I've got some tissues."

I pulled one out of my purse, wiped my eyes and took a deep breath. "I've asked the law firm I use to make discrete inquiries about what they think the land is worth," I said, "but any additional information would help. And I have a couple other ideas."

"I need to think about this," he said. "I don't want to get the Environmental League's hopes up. But if they could get that land through honest means, it would be a gift to future generations."

"It could help the farmers, too. They've got a real mess on their hands with that apple blight."

"I've been out there. It's a real disaster."

He was quiet. I was quiet. What next?

"You're full of surprises," he said.

"Good ones?"

He grabbed his backpack. "I'll get back to you, OK?"

"Don't you want to take the scones?"

"You keep 'em. You never did have enough food around for breakfast. Or dinner, either." He smiled. It was the only time he'd smiled during the whole conversation.

Chapter 44

So that's what I did. I wrote a letter to my clients saying I no longer would be serving them after the legislative session ended on July 31st. I left the envelopes on my desk overnight to give myself a final out, but the next morning when I walked through the rain to the mailbox, I was aware of a fresh, clean smell in the air.

Reactions ranged from annoyed, to disappointed, to "we wish you well in your new endeavor." The CFO of one of the solar energy companies I'd represented called to get a fuller story. When I told him my plans with the non-profits, he said it sounded like Davida going against Goliath, but he wished me well.

With the million four I was able to get for my condo (the real estate market was hot; I benefitted from a bidding war), I gave Maura a fully funded sabbatical. She deserved it. She said she was going to rent a cabin in the New Hampshire woods and give her mother a real holiday while she still was able to enjoy it. When I handed her the check, she did her little dance.

Maura and I agreed that, after I returned, together we would find a modest location for our new office, consistent with the capacities of my aspirational non-profit client-base.

In addition to lobbying, I hoped that I had absorbed some of my father's talents in public relations. I had enough confidence in myself to believe that, with time, I could pull it off. Most important, the office would be open only four days a week. At least that was my intention.

Before I left Boston I saw Dave Fish to iron out details about the conservation land. Thanks to Barbara's family connections, with an assist from Uncle Erich's bequest, the environmentalists in central Massachusetts were able to purchase the land in Apple Grove. In time, it would revert to pre-farmed wilderness. Dave reported that the apple growers were happy. Most of them planned to retire and move to Florida.

Piper Mangan was apoplectic.

Thus far, however, Susan O'Rourke's threats seemed to have restrained him.

Richard called before I left for Germany. He gave me the inside story about how his constituents had received the news and wished me safe travels, but the conversation was brief and antiseptic. Maybe he wasn't the right man for me after all. Still, I mourned. I had relinquished so much, some voluntarily, some beyond my control. It was a lot to process. Barbara said it would take time. How much time? I never was the patient sort.

The logistics of all the changes I was making were a welcome distraction. I found a small apartment near the Museum of Fine Arts, a "junior one bedroom with kitchenette," to tide me over until my financial situation became clearer. My furniture was in storage, to be retrieved after I returned. By the time I deposited my bag at the Lufthansa desk in Logan Airport, I felt lighter, and it wasn't because of the suitcase.

I had arranged to stay in a small, family owned bed and breakfast in Leipzig. I contracted with their teenage daughter to tutor me in German five times a week. Before long, I was able to make my way to the *Bushaltestelle* and navigate around the *Stadt* without too many awkward silences. Uncle Erich would have been impressed.

It took me a few weeks to ease into my non-working mode. I slept a lot—probably a delayed reaction from all the stress.

Almost every afternoon I went to Café-Central to sip *Kaffee mit Schlag* while I read the *Herald Tribune* and digested the latest political news from the States.

Maura sent me a picture with her arm around her mother's shoulder in front of a wooden A-frame surrounded by pine trees, a lake in the distance. She enclosed an article about the ribbon cutting ceremony at Apple Grove featured in the *Telegram and Gazette*. It included a picture of Richard standing behind Mrs. Tannenbaum's daughter. Maura attached a note that said "Well done!"

I tucked it in my wallet. My role in the process would remain anonymous, but I was surprised by how good it felt to give that money. Part of Uncle Erich was in that land, a gift for future generations. He would have been pleased. When I returned, I would arrange for a wooden bench with his name on a brass plaque to be placed somewhere on the grounds.

Barbara and I were in regular communication by email. The doctors were encouraged by how well Timmy was responding to therapy. The prognosis was good, thank God.

I often ran by the river in the *Clar-Zetkin-Park*, and after I discovered the *Botanischer Garten*, I used the binoculars Richard had given me to see birds flitting around the trees. I was hopeless at identifying them, but I enjoyed watching. Once I started to tag along behind a group of birders, but I had to stop. It reminded me too much of being with Richard on our Saturday morning jaunts.

The town where my grandmother grew up was about twenty-five kilometers from Leipzig. The first time I visited Grimma, I was excited to discover a sewing machine shop called Petersen's just off the square. I wondered whether I had located some distant third-generation relative, but after talking with the owner, a Herr Berthold Petersen, it appeared there was no connection. Still, I went back two more times to look at the sign. I took a picture.

By the third week of my stay at the *Gasthaus* of Herr and Frau Kohler, Frau Kohler began to treat me like one of the family. She offered to do my laundry, invited me to join them for Sunday dinner.

One September afternoon when I walked in the door, my pace slower than usual, I caught a yeasty fragrance in the air. Fine china and a silver coffee service had been arranged on the dining room table. Frau Kohler, Herr Kohler, and daughter Franzisa burst through the swinging door between kitchen and dining room and in unison said *"alles gute zum Geburtstag!"*

"How did you know it was my birthday?"

"Your passport," Frau Kohler said. "When you registered with us, I wrote it down on the calendar. *Ja, so,* here we are! I plum *kuchen* have made to celebrate!"

Franzisa presented me with a bilingual Sherlock Holmes adventure. "It has parallel columns," she said, "so if you get stuck in Deutsch you can check out the Englisch. You are making fine progress, though, and I don't think you'll need to do that too often."

It was the birthday kuchen, which tasted just like Grandma's, that made me feel like I'd crossed some kind of threshold. It wasn't only the *kuchen* I savored. It also was the taste of family, of friendship, of community. I wasn't sure how, but maybe I could learn from the way Uncle Erich had done it. It was a good beginning.

After two months went by, I took a risk and sent Richard a postcard of the Wartburg, with those timber frames he'd liked. I wrote the message in German, echoing the one he had translated for me: *"die Wartburg wo Luther die Biebel ubersezt hatte"* (the Wartburg where Luther translated the Bible). After the way we'd parted, I didn't know if I would hear from him again, but I wanted to try. He had been such a crucial part of my life. If he was willing, I wanted to build on what we had shared, flawed though it had been. One day when I went to the Leipzig American Express office to check my mail, there was a card from Richard. He said he'd seen Barbara. Actually, Barbara and Caleb had invited him over to dinner at least twice. My *yente* had been working overtime. And postcard by postcard, letter by letter, we wrote our way back. Or maybe I should say forward.

Three months later, when I burst through the Logan Airport customs doors in Terminal E, bleary eyed after eight hours in Lufthansa economy class, oh, what a gift, there was Richard.

Acknowledgments

Writing is a solitary enterprise, yet I have learned that it takes a community to create a book. I am indebted to several communities for feedback on *Conflicts of Interest*. Grub Street, a Boston based creative writing center for storytellers of every genre, has been a source of education, inspiration, and motivation for several years. I am especially grateful to Sophie Powell and Marjan Kamali, whose "Novel in progress" classes taught me about craft and offered counsel from first draft through countless revisions, as well as to students in each of their classes. Any deficiencies in this book are my own, and in no way a reflection of their superb teaching.

A friendship with one of the students, Claude Rothman, led to my participation in a writers' workshop she coordinates. I look forward to our monthly sessions, with appreciation to Sue Cnudde, Veronica Maria de Grieff, Suzanne Lipsky, Patrick Renzi, Ann Russell, Julie Vogel, and Terri Wise. Other friends who helped along the way were Gina Bovin, David Lucht, Monsignor Michael F. Groden (now of blessed memory), Fred Maples, S.J, Sherrie Ryan, Roberto Rodriguez, and Richard Roos, S.J. Special thanks go to Jerry Reilly, who began the process of transforming the text from computer to book format, to Jason Davis, who completed the process and designed the book jacket, and to Leah Abrahams, for her insightful and meticulous editorial guidance. I would have been lost without their help.

This is a work of fiction. The characters in this novel are products of my imagination. Some of the quotations from Uncle Erich's journal, however, I drew from a journal I began in 1981, the source of which, in at least one case, alas is lost in the mists of time. Where retrievable, I have noted the references. The insights of these writers have continued to guide and inspire me, as they did the characters in this novel.

Above all, I am grateful to my son Peter Kessler, Esq. He is a stellar writer who has a gentle way of asking questions which clarify and sharpen my thinking, usually over lunches of orange flavored chicken in a little Chinese restaurant near his office.

Suggested Questions
for Discussion Groups

Which characters in *Conflicts of Interest* did you especially like, and why?

Did you identify with Claire in certain ways? Other ways that you didn't?

Did Piper Mangan have any redeeming qualities, or was he a pure villain?

Did the friendship between Claire and Barbara feel familiar to you? Can you share an example? Why do you think Claire didn't have more friends?

How did Claire's childhood experiences shape the choices she has made as an adult?

Are there similarities in the values that Richard and Uncle Erich hold? What are they?

Uncle Erich says "If you don't mourn right, you don't live right." What do you think he meant? Do you agree?

In what contexts does Claire most clearly experience the power of community? How does it influence her choices?

Have you had an experience interacting with people of another culture, as Claire did when she went to Germany for her sabbatical?

What was that like? What did you learn?